THE FIRE
IN THE FLINT

THE FIRE
IN THE FLINT

WALTER WHITE

Foreword by R. Baxter Miller

BROWN THRASHER BOOKS

The University of Georgia Press

ATHENS & LONDON

Published in 1996 as a Brown Thrasher Book
by the University of Georgia Press, Athens, Georgia 30602
© 1924 by Alfred A. Knopf, Inc.
Brown Thrasher Edition © 1996 by the University of Georgia Press

The paper in this book meets the guidelines for permanence and
durability of the Committee on Production Guidelines for Book
Longevity of the Council on Library Resources.

Printed in the United States of America

00 99 98 97 96 P 5 4 3 2

Library of Congress Cataloging in Publication Data

White, Walter Francis, 1893–1955.
The fire in the flint / Walter White ; foreword by R. Baxter Miller.
p.   cm.
ISBN 0-8203-1742-X (pbk.: alk. paper)
1. Afro-American physicians—Georgia—Fiction.   2. City and town
life—Georgia—Fiction.   3. Georgia—Race relations—Fiction.
4. Young men—Georgia—Fiction.   I. Title.
PS3545.H6165F52   1996
813'.52—dc20   95-35218

British Library Cataloging in Publication Data available

TO
MY WIFE

"The fire in the flint never shows until it is struck."

—*Old English Proverb.*

THE FIRE
IN THE FLINT

FOREWORD

R. Baxter Miller

As a timely reassessment by the University of Georgia Press makes clear, the lasting impact of the life and work of Walter White is enormous. White was a political man of letters even more than Langston Hughes and Countée Cullen, those "purer" writers of greater youth. White lacked the folk flair and bold experimentation in African American southern idiom that would make Zora Neale Hurston a beacon to feminists and so many others beyond her time. Furthermore, White would not become, as Dorothy West, the last living testimony of his age. If the stream of consciousness in Jean Toomer's *Cane* (1923) were indeed the high standard of plasticity in language, White's *The Fire in the Flint* (1924) would seem almost pedestrian in comparison—nearly a regression to the delicate, stilted prose of the gilded age. Walter White was literally a fair child of the late nineteenth century.

Walter Francis White, one of seven children, was born a blue-eyed blond of African ancestry to Madeline and George White on 1 July 1893. His mother had formerly been a school teacher, and his father was a mail carrier. In the Atlanta race riots of 1906, the thirteen-year-old Walter stood with rifle in hand beside his father. In Atlanta, White came of age in the public schools. He earned a bachelor's degree from Atlanta University in 1916. While working at the Atlanta Life Insurance Company for many years, White became a resourceful leader for the NAACP and won the attention of James Weldon Johnson, the national field secretary. In 1918 he moved to New York City to become assistant secretary to Johnson.

[1]

FOREWORD

Able to cross the color line without difficulty, White infiltrated many supremacist groups in order to enlighten the nation on racial lynching. Once authorized as a deputy sheriff in Arkansas and later in Oklahoma, he was openly encouraged to murder blacks. Through the teens and twenties, he derived from his own social reports rich material for documentary essays and fiction. Along with James Weldon Johnson, Charles S. Johnson, Alain Locke, Jessie Fauset, and others, White championed the development of young writers such as Countée Cullen, Claude McKay, Langston Hughes, Rudolph Fisher, and Zora Neale Hurston. A strong supporter of the New Negro movement as popularized by Alain Locke in 1925, White joined ranks with Locke to establish a Negro Foreign Fellowship fund for young blacks to experience the artistic atmosphere of Europe. Through his political connections, White helped aspiring young black writers to meet editors and publishers as well.

Along with Johnson, White shared the belief that creative writing might serve to uplift the black race. After meeting with H. L. Mencken, an eminent intellectual of the white left, White was invited to assess the authenticity of *Birthright* (1922), a racial novel by T. S. Stribling. In a painfully long reply, White responded that Stribling had written outside the richness of African American experience, and Mencken replied, "Why don't you do the right kind of novel? You could do it, and it would create a sensation." White, who had rarely considered creative writing, discussed the invitation with colleagues. Eventually he accepted the request by Mary White Ovington, a friend and fellow member of the NAACP, to draft the novel at her cottage in Great Barrington, Massachusetts. White had recently married Gladys Powell, and on 15 February 1922 they packed for a two-week stay in New England during which time he completed *The Fire in the Flint*. Although one of the "most successful exposes of lynching in American fiction," according to Barksdale and Kinnamon, the plot is only a stock device.

In *The Fire in the Flint*, after four years of study at Atlanta

University, Kenneth Harper attends medical school before returning to his home town of Central City. A flourishing town in South Georgia, Central City, once an informal name for Macon, is less prominant than historic Atlanta, and more "central" to the mainstream southern values of the time. Kenneth deliberates over sacrificing the life of Mary Ewing, a secret white patient and the daughter of a prominent store owner, Roy Ewing, but saves her life instead. Elsewhere in the novel history proves more stereotypical: "Back to the public square. In the open space before the Confederate Monument, wood and excelsior had been piled. Nearby stood cans of kerosene. On the crude pyre they threw the body. Saturated it and wood with oil. A match applied. In the early morning sunlight the fire leaped higher and higher. Mingled with the flames and smoke the exulting cries of those who had done their duty—they had avenged and upheld white civilization."

Kenneth had come home to the corner of Lee and State Streets after a tour of military service in World War I. Some black men of the time straightened their naturally woolly hair with pomade, and it was not uncommon for the Black Maria, or patrol wagon, to carry those in possession of whiskey off to jail. If Walter White had written only documentary of this sort, his influence on literary history would not require reassessment. But at least two other figures—two gems of crystallized meaning—distinguish him in the evolution of black southern literature. First, during the Klan's frenzied, ritual meetings, "The droning voices ended the monotonous recital. The flickering torches gave forth a weird light that was lost in the darkness cast by the trees. The pungent odor of burning resin and the thick stifling smoke were blown by vagrant breezes into the faces of the hooded figures, causing a constant accompaniment of coughs, sneezes, and curses to the mumbled words. A recent rainstorm had left the low-lying gound soggy and damp and mightily uncomfortable underfoot." Without any value for individuating styles, the personal self disappears into the anonymous herd. As a metaphor for the group, the light is "weird" and unsteady. Ultimately, the climate—the very dehumanized air—has reduced human language to "mumbled words." Whatever their position in relation to the fire, they inhale the smoke of their own creation. Second, against the darkened landscape of sinking ground, their primitive acts deter all human conscience as proud and loyal Americans scheme to kill another American of a different color:

Fifteen men sat around a table in an office on Lee Street. There was above them a single electric-light bulb, fly-specked, without a shade over it. At eleven o'clock they had silently crept up the stairs after looking cautiously up and down the deserted expanse of Lee Street to see if they were observed. Like some silent, creeping, wolf-like denizen of the forest, each had stolen as noiselessly as possible up the stairs. The window carefully covered, no ray of light could be seen from the outside. Though unsigned, the mysterious note each of the fifteen had received that morning had brought them all together promptly. Though there was none to hear or see, they dispersed with silent and cautious movements and voices. They crept down the unlighted stairs, hands extended, fingers touching the walls on either side to aid them in making as little noise as possible.

All of the southern space in the text takes measure from the originating statue of the Confederate dead in Central City. But what lasting honor derives from either the fictive or historical world in which Robert E. Lee Street finds itself silently figured as an urban desert prowled upon by human wolves?

In White's literary world, grim economic necessity makes for blurred race relations in the southern United States. As store owners, both Roy Ewing and Ralph Minor would suffer financial reprisals for promoting racial equality. George Baird, president of the Bank of Central City, and Fred Griswold, president of Smith County Farmer's Bank, fear the loss of prominent customers due to opposing racial views. Nat Phelps, the proprietor of the Central City *Dispatch*, desperately needs to keep his cherished subscribers, and all the businessmen want to avoid having their wives and daughters ostracized. Apparently, ideals come much more easily than deeds. Even Kenneth Harper fails to see Dr. Scott properly as a decent white man with little intellect and few opportunities for religious enlightenment. Kenneth also misreads John Anthony, a lawyer and businessman, for Kenneth "was too young to know that the more largely a man profits from a liberal cause, the more loyal will be his support for that cause and the lesser likelihood of his defection when difficulties arise." An intrusive narration persists: "In his agonized fulmination against the whites . . . Kenneth forgot those who had been and were true friends of the black man—who had suffered and died that *he* might be free."

Judge Stevenson, a white supporter of Kenneth, sees the decade of the twenties in a different light and asks, "Why couldn't they see even then that they are doing more harm to themselves than they could ever do to the Negro? With all its rich natural resources, with its fertile soil and its wonderful climate, the South is farther behind in civilization than any other part of the United States—or the world, for that matter." In walking home from Judge Stevenson's house, Kenneth thinks about the moral cowardice of those who will not "call their souls their own. . . . [who are] creatures of the Frankenstein monster their own people had created." Indeed, the Judge sounds very similar in thought to Sterling Brown, a leading African American poet of the thirties: "Hope this thing turns out all right. Hope he don't get in no trouble. But even if he does, there'll be more like him coming on—and they got too much sense to stand for what nigras been made to suffer."

The lynch mob fails to recognize the basic humanity of Kenneth Harper. When he goes to Roy Ewing's to save Mary's life, the group conjures up fantasies of sexual infidelity involving Mrs. Ewing. Indeed, the whole novel exposes the failure of the lynchers to have any sustained or innovative vision. They focus on an upstairs bedroom in the second floor of the Ewing home simply because the family shades are lowered there. Kenneth suspects that even Judge Ewing would not grasp the theatrical irony if he were simply to let Mary die out of racial vengeance. "They wouldn't understand," he thought. "They'd never seen great actors on the stage . . . like casting pearls before swine. They'd never appreciate the wonder." Walter White does value the diverse ways through which the two races interpret the text of southern history. Sheriff Parker, Exalted Cyclops of the Ku Klux Klan, sets the scene for depravity:

Stodgy, phlegmatic, stupid citizens by day, these by night went through the discomforts of so unprepared a meeting-place, and through the absurdities of the rites imposed upon them by clever rogues who extracted from them fees and donations for the privilege of being made to appear more silly than is usually apparent. Add to that gullibility a natural love of the mysterious and adventurous and an instinct towards brute action restrained only by fear of punishment, by a conjuring of bogies and other malevolent dangers, and one understands, at least in part, the presence of these three hundred "white, Gentile, Protestant" citizens of Central City at this meeting.

Here the daytime citizen degenerates into a nighttime primitive. "Meeting-place" suggests an evil covenant across time in which even klansmen play out their assigned scripts as exploited actors. The presence of the fearful lynchers becomes a unifying metaphor for Central City, America, across both time and space. The courageous acts of Kenneth are ironic, for although he saves Mary's life, the men of her race plot his own murder. This quality of courage initiates a chain of events climaxed by the death of the brother James, who certainly never chooses martyrdom as a desirable end, and who pauses, as if to laugh at death, "cheating the howling pack," the mob.

Walter White, essayist, autobiographer, novelist, and nonfiction writer, was one of the most significant figures in the New Negro movement of the twenties, and his influence extended well into mid-century. White lived his life aligned spiritually with the folk masses. A native Georgian who personally experienced a violent South, White managed to maintain an incurable optimism toward overcoming racism so that even white reviewers recognized his extraordinary spirit. Though he was often genteel in his literary style, his drive to end the dehumanization of blacks was quite aggressive, and his interest in the rituals of consciousness was distinctly modern.

In manner White was somewhat Victorian, yet in concept he was quite innovative. As an effective lobbyist in Washington, D.C., he advised Presidents Franklin D. Roosevelt and Harry Truman. Furthermore, he helped facilitate the Gavan Bill against lynching and to defeat the nomination of John J. Parker, a segregationist, to the Supreme Court. In the literary reformation of the thirties, he called more for a social activism than for a polite aesthetic. Near the end of the forties, as the Jazz Age of the twenties met the postwar world of the forties, White articulated the need for a convergence of his two passions, art and activism, as Gwendolyn Brooks, Alice Childress, James Baldwin, and Ralph Ellison continued to emerge as strong voices of the African American community.

With spirit White called for exceptional talents that might survive the American melting pot of banality, and he helped to pave the way for new innovators of racial self-definition. Regardless of his own preferences, he encouraged new literary forms. Indeed, he helped to harvest African American arts in many ways, far beyond what he personally authored.

White recognized that a literary instant exists in which all people can choose their own way. In his autobiography, *A Man Called White*, he wrote of the 1906 Atlanta race riots: "I was sick with loathing for the hatred which had flared before me that night and come so close to making me a killer; but I was glad I was not one of those who hated; I was glad I was not one of those made sick and murderous by pride. I was glad I was not one of those whose story is the history of the world, a record of bloodshed, rapine, and pillage; I was glad my mind and spirit were part of the races that had not fully

awakened, and who therefore had still before them the opportunity to write a record of virtue as a memorandum to Arma-
geddon." As White watched the riot fires as a young boy, a
sense of racial justice sparked within him. The spark would
ignite a lifetime dedicated to ending racial hatred and writing
stories for the future of Georgia.

As testimony to his next title, *How Far the Promised Land?*
(1955), he had almost prophesied what would become the
dominant metaphor for Martin Luther King Jr., who had only
begun to lead the bus boycott in Montgomery. Indeed,
Francis Hackett has viewed White as "possessed by one of
those mastering passions to which no wise American can refuse heed and no good citizen refuse sympathy." Ralph J.
Bunche, a representative to the United Nations, added, "We
do not go backward, we do not stand still, he said; American
democracy moves forward. There is an ever-stronger current
of democracy which eventually will carry all Americans into
the 'Promised Land.'"

White's *The Fire in the Flint*, which exerted a conscien-
tious force on its era, impressed Sinclair Lewis, who ranked
the book along with *A Passage to India* by E. M. Forster as
the best two novels for 1924. On 10 October 1924, an un-
usually sensitive review by Jonathan Daniels in the *Raleigh
News and Observer* prompted disbelief from White, who confessed amazement to Benjamin Brawley that a southern paper
could be so favorable. Meanwhile, *The Fire in the Flint*
linked bold new alliances in an interracial chain for civil
rights from Macon and Athens all the way to New York City.
A. B. Brand, an unorthodox Jewish columnist for the *Macon
Telegraph*, wrote on 30 November 1924: "The *Red and the
Black* is a weekly publication from the University of Georgia,
where now John Wade and Roosevelt Walker (of the English
Department) and one [E. Merton] Coulter (History) are working such wonders that I continually fear the Board of Trustees
must hear about them and forthwith fire them."

Though Brand seemed to envy John Stallings, an editor

for the *New York World*, who had escaped the region, his un-published manuscript helped pave the way for cultural diversity much later: "I don't think that I ever wrote you [White] the details of the Revolt. That was the article which first prompted me to write you, a few months ago. It attempted to show that the rebellion of you five literati—as listed in this column—was induced by the repressions, outlined the revolt, and gave testimony of Georgia's reception thereto. . . . Fearing for my life, I submitted the piece first to several typical enlightened Georgians. . . . The Revolt now reposes in my desk drawer and shall never see the light of day." On 16 March 1926, Alfred A. Knopf Jr., vice-president of the publishing company named for his family, recollected about the lasting impact of White's first book. Sinclair Lewis had called the volume "splendidly courageous, rather terrifying and of the highest significance." Lawrence Stallings had intoned, "Few novels have been needed more." Lydia Gibson had recognized the volume in *The Liberator* as "one of the first of a great literature expressing the dreams, the resentments, and the affirmations of a rising people." Finally, Robert W. Bagnal had qualified in *The Messenger* that the White story was "melodramatic but true; bitter but fair," while Jim Tully had lauded *Fire* in the *International Book Review* as the "greatest novel yet written by a Negro in the United States." In hindsight, the praise may seem exaggerated. But Louis Marshall, whose firm of Guggenheimer, Untermeyer, and Marshall was at 180 Broadway, had already written White on 12 September 1924: "Your eloquent and moving tale bears the impress of truth and carries conviction to the hearts of those who honestly believe in the equality of all men before the Almighty and in the eye of the law."

Although White rarely wrote or thought in theoretical terms, his life's work implies them. Long before the challenges that would come from Shelby Steele and Dan Quayle, he vindicated African American character with these lasting words:

FOREWORD

My best friends and my enemies have accused me at various times of a great many things but not yet has there come to my ears the charge that I failed to take advantage of every opportunity for advancement. Opportunity herself has never knocked on my door. The poor girl never had the chance for I always have lain in wait for her. Whenever she happened anywhere near I reached out and yanked her in even before she could put her knuckles on my portal.

WORKS CONSULTED

Broun, Heywood. "It Seems to Heywood Broun." *Nation* 21 May 1930, 591.

Cannon, Poppy. *A Gentle Knight: My Husband Walter White*. New York: Rinehart, 1956.

Du Bois, W. E. B. *Collected Published Works of W. E. B. Du Bois*. Ed. Herbert Aptheker. Milwood, N.J.: Kraus-Thomson, 1977.

Cooney, Charles F. "Walter White and the Harlem Renaissance." *Journal of Negro History* 57 (July 1972): 231–40.

Gustafson, Alrik. *Six Scandinavian Novelists*. Minneapolis: University of Minnesota Press, 1966.

NAACP papers. James Madison Branch of the Library of Congress. Washington, D.C.

Scruggs, Charles W. "Alain Locke and Walter White: Their Struggle for Control of the Harlem Renaissance." *Black American Literature Forum* 14 (September 1980): 91–99.

Waldron, Edward E. *Walter White and the Harlem Renaissance*. Minneapolis: University of Minnesota Press, 1966.

White, Walter. *Flight*. New York: Knopf, 1926

———. *A Man Called White: The Autobiography of Walter White*. 1924. Reprint, Athens: University of Georgia Press, 1995.

Wilkins, Roy. "Walter White." In *Rising Above Color*, ed. Philip Henry Lotz. New York: Association Press, 1943.

CHAPTER I

KENNETH HARPER gazed slowly around his office. A smile of satisfaction wreathed his face, reflecting his inward contentment. He felt like a runner who sees ahead of him the coveted goal towards which he has been straining through many gruelling miles. Kenneth was tired but he gave no thought to his weariness. Two weeks of hard work, countless annoyances, seemingly infinite delays—all were now forgotten in the warm glow which pervaded his being. He, Kenneth B. Harper, M.D., was now ready to receive the stream of patients he felt sure was coming.

He walked around the room and fingered with almost loving tenderness the newly installed apparatus. He adjusted and readjusted the examining-table of shining nickel and white enamel which had arrived that morning from New York. He arranged again the black leather pads and cushions. With his handkerchief he wiped imaginary spots of dust from the plate glass door and shelves of the instrument case, though his sister Mamie had polished them but half an hour before until they shone with crystal clearness. Instrument after instrument he fondled with the air of a connoisseur examining a rare bit of porcelain. He fingered critically their various parts to see if all were in perfect condition. He tore a stamp from an old letter and placed it under the lens of the expensive microscope adjusting and re-adjusting until every feature of the stamp stood out clearly even to the most minute detail. He raised and lowered half a dozen times or more the lid of the nickelled sterilizer. He set at various angles the white screen which surrounded the examining-table, viewed it each time from different corners of the room, and rearranged it until it was set just right. He ran his hand over the card index files in his small desk. He looked at the clean white cards with the tabs on them—the cards which, though innocent now of writing, he hoped and expected would soon be filled with the names of innumerable sick people he was treating.

His eye caught what he thought was a pucker in the grey-and-blue-chequered linoleum which covered the floor. He went over and moved the sectional book-case containing his volumes on obstetrics, on gynæcology, on *materia medica,* on the diseases he knew he would treat as a general practitioner of medicine in so small a place as Central City. No, that wasn't a pucker—it was only the light from the window striking it at that angle.

"Dr. Kenneth B. Harper, Physician and Surgeon." He spelled out the letters which were painted on the upper panes of the two windows facing on State Street. It thrilled him that eight years of hard work had ended and he now was at the point in his life to-wards which he had longingly looked all those years.

Casting his eyes again around the office, he went into the adjoining reception room.

Kenneth threw himself in utter exhaustion into one of the comfortable arm-chairs there. His hands, long-fingered, tapering to slender points, the hands of a pianist, an artist, whether of brush or chisel or scalpel, hung over the sides in languid fashion. He was without coat or vest. His shirt-sleeves were rolled back above his elbows, revealing strongly muscled dark brown arms. His face was of the same richly coloured brown. His mouth was sensitively shaped with evenly matched strong white teeth. The eyes too were brown, usually sober and serious, but flashing into a broad and friendly smile when there was occasion for it. Brushed straight back from the broad forehead was a mass of wavy hair, brown also but of a deeper shade, almost black. The chin was well shaped.

As he lounged in the chair and looked around the reception room, he appeared to be of medium height, rather well-proportioned, almost stocky. Three years of baseball and football, and nearly two years of army life with all its hardships, had thickened up the once rather slender figure and had given to the face a more mature appearance, different from the youthful, almost callow look he had worn when his diploma had been handed him at the end of his college course.

The reception room was as pleasing to him as he sat there as had been the private office. There were three or four more chairs like the one in which he sat. There was a couch to match. The wall-paper was a subdued tan, serving as an excellent background for four brightly coloured reproductions of good pictures. Their brightness was matched by a vase of deep blue that stood on the table. Beside the vase were two rows of magazines placed there for perusal by his patients as they waited admittance to the more austere room beyond. It was comfortable. It was in good taste—almost too good taste, Kenneth thought, for a place like Central City in a section like the southernmost part of Georgia. Some of the country folks and even those in town would probably say it was too plain—didn't have enough colour about it. Oh, well, that wouldn't matter, Kenneth thought. They wouldn't have to live there. Most of them would hardly notice it, if they paid any attention at all to relatively minor and unimportant things like colour schemes.

Kenneth felt that he had good reason to feel content with the present outlook. He lighted a cigarette and settled himself more comfortably in the deep chair and let his mind wander over the long trail he had covered. He thought of the eight happy years he had spent at Atlanta University—four of high school and four of college. He remembered gratefully the hours of companionship with those men and women who had left comfortable homes and friends in the North to give their lives to the education of coloured boys and girls in Georgia. They were so human—so sincere—so genuinely anxious to help. It wasn't easy for them to do it, either, for it meant ostracism and all its attendant unpleasantnesses to teach coloured children in Georgia anything other than industrial courses. And they were so different from the white folks he knew in Central City. Here he had always been made to feel that because he was a "nigger" he was predestined to inferiority. But there at Atlanta they had treated him like a human being. He was glad he had gone to Atlanta University. It had made him realize that all white folks weren't bad—that there were decent ones, after all.

And then medical school in the North! How eagerly he had looked forward to it! The bustle, the air of alert and eager determination, the lovely old ivied walls of the buildings where he attended classes. He laughed softly to himself as he remembered how terribly lonesome he had been that first day when as an ignorant country boy he found himself really at a Northern school. That had been a hard night to get through. Everybody had seemed so intent on doing something that was interesting, going so rapidly towards the places where those interesting things were to take place, greeting old friends and acquaintances affectionately and with all the boisterous bonhomie that only youth, and college youth at that, seem to be able to master. It had been a bitter pill for him to swallow that he alone of all that seething, noisy, tremendous mass of students, was alone—without friend or acquaintance—the one lonely figure of the thousands around him.

That hadn't lasted long though. Good old Bill

Van Vleet! That's what having family and money and prestige behind you did for a fellow! It was a mighty welcome thing when old Bill came to him there as he sat dejectedly that second morning on the campus and roused him out of his gloom. And then the four years when Bill had been his closest friend. He had been one wonderful free soul that knew no line of caste or race.

His friendship with Van Vleet seemed to Kenneth now almost like the memory of a pleasant dream on awaking. Even then it had often seemed but a fleeting, evanescent experience—a wholly temporary arrangement that was intended to last only through the four years of medical school. Those times when Bill had invited him to spend Christmas holidays at his home—they had been hard invitations to get out of. Bill had been sincere enough, no doubt of that. But Bill's father—his mother—their friends—would they—old Pennsylvania Dutch family that they were —would they be as glad to welcome a Negro into their home? He had always been afraid to take the chance of finding that they wouldn't. Decent enough had they been when Bill introduced him to them on one of their visits to Philadelphia. But—and this was a big "but"—there was a real difference between being nice to a coloured friend of Bill's at school and treating that same fellow decently in their own home. Kenneth was conscious of a vague feeling even now that he had not treated them fairly in judging them by the white people of Central City. Yet, white folks were white folks—and that's that! Hadn't his father always told him that the best way to get along with white people was to stay away from them and let them alone as much as possible?

Through his mind passed memories of the many conversations he had had with his father on that subject. Especially that talk together before he had gone away to medical school. He didn't know then it was the last time he would see his father alive. He had had no way of knowing that his father, always so rugged, so buoyantly healthy, so uncomplaining, would die of appendicitis while he, Kenneth, was in France. If he had only been at home! He'd have known it wasn't a case of plain cramps, as that old fossil, Dr. Bennett, had called it. What was the exact way in which his father had put his philosophy of life in the South during that last talk they had had together? It had run like this: Any Negro can get along without trouble in the South if he only attends to his own business. It was unfortunate, mighty unpleasant and uncomfortable at times, that coloured people, no matter what their standing, had to ride in Jim Crow cars, couldn't vote, couldn't use the public libraries and all those other things. Lynching, too, was bad. But only bad Negroes ever got lynched. And, after all, those things weren't all of life. Booker Washington was right. And the others who were always howling about rights were wrong. Get a trade or a profession. Get a home. Get some property. Get a bank account. Do something! Be somebody! And then, when enough Negroes had reached that stage, the ballot and all the other things now denied them would come. White folks then would see that the Negro was deserving of those rights and privileges and would freely, gladly give them to him without his asking for them.

That was the way he felt. When Bill Van Vleet had urged him to go with him to dinners or the theatre, he had had always some excuse that Bill had to accept whether he had believed it or not. Good Old Bill! They never knew during those more or less happy days what was in store for them both. Neither of them had known that the German Army was going to sweep down through Belgium. Nor did they know that Bill was fated to end his short but brilliant career as an aviator in a blazing, spectacular descent behind the German lines, the lucky shot of a German anti-aircraft gun.

Graduation. The diploma which gave him the right to call himself "Dr. Kenneth B. Harper." And then that stormy, yet advantageous year in New York at Bellevue. Hadn't they raised sand at his, a Negro's presumption in seeking that interneship at Bellevue! He'd almost lost out. No Negro interne had ever been there before. If it hadn't been for Dr. Cox, to whom he had had a letter of introduction from his old professor of pathology at school, he never would have got the chance. But it had been worth it.

Kenneth lighted another cigarette and draped his legs over the arm of the chair. It wasn't bad at all to think of the things he had gone through—now that they were over. Especially the army. Out of Bellevue one week when the chance came to go to the Negro officers' training-camp at Des Moines. First lieutenant's bars in the medical corps. Then the long months of training and hard work at Camp Upton, relieved by occasional pleasant trips to New York. Lucky he'd been assigned to the 367th of the 92nd Division. Good to be near a real town like New York.

That had been some exciting ride across. And then the Meuse, the Argonne, then Metz. God, but that was a terrible nightmare! Right back of the lines had he been assigned. Men with arms and legs shot off. Some torn to pieces by shrapnel. Some burned horribly by mustard gas. The worst night had been when the Germans made that sudden attack at the Meuse. For five days they had been fighting and working. That night he had almost broken down. How he had cursed war! And those who made war. And the civilization that permitted war —even made it necessary. Never again for him! Seemed like a horrible dream—a nightmare worse than any he had ever known as a boy when he'd eaten green apples or too much mince pie.

That awful experience he had soon relegated to the background of his mind. Especially when he was spending those blessed six months at the Sorbonne. That had been another hard job to put over. They didn't want any Negroes staying in France. They'd howled and they'd brought up miles of red tape. But he had ignored the howls and unwound the red tape.

And now, Central City again. It *was* good to get back. Four—eight—sixteen years had he spent in preparation. Now he was all ready to get to work at his profession. For a time he'd have to do general practising. Had to make money. Then he'd specialize in surgery—major surgery. Soon's he got enough money ahead, he'd build a sanitarium. Make of it as modern a hospital as he could afford. He'd draw on all of South Georgia for his patients. Nearest one now is Atlanta. All South Georgia—most of Florida—even from Alabama. Ten years from now he'd have a place known and patronized by all the coloured people in the South. Something like the Mayo Brothers up in Rochester, Minnesota!

"Pretty nifty, eh, Ken?"

Kenneth, aroused suddenly from his retrospection and day-dreams, jumped at the unexpected voice behind him. It was his younger brother, Bob. He laughed a little shamefacedly at his having been startled. Without waiting for a reply, Bob entered the room and sat on the edge of the table facing Kenneth.

"Yep! Things are shaping up rather nicely. Everything's here now but the patients. And those'll be coming along pretty soon, I believe," replied Kenneth confidently. He went on talking enthusiastically of the castles in the air he had been building when Bob entered the room—of the hospital he was going to erect—how he planned attending the State Medical Convention every year to form contacts with other coloured doctors of Georgia—how he was in-

[20]

tending to visit during the coming year all the coloured physicians within a radius of a hundred miles
of Central City to enlist their support. He discussed
the question of a name for the hospital. How would
Harper's Sanitarium sound? Or would the Central
City Infirmary be better? Or the Hospital of South
Georgia?

On and on Kenneth rambled, talking half to Bob,
half in audible continuation of his reverie before
Bob had entered. But Bob wasn't listening to him.
On his face was the usual half-moody, half-
discontented expression which Kenneth knew so well.
Bob was looking down the dusty expanse of the road
which bore rather poorly the imposing title of State
Street. The house was located at the corner of Lee
and State Streets. It was set back about fifty feet
from the streets, and the yard outside showed the
work of one who loved flowers. There was an expanse of smooth lawn, dotted here and there with
flowering beds of pansies, of nasturtiums. There
were several abundantly laden rose-bushes and two
of "cape jessamine" that filled the air with an intoxi-
cating, almost cloying sweetness.

Though it was a balmy October afternoon, the air
languorous and caressing, Bob shared none of the
atmosphere's lazy contentment. All this riot of colours and odours served in no manner to remove from
his face the dissatisfied look that covered it. He listened to Kenneth's rhapsodies of what he intended
accomplishing with what was almost a grimace of
distaste. He was taller than Kenneth, of slighter

build, but of the same rich colouring of skin and with the same hair and features.

In spite of these physical resemblances between the two brothers, there was a more intangible difference which clearly distinguished the two. Kenneth was more phlegmatic, more of a philosophic turn of mind, more content with his lot, able to forget himself in his work, and when that was finished, in his books. Bob, on the other hand, was of a highly sensitized nature, more analytical of mind, more easily roused to passion and anger. This tendency had been developed since the death of his father just before he completed his freshman year at Atlanta. The death had necessitated his leaving school and returning to Central City to act as administrator of his father's estate. His experiences in accomplishing this task had not been pleasant ones. He had been forced to deal with the tricksters that infested the town. He had come in contact with all the chicanery, the petty thievery, the padded accounts, that only petty minds can devise. The utter impotence he had felt in having no legal redress as a Negro had embittered him. Joe Harper, their father, had been exceedingly careful in keeping account of all bills owed and due him. Yet Bob had been forced to pay a number of bills of which he could find no record in his father's neatly kept papers. These had aggregated somewhere between three and four thousand dollars. Various white merchants of the town claimed that Joe Harper, his father, owed them. Bob knew they were lying. Yet he could do nothing. No court in South Georgia would have listened to his side of the story or paid more than perfunctory attention to him. It was a case of a white man's word against a Negro's, and a verdict against the Negro was sure even before the case was opened.

Kenneth, on the other hand, had been a favourite of their quiet, almost taciturn father. Always filled with ambition for his children, Joe Harper had furnished Kenneth, as liberally as he could afford, the money necessary for him to get the medical education he wanted. He had not been a rich man but he had been comfortably fixed financially. Starting out as a carpenter doing odd jobs around Central City, he had gradually expanded his activities to the building of small houses and later to larger homes and business buildings. Most of the two-story buildings that lined Lee Street in the business section of Central City had been built by him. White and coloured alike knew that when Joe Harper took a contract, it would be done right. Aided by a frugal and economical wife, he had purchased real estate and, though the profits had been slow and small, had managed with his wife to accumulate during their thirty-five years of married life between twenty and twenty-five thousand dollars which he left at his death to his wife and three children.

Kenneth had been furnished with the best that his father could afford, while Bob, some ten years younger than his brother, had had to wait until Kenneth finished school before he could begin his course. Bob felt no jealousy of his favoured brother, yet the experiences that had been his in Central City while Kenneth was away had tended towards a bitterness which frequently found expression on his face. He was the natural rebel, revolt was a part of his creed. Kenneth was the natural pacifist—he never bothered trouble until trouble bothered him. Even then, if he could avoid it, he always did. It was not strange, therefore, that he should have come home believing implicitly that his father was right when he had said Kenneth could get along without trouble in Central City as long as he attended to his own business.

Kenneth talked on and on, unfolding the plans he had made for the extending of the influence of his hospital throughout the South. Bob, occupied with his own thoughts, heard but little of it. Suddenly he interrupted Kenneth with a sharply put question.

"Ken, why did you come back to Central City?" he asked. He went on without waiting for a reply. "If I had had your chances of studying up North and in France, and living where you don't have to be afraid of getting into trouble with Crackers all the time, I'd rather've done anything else than to come back to this rotten place to live the rest of my life."

Kenneth laughed easily, almost as though a five-year-old had asked some exceedingly foolish question.

"Why did I come back?" he repeated. "That's easy. I came back because I can make more money here than anywhere else."

"But that isn't the most important thing in life!"
Bob exclaimed.

"Maybe not the most important," Kenneth
laughed, "but a mighty convenient article to have
lying around. I came back here where the bulk of
coloured people live and where they make money off
their crops and where there won't be much trouble
for me to build up a big practice."

"That's an old argument," retorted Bob. "Nearly
a million coloured people went North during the war
and they're making money there hand over fist. You
could make just as much money, if not more, in a
city like Detroit or Cleveland or New York, and you
wouldn't have to be always afraid you've given offence to some of these damned ignorant Crackers
down here."

"Oh, I suppose I could've made money there. Dr.
Cox at Bellevue told me I ought to stay there in New
York and practise in Harlem, but I wanted to come
back home. I can do more good here, both for myself and for the coloured people, than I could up
there." He paused and then asserted confidently:
"And I don't think I'll have any trouble down here.
Papa got along all right here in this town for more
than fifty years, and I reckon I can do it too."

"But, Ken," Bob protested, "the way things were
when he came along are a lot different from the way
they are now. Just yesterday Old Man Mygatt down
to the bank got mad and told me I was an 'impudent
young nigger that needed to be taught my place' be-

[25]

cause I called his hand on a note he claimed papa owed the bank. He knew I knew he was lying, and that's what made him so mad. They're already saying I'm not a 'good nigger' like papa was and that education has spoiled me into thinking I'm as good as they are. Good Lord, if I wasn't any better than these ignorant Crackers in this town, I'd go out and jump in the river."

Bob was working himself into a temper. Kenneth interrupted him with a good-natured smile as he said:

"Bob, you're getting too pessimistic. You've been reading too many of these coloured newspapers published in New York and Chicago and these societies that're always playing up some lynching or other trouble down here——"

"What if I have? I don't need to read them to know that things are much worse to-day than they were a few years back. You haven't lived down here for nearly nine years and you don't know how things are changed."

"It's you who have changed—not conditions so much!" Kenneth answered. "What if there are mean white folks? There are lots of other white people who want to see the Negro succeed. Only this morning Dr. Bennett told mamma he was glad I came back and he'd do what he could to help me. And there're lots more like——"

"That's nice of Dr. Bennett," interjected Bob. "He can afford to talk big—he's got the practice of this town sewed up. And, most of all, he's a white man. Suppose some of these poor whites get it into their heads to make trouble because you're getting too prosperous—what then? Dr. Bennett and all the rest of the good white folks around here can't help you!"

"Oh, yes, they can," Kenneth observed with the same confident smile. "Judge Stevenson and Roy Ewing and Mr. Baird at the Bank of Central City and a lot others run this town and they aren't going to let any decent coloured man be bothered. Why, I'll have a cinch around this part of Georgia! There aren't more than half a dozen coloured doctors in all this part of the country who've had a decent medical education and training. All they know is ladling out pills and fake panaceas. In a few years I'll be able to give up general practising and give all my time to major surgery. I'll handle pretty nearly everything in this part of the State. And then you'll see I'm right!"

"Have it your own way," retorted Bob. "But I'm telling you again, you haven't been living down here for eight or nine years and you don't know. When all these Negroes were going North, some of these same 'good white folks' you're depending on started talking about 'putting niggers in their place' when they couldn't get servants and field hands. You'll find things a lot different from the way they were when you went up North to school."

"What're you boys fussing about? What's the trouble?"

Bob and Kenneth turned at the voice from the doorway behind them. It was their mother.

"Nothing, mamma, only Bob's got a fit of the blues to-day."

Mrs. Harper came in and looked from one to the other of her sons. She was a buxom, pleasant-faced woman of fifty-odd years, her hair once brown now flecked with grey. She wiped the perspiration from her forehead with the corner of her apron, announcing meanwhile that supper was ready. As he rose, Kenneth continued his explanation of their conversation.

"Bob's seeing things like a kid in the dark. He thinks I'll not be able to do the things I came back here to accomplish. Thinks the Crackers won't let me! I'm going to solve my own problem, do as much good as I can, make as much money as I can! If every Negro in America did the same thing, there wouldn't be any 'race problem.' "

Mrs. Harper took an arm of each of her sons and led them into the dining-room where their sister Mamie was putting supper on the table.

"You're right, Kenneth," Mrs. Harper remarked as she sat down at the table. "Your father and I got along here together in Central City without a bit of trouble for thirty-five years, and I reckon you can do it too."

"But, mamma," Bob protested, "I've been telling Ken things are not what they were when you and papa came along. Why——"

"Let's forget the race problem for a while," Kenneth interrupted. "I 'm too hungry and tired to talk about it now."

"That's right," was Mrs. Harper's comment. "Draw your chairs up to the table. You're not goin' to have any trouble here in town, Ken, and we're mighty glad you came back. Mrs. Amos was in this afternoon and she tells me they're having some trouble out near Ashland between the coloured share-croppers and their landlords, but that'll blow over—just as it's always done."

"What's the trouble out there?" asked Kenneth. He wasn't much interested, for he could hear Mamie, in the kitchen beyond, singing some popular air to the accompaniment of chicken-frying.

"It's a case where coloured farmers claim they can't get fair settlements from their landlords for their crops at the end of the year," explained his mother.

"Why don't they hire a lawyer?" Kenneth asked, with little interest.

"That shows you've forgotten all about things in the South," said Bob with mingled triumph and despair at his brother's ignorance. "There isn't a white lawyer in Georgia who'd take a case like this. In the first place, the courts would be against him because his client's a Negro, and in the second place, he'd have to buck this combination of landlords, store-keepers, and bankers who are getting rich robbing Negroes. If a white lawyer took a case of a Negro share-cropper, he'd either sell out to the landlord or be scared to death before he ever got to court. And as for a Negro lawyer," here Bob laughed sardonically, "he'd be run out of town by the Ku Klux

[29]

Klan or lynched almost before he took the case!"

"Oh, I don't know so much about that!" Kenneth
replied. "There are landlords, without doubt, who
rob their tenants, but after all there are only a few
of them. And furthermore," he declared as Mamie
entered the room with a platter of fried chicken in
one hand and a plate of hot biscuits in the other,
"supper looks just a little bit more interesting to me
right now than landlords, tenants, or problems of
any kind."

Mamie divested herself of her apron and sat down
to the table. She was an attractive girl of twenty-
two or twenty-three, more slender than Bob, and
about Kenneth's height. Her hair was darker than
that of either of her brothers, was parted in the
middle and brushed down hard on either side.
Though not a pretty girl, she had an air about her as
though she was happy because of the sheer joy of
living. She had graduated from Atlanta University
two years before, and with two other girls had been
teaching the seven grades in the little ramshackle
building that served as a coloured school in the
town. That hard work had not as yet begun to tell
on her. She seemed filled with buoyant good health
and blessed with a lively good nature. Yet she too
was inclined to spells of depression like Bob's. She
resembled him more nearly than Kenneth. As has
every comely coloured girl in towns of the South like
Central City, she had had many repulsive experiences
when she had to fight with might and main to ward
off unwelcome attentions—both of the men of her

own race and of white men. Especially had this been true since the death of her father. Often her face overclouded as she thought of them. She, like Bob, felt always as though they were living on top of a volcano—and never knew when it might erupt. . . .

The four sat at supper. Forgotten were problems other than the immediate one of Kenneth's in getting his practice under way. Eagerly they talked of his plans, his prospects, his ambitions. Bob said nothing until they began to discuss him and his plans for returning to school the following fall, now that Kenneth was back to complete the settling of the small details that remained in connection with Joe Harper's estate. . . .

It was a happy and reasonably prosperous, intelligent family group—one that can be duplicated many, many times in the South.

CHAPTER II

SITUATED in the heart of the farming section of the State, with its fertile soil, its equable climate, its forests of pine trees, Central City was one of the flourishing towns of South Georgia. Its population was between eight and ten thousand, of which some four thousand were Negroes. The wealth and prosperity of the town depended not so much on the town itself as it did on the farmers of the fertile lands surrounding it. To Central City they came on Saturday afternoons to sell their cotton, their corn, their hogs and cows, and to buy in turn sugar, cloth, coffee, farming-implements, shoes, and amusement. It was divided into four nearly equal sections by the intersection of the tracks of the Central of Georgia Railroad and of the Georgia, Southern and Florida Railway. Drowsy, indolent during the first six days of the week, Central City awoke on Saturday morning for "goin' t' town" day with its bustle and excitement and lively trade. Then the broad dustiness of Lee Street was disturbed by the Fords and muddied wagons of farmers, white and black. In the wagons were usually splint-bottom chairs or boards stretched from side to side, occupied by scrawny, lanky "po' whites" with a swarm of children to match, clad in single-piece garments, once

[32]

red in colour and now, through many washings with lye soap, an indeterminate reddish brown. Or, if the driver was a Negro, he generally was surrounded by just as many little black offspring, clad also in greyish or reddish-brown garments, and scrambling over the farm products being brought to town for sale or exchange for the simple and few store products needed. And beside him the usually buxom, ample-bodied wife, clad in her finest and most gaudy clothing to celebrate the trip to town looked forward to eagerly all the week.

Crowded were the streets with vehicles and the sidewalks with the jostling, laughing, loudly talking throng of humans. After the noonday whistle had blown signalling release to the hordes of whites working in the cotton mill over beyond the tracks, the crowd was augmented considerably, the new-comers made up of those who had deserted the country districts, discouraged by the hard life of farming, by rainy and unprofitable seasons, by the ravages of the boll weevil and of landlords, both working dire distress on poor white and black alike. Discouraged, they had come to "the city" to work at small wages in the cotton mill.

All the trading done on these days did not take place over the counters of the stores that lined Lee Street. In the dirty little alleyways from off the main street, men with furtive eyes but bold ways dispensed synthetic gin, "real" rye whisky, and more often "white mule," as the moonshine corn whisky is called. Bottles were tilted and held to the mouth a long time—and later the scene would be enlivened by furious but shortlived fights. Guns, knives, all sorts of weapons appeared with miraculous speed— the quarrel was settled, the wounded or killed removed, and the throng forgot the incident in some new joyous and usually commonplace or sordid adventure.

When darkness began to approach, the wagons and Fords, loaded with merchandise for the next week, and with the children clutching sticky and brightly coloured candies, began to rumble countrywards, and Central City by nightfall had resumed its sleepy, indolent, and deserted manner.

From the corner where Oglethorpe Avenue crossed Lee Street and where stood the monument to the Confederate Dead, the business section extended up Lee Street for three blocks. Here the street was dignified with a narrow "park," some twenty feet in width, which ran the length of the business thoroughfare. Over beyond the monument lay the section of Central City where lived the more well-to-do of its white inhabitants. Georgia Avenue was here the realm of the socially elect. Shaded by elms, it numbered several more or less pretentious homes of two stories, some of brick, the majority of frame structure. Here were the homes of Roy Ewing, president of the local Chamber of Commerce and owner of Ewing's General Merchandise Emporium; of George Baird, president of the Bank of Central City; of Fred Griswold, occupying the same relation to Central City's other bank, the Smith County Farmers' Bank; of

Ralph Minor, owner and manager of the Bon Ton Store.

Here too were the wives of these men, busying themselves with their household duties and the minor social life of the community. In the morning they attended to the many details of housekeeping; in the afternoon and early evening they sat on their front porches or visited neighbours or went for a ride. Placid, uneventful, stupid lives they led with no other interests than the petty affairs of a small and unprogressive town.

The young girls of Central City usually in the afternoon dressed in all their small-town finery and strolled down to Odell's Drug Store where the young men congregated. Having consumed a frothy soda or a gummy, sweetish sundae, they went to the Idle Hour Moving Picture Palace to worship at the celluloid shrine of a favourite film actor, usually of the highly romantic type. Then the stroll homewards, always past the Central City Hotel, a two-storied frame structure located at the corner of Lee Street and Oglethorpe Avenue opposite the Confederate monument. In front were arm-chairs, occupied in warm weather, which was nearly all the year round, by travelling salesmen or other transients. Often a sidelong glance and a fleeting, would-be-coy smile would cause one of the chair-occupants to rise as casually as he could feign, yawn and stretch, and with affected nonchalance stroll down Lee Street in the wake of the smiling one. . . .

At the other end of Lee Street from the residential

section of the well-to-do whites, past the business section of that main artery of the town, lay that portion
known generally as "Darktown." Fringing it were
several better-than-the-average homes, neat, well
painted, comfortable-looking, fronted with smooth
lawns and tidy, colourful flower-beds. It was one
of these at the corner of Lee and State Streets that
the Harpers owned and occupied.

After crossing State Street, an abrupt descent was
taken by Lee Street. Here lived in squalor and filth
and abject poverty the poorer class of Negroes. The
streets were winding, unpaved lanes, veritable seas
and rivers of sticky, gummy, discouraging mud in
rainy weather, into which the wheels of vehicles sank
to their hubs if the drivers of those conveyances were
indiscreet enough to drive through them. In summer these eddying wallows of muck and filth and
mud dry up and are transformed into swirling storms
of germ-laden dust when a vagrant wind sweeps over
them or a vehicle drives through them, choking the
throats of unlucky passers-by, and, to the despair of
the dusky housewives, flying through open windows.

The houses that bordered these roads were for the
most part of three and four rooms, the exteriors unpainted or whitewashed, the interiors gloomy and
smelly. But few of them had sanitary arrangements,
and at the end of the little patch of ground that was
back of each of them, in which a few discouraged
vegetables strove to push their heads above the
ground, there stood another unpainted structure,
small, known as "the privy." In front there was

nearly always some attempt at flower-cultivation, the
tiny beds bordered with bottles, shells, and bits of
brightly coloured glass. The ugliness of the houses
in many instances was hidden in summer-time by
vines and rambler roses that covered the porches and
sometimes the fronts of the houses.

Around these houses, in the streets, everywhere,
there played a seemingly innumerable horde of
black and brown and yellow children, noisy, quarrelsome, clad usually in one-piece dresses of the same
indeterminate shade of grey or red or brown that was
seen on the country children on Saturday. In front
of many of the houses, there sat on sunny days an
old and bent man or ancient woman puffing the omnipresent corn-cob pipe. . . .

A half-mile westward from "Darktown," and separated from it by the Central of Georgia Railroad
tracks, stood the Central City Cotton Spinning-Mill.
Clustered around its ugly red-brick walls stood dwellings that differed but little from those of "Darktown."
Here were the same dingy, small, unsanitary, un-
beautiful, and unpainted dwellings. Here were the
same muddy or dusty unpaved streets. Here were
the same squalor and poverty and filth and abject
ignorance. There were but few superficial or recog-
nizable differences. One was that the children wore,
instead of the brown plumpness of the Negro children, a pale, emaciated, consumptive air because of
the long hours in the lint-laden confines of the mills.
The men were long, stooped, cadaverous-appearing.
The women were sallow, unattractive, sad-looking,

each usually with the end of a snuff-stick protruding from her mouth. The children, when they played at all, did so in listless, wearied, uninterested, and apathetic fashion. The houses looked even more gaunt and bare than those in the quarter which housed the poorer Negroes, for the tiny patches of ground that fronted the houses here in "Factoryville" were but seldom planted with flowers. More often it was trampled down until it became a hard, red-clay, sun-baked expanse on which the children, and dogs as emaciated and forlorn, sometimes played.

Here there was but one strong conviction, but one firm rock of faith to which they clung—the inherent and carefully nurtured hatred of "niggers" and a belief in their own infinite superiority over their dark-skinned neighbours. Their gods were Tom Watson and Hoke Smith and Tom Hardwick and other demagogic politicians and office-seekers who came to them every two or four years and harangued them on the necessity of their upholding white civilization by re-electing them to office. But one appeal was needed—but one was used—and that one always successfully. Meanwhile, their children left school and entered the mill to work the few years that such a life gave them. And, in the meantime, the black children they hated so—deprived by prejudice from working in the mills, and pushed forward by often illiterate but always ambitious black parents—went to school. . . .

This, in brief, was the Central City to which Kenneth had returned. A typical Southern town—reasonably rich as wealth is measured in that part of Georgia—rich in money and lands and cotton—amazingly ignorant in the finer things of life. Noisy, unreflective, their wants but few and those easily satisfied. The men, self-made, with all that that distinctly American term implies. The women concerned only with their petty household affairs and more petty gossip and social intercourse. But, beyond these, life was and is a closed book. Or, more, a book that never was written or printed.

The companionship and inspiration of books was unknown. Music, even with the omnipresent Victrola, meant only the latest bit of cheap jazz or a Yiddish or Negro dialect song. Art, in its many forms was considered solely for decadent, effete "furriners." Hostility would have met the woman of the town's upper class who attempted to exhibit any knowledge of art. Her friends would have felt that she was trying "to put something over on them." As for any man of the town, at best he would have been considered a "little queer in the head," at the worst suspected of moral turpitude or perversion.

But two releases from the commonplace, monotonous life were left. The first, liquor. Bootlegging throve. The woods around Central City were infested with "moonshine" stills that seldom were still. The initiated drove out to certain lonely spots, deposited under well-known trees a jug or other container with a banknote stuck in its mouth. One then gave a certain whistle and walked away. Soon there would come an answering signal. One went back to the tree and found the money gone but the container filled with a colourless or pale-yellow liquid. . . . Or, the more affluent had it brought to them in town hidden under wagon-loads of fodder or cotton.

The other and even more popular outlet of un-fulfilled and suppressed emotions was sex. Central City boasted it had no red-light district like Macon and Savannah and Atlanta. That was true. All over the town were protected domiciles housing slatternly women. To them went by circuitous routes the merchants whose stores were on Lee Street. To them went the gangs from the turpentine camps on their periodic pilgrimages to town on pay-day. And a traveller on any of the roads leading from the town could see, on warm evenings, automobiles standing with engines stilled and lights dimmed on the side of the road. Down on Harris and Butler Streets in "Darktown" were other houses. Here were coloured women who seemed never to have to work. Here was seldom seen a coloured man. And the children around these houses were usually lighter in colour than in other parts of "Darktown."

Negro fathers and mothers of comely daughters never allowed them to go out unaccompanied after dark. There were too many dangers from men of their own race. And even greater ones from men of the other race. There had been too many disastrous consequences from relaxation of vigil by certain bowed and heart-broken coloured parents. And they had no redress at law. The laws of the State against intermarriage saw to it that there should be none.

Central City inhabitants knew all these things. But familiarity with them had bred the belief that they did not exist—that is, they were thought a natural part of the town's armament against scandal. One soon grew used to them—and forgot them. The town was no worse than any other—far better than most.

It was a rude shock to Kenneth when he began to see these things through an entirely different pair of eyes than those with which he had viewed them before he left Central City for the North. The sordidness, the blatant vulgarity, the viciousness of it all —especially the houses on Butler and Harris Streets —appalled and sickened him. Even more was he disgusted by the complacent acceptance of the whole miserable business by white and black alike. On two or three occasions he tentatively mentioned it to a few of those he had known intimately years before. Some of them laughed indulgently—others cautioned him to leave it alone. Finding no response, he shrugged his shoulders and dismissed the whole affair from his mind. "It was here long before I was born," he said to himself philosophically, "it'll probably be here long after I'm dead, and the best thing for me to do is to stick to my own business and let other people's morals alone."

CHAPTER III

ENNETH came into contact with few others than his own people during the first month after his return to Central City. The first two weeks had been spent in getting his offices arranged with the innumerable details of carpentering, plastering, painting, and disposition of the equipment he had ordered in New York during the days he had spent there on his return from France.

During the early months of 1917, when through every available means propaganda was being used to whip into being America's war spirit, one of the most powerful arguments heard was that of the beneficial effect army life would have on the men who entered the service. Newspapers and magazines were filled with it, orators in church and theatre and hall shouted it, every signboard thrust it into the faces of Americans. Alluring pictures were painted of the growth, physical and mental, that would certainly follow enlistment "to make the world safe for democracy."

To some of those who fought, such a change probably did come, but the mental outlook of most of them was changed but little. The war was too big a thing, too terrible and too searing a catastrophe, to be adequately comprehended by the farmer boys, the clerks, and the boys fresh from school who chiefly made up the fighting forces. Their lives had been too largely confined to the narrow ways to enable them to realize the immensity of the event into which they had been so suddenly plunged. Their most vivid memories were of "that damned second loot" or of *beaucoup vin blanc* or, most frequently, of all-too-brief adventures with the *mademoiselles*. With the end of the war and demobilization had come the short periods of hero-worship and then the sudden forgetfulness of those for whom they had fought. The old narrow life began again with but occasional revolts against the monotony of it all, against the blasting of the high hopes held when the war was being fought. Even these spasmodic revolts eventually petered out in vague mutterings among men like themselves who let their inward dissatisfaction dissipate in thin air.

More deep-rooted was this revolt among Negro ex-service men. Many of them entered the army, not so much because they were fired with the desire to fight for an abstract thing like world democracy, but, because they were of a race oppressed, they entertained very definite beliefs that service in France would mean a more decent regime in America, when the war was over, for themselves and all others who were classed as Negroes. Many of them, consciously or subconsciously, had a spirit which might have been expressed like this: "Yes, we'll fight for democracy in France, but when that's over with we're going to expect and we're going to get some of that same democracy for ourselves right here in America." It was because of this spirit and determination that they submitted to the rigid army discipline to which was often added all the contumely that race prejudice could heap upon them.

Kenneth was of that class which thought of these things in a more detached, more abstract, more subconscious manner. During the days when, stationed close to the line, he treated black men brought to the base hospital with arms and legs torn away by exploding shells, with bodies torn and mangled by shrapnel, or with flesh seared by mustard gas, he had inwardly cursed the so-called civilization which not only permitted but made such carnage necessary. But when the nightmare had ended, he rapidly forgot the nausea he had felt, and plunged again into his beloved work. More easily than he would have thought possible, he forgot the months of discomfort and weariness and bloodshed. It came back to him only in fitful memories as of some particularly horrible dream.

To Kenneth, when work grew wearisome or when memories would not down, there came relaxation in literature, an opiate for which he would never cease being grateful to Professor Fuller, his old teacher at Atlanta. It was "Pop" Fuller who, with his benign and paternal manner, his adoration of the best of the world's literature, had sown in Kenneth the seed of that same love. He read and reread *Jean Christophe*, finding in the adventures and particularly in the mental processes of Rolland's hero many of his own reactions towards life. He had read the plays of Bernard Shaw, garnering here and there a morsel of truth though much of Shaw eluded him. Theodore Dreiser's gloominess and sex-obsession he liked though it often repelled him; he admired the man for his honesty and disliked his pessimism or what seemed to him a dolorous outlook on life. He loved the colourful romances of Hergesheimer, considering them of little enduring value but nevertheless admiring his descriptions of affluent life, enjoying it vicariously. Willa Cather's *My Antonia* he delighted in because of its simplicity and power and beauty.

The works of D. H. Lawrence, Kenneth read with conflicting emotions. Mystical, turgid, tortuous phrases, and meaning not always clear. Yet he revelled in Lawrence's clear insight into the bends and backwaters and perplexing twistings of the stream of life. Kenneth liked best of all foreign writers Knut Hamsun. He had read many times *Hunger*, *Growth of the Soil*, and other novels of the Norwegian writer. He at times was annoyed by their lack of plot, but more often he enjoyed them because they had none, reflecting that life itself is never a smoothly turned and finished work of art, its causes and effects, its tears and joys, its loves and hates neatly dovetailing one into another as writers of fiction would have it.

So too did he satisfy his love for the sea in the novels of Conrad—the love so many have who are born and grow to manhood far from the sea. Ken-

neth loved it with an abiding and passionate love—
loved, yet feared it for its relentless power and sav-
agery—a love such as a man would have for an alluring, yet tempestuous mistress of fiery and uncer-
tain temper. In Conrad's romances he lived by
proxy the life he would have liked had not fear of
the water and the circumstances of his life prevented
it. Flaubert, Zola, Maupassant he read and reread,
finding in the struggles of *Emma Bovary* and
Nana and other heroines and heroes of the French
realists mental counterparts of some of the coloured
men and women of his acquaintance in their struggles against the restrictions of stupid and crass and
ignorant surroundings. The very dissimilarities of
environment and circumstance between his own acquaintances and the characters in the novels he read,
seemed to emphasize the narrowness of his own life
in the South. So does a bedridden invalid read with
keen delight the adventurous and rococo romances of
Zane Grey or Jack London.

But perhaps most of all he admired the writing of
Du Bois—the fiery, burning philippics of one of his
own race against the proscriptions of race prejudice.
He read them with a curious sort of detachment—
as being something which touched him in a more or
less remote way but not as a factor in forming his
own opinions as a Negro in a land where democracy
often stopped dead at the colour line.

It was in this that Kenneth's attitude towards life
was most clearly shown. His was the more philosophic viewpoint on the race question, that problem so

close to him. The proscriptions which he and others of his race were forced to endure were inconvenient, yet they were apparently a part of life, one of its annoyances, a thing which had always been and probably would be for all time to come. Therefore, he reasoned, why bother with it any more than one was forced to by sheer necessity? Better it was for him if he attended to his own individual problems, solved them to the best of his ability and as circumstances would permit, and left to those who chose to do it the agitation for the betterment of things in general. If he solved his problems and every other Negro did the same, he often thought, then the thing we call the race problem will be solved. Besides, he reasoned, the whole thing is too big for one man to tackle it, and if he does attack it, more than likely he will go down to defeat in the attempt. And what would be gained? . . .

His office completed, Kenneth began the making of those contacts he needed to secure the patients he knew were coming. In this his mother and Mamie were of invaluable assistance. Everybody knew the Harpers. It was a simple matter for Kenneth to renew acquaintances broken when he had left for school in the North. He joined local lodges of the Grand United Order of Heavenly Reapers and the Exalted Knights of Damon. The affected mysteriousness of his initiation into these fraternal orders, the secret grip, the passwords, the elaborately worded rituals, all of which the other members took so seriously, amused him, but he went through it all with an outwardly solemn demeanour. He knew it was good business to affiliate himself with these often absurd societies which played so large a part in the lives of these simple and illiterate coloured folk. Along with the strenuous emotionalism of their religion, it served as an outlet for their naturally deep feelings.

In spite of the renewal of acquaintances, the careful campaign of winning confidence in his ability as a physician, Kenneth found that the flood of patients did not come as he had hoped. The coloured people of Central City had had impressed upon them by three hundred years of slavery and that which was called freedom after the Emancipation Proclamation was signed, that no Negro doctor, however talented, was quite as good as a white one. This slave mentality, Kenneth now realized, inbred upon generation after generation of coloured folk, is the greatest handicap from which the Negro suffers, destroying as it does that confidence in his own ability which would enable him to meet without fear or apology the test of modern competition.

Kenneth's youthful appearance, too, militated against him. Though twenty-nine years old, he looked not more than a mere twenty-four or twenty-five. "He may know his stuff and be as smart as all outdoors," ran the usual verdict, "but I don't want no boy treating me when I'm sick."

Perhaps the greatest factor contributing to the coloured folks' lack of confidence in physicians of their own race was the inefficiency of Dr. Williams, the only coloured doctor in Central City prior to

[48]

Kenneth's return. Dr. Williams belonged to the old school and moved on the theory that when he graduated some eighteen years before from a medical school in Alabama, the development of medical knowledge had stopped. He fondly pictured himself as being the most prominent personage of Central City's Negro colony, was pompous, bulbous-eyed, and exceedingly fond of long words, especially of Latin derivation. He made it a rule of his life never to use a word of one syllable if one of two or more would serve as well. Active in fraternal order circles (he was a member of nine lodges), class-leader in Central City's largest Methodist church, arbiter supreme of local affairs in general, he filled the rôle with what he imagined was unsurpassable éclat. His idea of complimenting a hostess was ostentatiously to loosen his belt along about the middle of dinner. Once he had been introduced as the "black William Jennings Bryan," believed it thereafter, and thought it praise of a high order.

He was one of those who say on every possible occasion: "I am kept so terribly busy I never have a minute to myself." Like nine out of ten who say it, Dr. Williams always repeated this stock phrase of those who flatter themselves in this fashion—so necessary to those of small minds who would be thought great—not because it was true, but to enhance his pre-eminence in the eyes of his hearers—and in his own eyes as well.

He always wore coats which resembled morning coats, known in local parlance as "Jim-swingers."

He kept his hair straightened, wore it brushed straight back from his forehead like highly polished steel wires, and, with pomades and hair oils liberally applied, it glistened like the patent leather shoes which adorned his ample feet.

His stout form filled the Ford in which he made his professional calls, and it was a sight worth seeing as he majestically rolled through the streets of the town bowing graciously and calling out loud greetings to the acquaintances he espied by the way. Always his bows to white people were twice as low and obsequious as to those of darker skin. Until Kenneth returned, Dr. Williams had had his own way in Central City. Through his fraternal and church connections and lack of competition, he had made a little money, much of it through his position as medical examiner for the lodges to which he belonged. As long as he treated minor ailments—cuts, colic, childbirths, and the like—he had little trouble. But when more serious maladies attacked them, the coloured population sent for the old white physician, Dr. Bennett, instead of for Dr. Williams.

The great amount of time at his disposal irritated Kenneth. He was like a spirited horse, champing at the bit, eager to be off. The patronizing air of his people nettled him—caused him to reflect somewhat bitterly that "a prophet is not without honour save in his own country." And when one has not the gift of prophecy to foretell, or of clairvoyance to see, what the future holds in the way of success, one is not likely to develop a philosophic calm which enables him to await the coming of long-desired results.

He was seated one day in his office reading when his mother entered. Closing his book, he asked the reason for her frown.

"You remember Mrs. Bradley—Mrs. Emma Bradley down on Ashley Street—don't you, Kenneth?" Without waiting for a reply, Mrs. Harper went on: "Well, she's mighty sick. Jim Bradley has had Dr. Bennett in to see what's the matter with her but he don't seem to do her much good."

Kenneth remembered Mrs. Bradley well indeed. The most talkative woman in Central City. It was she who had come to his mother with a long face and dolorous manner when he as a youngster had misbehaved in church. He had learned instinctively to connect Mrs. Bradley's visits with excursions to the little back room accompanied by his mother and a switch cut from the peach-tree in the back yard— a sort of natural cause and effect. Visions of those days rose in his mind and he imagined he could feel the sting of those switches on his legs now.

"What seems to be the trouble with her?" he asked.

"It's some sort of stomach-trouble—she's got an awful pain in her side. She says it can't be her appendix because she had that removed up to Atlanta when she was operated on there for a tumour nearly four years ago. Dr. Bennett gave her some medicine but it doesn't help here any. Won't you run down there to see her?"

"I can't, mamma, until I am called in professionally. Dr. Bennett won't like it. It isn't ethical.

Besides, didn't Mrs. Bradley say when I came back that she didn't want any coloured doctor fooling with her?"

"Yes, she did, but you mustn't mind that. Just run in to see her as a social call."

Kenneth rose and instinctively took up his bag. Remembering, he put it down, put on his hat, kissed his mother, and walked down to Mrs. Bradley's. Outside the gate stood Dr. Bennett's mud-splashed buggy, sagging on one side through years of service in carrying its owner's great bulk. Between the shafts stood the old bay horse, its head hung dejectedly as though asleep, which Central City always connected with its driver.

Entering the gate held by one hinge, Kenneth made his way to the little three-room unpainted house which served as home for the Bradleys and their six children. On knocking, the door was opened by Dr. Bennett, who apparently was just leaving. He stood there, his hat on, stained by many storms, its black felt turning a greenish brown through years of service and countless rides through the red dust of the roads leading out of Central City. Dr. Bennett himself was large and flabby. His clothes hung on him in haphazard fashion and looked as though they had never been subjected to the indignity of a tailor's iron. A Sherlock Holmes, or even one less gifted, could read on his vest with little difficulty those things which its wearer had eaten for many meals past. Dr. Bennett's face was red through exposure to many suns, and covered with the bristle of a three days' growth of beard. Small eyes set close together, they belied a bluff good humour which Dr. Bennett could easily assume when there was occasion for it. The corners of the mouth were stained a deep brown where tobacco juice had run down the folds of the flesh.

Behind him stood Jim Bradley with worried face, his ashy black skin showing the effects of remaining all night by the bedside of his wife.

Dr. Bennett looked at Kenneth inquiringly.

"Don't you remember me, Dr. Bennett? I'm Kenneth Harper."

"Bless my soul, so it is. How're you, Ken? Le's see—it's been nigh on to eight years since you went No'th, ain't it? Heard you was back in town. Hear you goin' to practise here. Come 'round to see me some time. Right glad you're here. I'll be kinder glad to get somebody t' help me treat these niggers for colic or when they get carved up in a crap game. Hope you ain't got none of them No'then ideas 'bout social equality while you was up there. Jus' do like your daddy did, and you'll get along all right down here. These niggers who went over to France and ran around with them Frenchwomen been causin' a lot of trouble 'round here, kickin' up a rumpus, and talkin' 'bout votin' and ridin' in the same car with white folks. But don't you let them get you mixed up in it, 'cause there'll be trouble sho's you born if they don't shut up and git to work. Jus' do like your daddy did, and you'll do a lot to keep the white folks' friendship."

Dr. Bennett poured forth all this gratuitous advice between asthmatic wheezes without waiting for Kenneth to reply. He then turned to Jim Bradley with a parting word of advice.

"Jim, keep that hot iron on Emma's stomach and give her those pills every hour. 'Tain't nothin' but the belly-ache. She'll be all right in an hour or two."

Turning without another word, he half ambled, half shuffled out to his buggy, pulled himself up into it with more puffing and wheezing, and drove away.

Jim Bradley took Kenneth's arm and led him back on to the little porch, closing the door behind him.

"I'm pow'ful glad t' see you, Ken. My, but you done growed sence you went up No'th! Befo' you go in dar, I want t' tell you somethin'. Emma's been right po'ly fuh two days. Her stomach's swelled up right sma't and she's been hollering all night. Dis mawning she don't seem jus' right in de haid. I tol' her I was gwine to ast you to come see her, but she said she didn't want no young nigger doctah botherin' with her. But don't you min' her. I wants you to tell me what to do."

Kenneth smiled.

"I'll do what I can for her, Jim. But what about Dr. Bennett?"

"Dat's a' right. He give her some med'cine but it ain't done her no good. She's too good a woman fuh me to lose her, even if she do talk a li'l' too much. You make out like you jus' drap in to pass the time o' day with her."

Kenneth entered the dark and ill-smelling room. Opposite the door a fire smouldered in the fire-place, giving fitful spurts of flame that illumined the room and then died down again. There was no grate, the pieces of wood resting on crude andirons, blackened by the smoke of many fires. Over the mantel there hung a cheap charcoal reproduction of Jim and Emma in their wedding-clothes, made by some local "artist" from an old photograph. One or two nondescript chairs worn shiny through years of use stood before the fire. In one corner stood a dresser on which were various bottles of medicine and of "Madame Walker's Hair Grower." On the floor a rug, worn through in spots and patched with fragments of other rugs all apparently of different colours, covered the space in front of the bed. The rest of the floor was bare and showed evidences of a recent vigorous scrubbing. The one window was closed tightly and covered over with a cracked shade, long since divorced from its roller, tacked to the upper ledge of the window.

On the bed Mrs. Bradley was rolling and tossing in great pain. Her eyes opened slightly when Kenneth approached the bed and closed again immediately as a new spasm of pain passed through her body. She moaned piteously and held her hands on her side, pressing down hard one hand over the other.

At a sign from Jim, Kenneth started to take her pulse.

"Go way from here and leave me 'lone! Oh,

Lawdy, why is I suff'rin' this way? I jus' wish I was daid! Oh—oh—oh!"

This last as she writhed in agony. Kenneth drew back the covers, examined Mrs. Bradley's abdomen, took her pulse. Every sign pointed to an attack of acute appendicitis. He informed Jim of his diagnosis.

"But, Doc, it ain't dat trouble, 'cause Emma says dat was taken out a long time ago."

"I can't help what she says. She's got appendicitis. You go get Dr. Bennett and tell him your wife has got to be operated on right away or she is going to die. Get a move on you now! If it was my case, I would operate within an hour. Stop by my house and tell Bob to bring me an ice bag as quick as he can."

Jim hurried away to catch Dr. Bennett. Kenneth meanwhile did what he could to relieve Mrs. Bradley's suffering. In a few minutes Bob came with the ice bag. Then Jim returned with his face even more doleful than it had been when Kenneth had told him how sick his wife was.

"Doc Bennett says he don't care what you do. He got kinder mad when I told him you said it was 'pendicitis, and tol' me dat if I couldn't take his word, he wouldn't have anything mo' to do with Emma. He seemed kinder mad 'cause you said it was mo' than a stomach-ache. Said he wa'n't goin' to let no young nigger doctor tell him his bus'ness. So, Doc, you'll have t' do what you thinks bes'."

"All right, I'll do it. First thing, I'm going to

move your wife over to my office. We can put her up in the spare room. Bob will drive her over in the car. Get something around her and you'd better come on over with her. I'll get Dr. Williams to help me."

Kenneth was jubilant at securing his first surgical case since his return to Central City, though his pleasure was tinged with doubt as to the ethics of the manner in which it had come to him. He did not let that worry him very long, however, but began his preparations for the operation.

First he telephoned to Mrs. Johnson, who, before she married and settled down in Central City, had been a trained nurse at a coloured hospital at Atlanta. She hurried over at once. Neat, quiet, and efficient, she took charge immediately of preparations, sterilizing the array of shiny instruments, preparing wads of absorbent cotton, arranging bandages and catgut and hæmostatics.

Kenneth left all this to Mrs. Johnson, for he knew in her hands it would be well done. He telephoned to Dr. Williams to ask that he give the anæsthesia. In his excitement Kenneth neglected to put in his voice the note of asking a great and unusual favour of Dr. Williams. That eminent physician, eminent in his own eyes, cleared his throat several times before replying, while Kenneth waited at the other end of the line. He realized his absolute dependence on Dr. Williams, for he knew no white doctor would assist a Negro surgeon or even operate with a coloured assistant. There was none other in Central

City who could give the ether to Mrs. Bradley. It made him furious that Dr. Williams should hesitate so long. At the same time, he knew he must restrain the hot and burning words that he would have used. The pompous one hinted of the pressure of his own work—work that would keep him busy all day. Into his words he injected the note of affront at being asked—he, *the* coloured physician of Central City—to assist a younger man. Especially on that man's first case. Kenneth swallowed his anger and pride, and pleaded with Dr. Williams at least to come over. Finally, the older physician agreed in a condescending manner to do so.

Hurrying back to his office, Kenneth found Mrs. Bradley arranged on the table ready for the operation. Examining her, he found she was in delirium, her eyes glazed, her abdomen hard and distended, and she had a temperature of 105 degrees. He hastily sterilized his hands and put on his gown and cap. As he finished his preparations, Dr. Williams in leisurely manner strolled into the room with a benevolent and patronizing "Howdy, Kenneth, my boy. I won't be able to help you out after all. I've got to see some patients of my own."

He emphasized "my own," for he had heard of the manner by which Kenneth had obtained the case of Mrs. Bradley. Kenneth, pale with anger, excited over his first real case in Central City, stared at Dr. Williams in amazement at his words.

"But, Dr. Williams, you can't do that! Mrs. Bradley here is dying!"

The older doctor looked around patronizingly at the circle of anxious faces. Jim Bradley, his face lined and seamed with toil, the lines deepened in distress at the agony of his wife and the imminence of losing her, gazed at him with dumb pleading in his eyes, pleading without spoken words with the look of an old, faithful dog beseeching its master. Bob looked with a malevolent glare at his pompous sleekness, as though he would like to spring upon him. Mrs. Johnson plainly showed her contempt of such callousness on the part of one who bore the title, however poorly, of physician. In Kenneth's eyes was a commingling of eagerness and rage and bitterness and anxiety. On Emma Bradley's face there was nothing but the pain and agony of her delirious ravings. Dr. Williams seemed to enjoy thoroughly his little moment of triumph. He delayed speaking in order that it might be prolonged as much as possible. The silence was broken by Jim Bradley.

"Doc, won't you please he'p?" he pleaded. "She's all I got!"

Kenneth could remain silent no longer. He longed to punch that fat face and erase from it the supercilious smirk that adorned it.

"Dr. Williams," he began with cold hatred in his voice, "either you are going to give this anæsthesia or else I'm going to go into every church in Central City and tell exactly what you've done here today."

Dr. Williams turned angrily on Kenneth.

"Young man, I don't allow anybody to talk to me

like that—least of all, a young whippersnapper just
out of school . . ." he shouted.

By this time Kenneth's patience was at an end.
He seized the lapels of the other doctor's coat in
one hand and thrust his clenched fist under the nose
of the now thoroughly alarmed Dr. Williams.

"Are you going to help—or aren't you?" he demanded.

The situation was becoming too uncomfortable for
the older man. He could stand Kenneth's opposition but not the ridicule which would inevitably follow the spreading of the news that he had been beaten
up and made ridiculous by Kenneth. He swallowed
—a look of indecision passed over his face as he
visibly wondered if Kenneth really dared hit him—
followed by a look of fear as Kenneth drew back
his fist as though to strike. Discretion seemed the
better course to pursue—he could wait until a later
and more propitious date for his revenge—he agreed
to help. A look of relief came over Jim Bradley's
face. A grin covered Bob's as he saw his brother
showing at last some signs of fighting spirit. Without further words Kenneth prepared to operate. . . .

The patient under the ether, Kenneth with sure,
deft strokes made an incision and rapidly removed
the appendix. Ten—twelve—fifteen minutes, and
the work was done. He found Mrs. Bradley's peri-
toneum badly inflamed, the appendix swollen and
about to burst. A few hours' delay and it would
have been too late. . . .

The next morning Mrs. Bradley's temperature had

gone down to normal. Two weeks later she was
sufficiently recovered to be removed to her home.
Three weeks later she was on her feet again. Then
Kenneth for the first time in his life had no fault to
find with the vigour with which Mrs. Bradley could
use her tongue. Glorying as only such a woman
can in her temporary fame at escape from death by
so narrow a margin, she went up and down the streets
of the town telling how Kenneth had saved her life.
With each telling of the story it took on more embel-
lishments until eventually the simple operation
ranked in importance in her mind with the first
sewing-up of the human heart.

Kenneth found his practice growing. His days
were filled with his work. One man viewed his
growing practice with bitterness. It was Dr. Williams, resentful of the small figure he had cut in
the episode in Kenneth's office, which had become
known all over Central City. Of a petty and vindictive nature, he bided his time until he could force
atonement from the upstart who had so presumptu-
ously insulted and belittled him, the Beau Brummel,
the leading physician, the prominent coloured citizen. But Kenneth, if he knew of the hatred in the
man's heart, was supremely oblivious of it.

The morning after his operation on Mrs. Bradley,
he added another to the list of those who did not wish
him well. He had taken the bottle of alcohol containing Mrs. Bradley's appendix to Dr. Bennett to
show that worthy that he had been right, after all, in
his diagnosis. He found him seated in his office.

Dr. Bennett, with little apparent interest, glanced at the bottle.

"Humph!" he ejaculated, aiming at the cuspidor and letting fly a thin stream of tobacco juice which accurately met its mark. "You never can tell what's wrong with a nigger anyhow. They ain't got nacheral diseases like white folks. A hoss doctor can treat 'em better'n one that treats humans. I always said that a nigger's more animal than human. . . ."

Kenneth had been eager to discuss the case of Mrs. Bradley with his fellow practitioner. He had not even been asked to sit down by Dr. Bennett. He realized for the first time that in spite of the superiority of his medical training to that of Dr. Bennett's, the latter did not recognize him as a qualified physician, but only as a "nigger doctor." Making some excuse, he left the house. Dr. Bennett turned back to the local paper he had been reading when Kenneth entered, took a fresh chew of tobacco from the plug in his hip pocket, grunted, and remarked: "A damned nigger telling me *I* don't know medicine!"

CHAPTER IV

Two months passed by. Kenneth had begun to secure more patients than he could very well handle. Already he was kept busier than Dr. Williams though there was enough practice for both of them. Kenneth soon began to tire of treating minor ailments and longed to reach the time when he could give up his general practice and devote his time to surgery. Except for the delivery of the babies that came with amazing rapidity in the community, he did little else than treat colic, minor cuts, children's diseases, with an occasional case of tuberculosis. More frequently he treated for venereal diseases, though this latter was even more distasteful to him than general practice while at the same time more remunerative.

A new source of practice and revenue began gradually to grow. The main entrance to his office was on Lee Street. This door was some fifty feet back from Lee Street, and the overhanging branches of the elms cut off completely the light from the street lamp at the corner. One night, as he sat reading in his office, there came a knock at his door. Opening it, he found standing there Roy Ewing. Ewing had inherited the general merchandise store bearing his name from his father, was a deacon in the largest

Baptist Church in Central City, was president of the
Central City Chamber of Commerce, and was regarded as a leading citizen.

Kenneth gazed at his caller in some surprise.

"Hello, Ken. Anybody around?"

On being assured that he was alone, Ewing entered, brushing by Kenneth to get out of the glare of
the light. Kenneth followed him into the office,
meanwhile asking his caller what he could do for
him.

"Ken, I've got a little job I want you to do for me.
I'm in a little trouble. Went up to Macon last month
with Bill Jackson, and we had a little fun. I guess
I took too much liquor. We went by a place Bill
knew about where there were some girls. I took a
fancy to a little girl from Atlanta who told me she
had slipped away from home and her folks thought
she was visiting her cousins at Forsyth. Anyhow, I
thought everything was all right, but I'm in a bad
way and I want you to treat me. I can't go to Dr.
Bennett 'cause I don't want him to know about it.
I'll take care of you all right, and if you get me fixed
up I'll pay you well."

Kenneth looked at him in amazement. Roy Ewing, acknowledged leader of the "superior race"!
He knew too much of the ways of the South, however,
to make any comment or let too much of what was
going on in his mind show on his face. He gave the
treatment required. That was Kenneth's introduction to one part of the work of a coloured physician

in the South. Many phases of life that he as a youth
had never known about or, before his larger experience in the North and in France, had passed by him
unnoticed, he now had brought to his attention.
This was one of them. He began to see more clearly
that his was going to be a difficult course to pursue.
He determined anew that as far as possible he would
keep to his own affairs and meddle not at all with the
life about him.

When Ewing had gone, Kenneth returned to his
reading. Hardly had he started again when Bob
came in.

"Can you stop for a few minutes, Ken? I want
to talk with you."

With a look of regret at his book, Kenneth settled
back and prepared to listen.

"What world problem have you got on your mind
now, Bob?"

"Don't start to kidding me, Ken. I don't see how
you can shut your eyes to how coloured people are
being treated here."

"What's wrong? Everything seems to me to be
getting along as well as can be expected."

"That's because you don't go out of the house unless you are hurrying to give somebody a pill or a
dose of medicine. To-day I came by the school to
get Mamie and bring her home. You ought to see
the dump they call a school building. It's a dirty
old building that looks like it'll fall down any time
a hard wind comes along. All that's inside is a

rickety table, and some hard benches with no desks, and when it rains they have to send the children home, as the water stands two or three inches deep on the floor. Outside of Mamie they haven't one teacher who's gone any higher than the sixth or seventh grade—they have to take anybody who is willing to work for the twelve dollars a month they pay coloured teachers."

Bob's face had on it the look of discontent and resentment that was almost growing chronic.

"Well, what can we do about it? I'm afraid you're getting to be a regular Atlas, trying to carry all the burdens of the world on your shoulders. I know things aren't all they ought to be, but you and I can't solve the problems. The race problem will be here long after we're dead and gone."

"Oh, for goodness' sake, shut up that preachy tone of long-suffering patience, will you?—and forget your own little interests for a while. I know you think I'm silly to let these things worry me. But the reason why things are as bad as they are is just because the majority of Negroes are like you—always dodging anything that may make them unpopular with white folks. And that isn't all. There's a gang of white boys that hang around Ewing's Store that meddle with every coloured girl that goes by. I was in the store to-day when Minnie Baxter passed by on her way to the post office, and that dirty little Jim Archer said something that made me boil all over. And it didn't help any to know that if I had said a word to him, there would have been a fight,

[66]

and I would have been beaten half to death if I hadn't been killed."

"Yes, I've seen that, too. What we ought to do is to try and keep these girls off of Lee Street, unless someone is with them. If we weren't living in the South, we might do something. But here we are, and as long as we stay here, we've got to swallow a lot of these things and stay to ourselves."

"But, Ken, it isn't always convenient for someone to go downtown with them. I'll tell you what let's do. Let's get the better class of coloured people together like Reverend Wilson, Mr. Graham, Mr. Adams, and some others, and form a Coloured Protective League here in Central City. We can then take up these cases and see if something can't be done to remedy them."

Bob leaned forward in his eagerness to impress Kenneth with his idea.

"You see, if any one or two of us takes up a case we are marked men. But if there are two or three hundred of us they can't take it out on all of us."

"That's true. But what about the effect on the white people whose actions you want to check? If Negroes start organizing for any purpose whatever, there'll always be folks who'll declare they are planning to start some trouble. No, I don't think we ought to do anything just now. I tell you what I'll do. The next time I see Roy Ewing, I'll speak to him and ask him to stop those fellows from annoying our girls. The fellows can take care of themselves."

Bob rose and shrugged his shoulders and said nothing more. Kenneth after a minute or two returned to his book.

Nothing further was said on the subject for several days. When Mr. Ewing called the following week, Kenneth brought the matter up, and told him what Bob had said about the boys in front of Ewing's store.

"I've seen them doing it, Ken, and I spoke to them only to-day about it. But you know, boys will be boys, and they haven't done any harm to the girls. Their talk is a little rough at times, but as long as it stops there, I don't see why anybody should object."

"But, Mr. Ewing, Bob tells me that they say some pretty raw things. Suppose one of them said the same things to Mrs. Ewing, how would you feel then?"

Ewing flushed.

"That's different. Mrs. Ewing is a white woman."

"But can't you see that we feel towards our women just as you do towards yours? If one of those fellows ever spoke to my sister, there'd be trouble, and the Lord knows I want to get along with all the people here, if I can. If this thing called democracy that I helped fight for is worth anything at all, it ought to mean that we coloured people should be protected like anybody else."

Mr. Ewing looked at Kenneth sharply.

"I know that things aren't altogether as they ought to be. It's pretty tough on fellows like you, Ken, who have had an education. While you were away, a bunch of these mill hands 'cross the tracks got Jerry Bird, a nigger that'd been working for me nearly five years. He came here from down the country some place after you left for up North. Jerry was as steady a fellow as I've ever seen—as honest as the day was long. I trusted Jerry anywhere, lots quicker than I would've some of these white people 'round here. He had a black skin but his heart was white. One night Jerry was over to my house helping Mrs. Ewing until nearly ten o'clock. On his way home this bunch of roughnecks from "Factoryville" stopped him while they were looking for a nigger that'd scared a white girl. When Jerry got scared and started to run, they took out after him and strung him up to a tree. And he wasn't any more guilty of touching that white girl than you or me."

"What did you do about it?" asked Bob.

"Nothing. Suppose I had kicked up a ruckus about it. They found out afterwards that the girl hadn't been bothered at all. But just suppose I had gone and cussed out the fellows who did the lynching. Most of them trade at my store. Or if they don't, a lot of their friends do. They'd have taken their trade to some other store and I'd 'a' gained nothing for my trouble."

"But surely you don't believe that lynching ever helps, do you?"

"Yes and no. Lynching never bothers folks like you. Why, your daddy was one of the most respected folks in this town. But lynching does keep some of these young nigger bucks in check."

"Does it? It seems to me that there isn't much less so-called rape around here or anywhere else in the South, even after forty years of lynching. Mr. Ewing, why don't you and the other decent white people here come out against lynching?"

"Who? Me? Never!" Ewing looked his amazement at the suggestion. "Why, it would ruin my business, my wife would begin to be dropped by all the other folks of the town, and it wouldn't be long before they'd begin calling me a 'nigger-lover.' No, sir-ee! I'll just let things rock along and let well enough alone."

"Mr. Ewing, if fifty men like you in this town banded together and came out flat-footedly against lynching, there are lots more who would join you gladly."

"That may be true," Ewing answered doubtfully. "But then again it mightn't. Let's see who might be some of the fifty. There's George Baird, he's president of the Bank of Central City, and Fred Griswold, president of the Smith County Farmers' Bank. You can count them out because they'd be afraid of losing their depositors. Then there's Ralph Minor who owns the Bon Ton Store. He's out for the same reason that I am. Then there's Nat Phelps, who runs the Central City *Dispatch*. He has a hard enough time as it is. If he lost a couple of hundred subscribers, he'd have to close up shop. And so it goes."

"What about the preachers? It doesn't seem much of a religion they're preaching if the commandment, 'Thou shalt not kill,' doesn't form part of their creed."

"Oh, you needn't look for nothing much from them. Three years ago old Reverend Adams down to the First Methodist took it into his head he was going to tackle something easy—nothing like the race problem. He started in to wipe out the bootleggers 'round here, thinking he could get a lot of support. But he didn't, because most of the folks he figgered on lining up with him were regular customers of the fellows he was after." Ewing chuckled at the memory of the crusade that had died "aborning." "When the next quarterly conference was held, they elected a new pastor for the First Methodist. No, Ken, it ain't so easy as it looks. You're asking me to do something that not a Southern white man has done since the Civil War——"

Rising, he walked towards the door and remarked:

"My advice to you is to stay away from any talk like this with anybody else. There probably ain't another man in town who would've talked to you like this, and if the boys in the Ku Klux Klan knew I had been running along like this with a coloured man, I don't know what'd happen to *me*. See you later. So long!"

Kenneth walked up and down the room with his hands stuffed deep into his pockets, his thoughts rushing through his head in helter-skelter fashion.

He was suddenly conscious of a feeling that he

had been thrust into a tiny boat and forced to em-
bark on a limitless sea, with neither compass nor
chart nor sun nor moon to guide him. Would he
arrive? Or would he go down in some squall which
arose from he knew not where or when? The whole
situation seemed so vast, so sinister, so monstrous,
that he shuddered involuntarily, as he had done as a
child when left alone in a dark room at night. Religion, which had been the guide and stay of his
father in like circumstances, offered him no solace.
He thought with a faint smile of the institution known
as the Church. What was it? A vast money ma-
chine, interested in rallies and pastors' days and
schemes to milk more dollars from its communicants. In preparing people to die. He wasn't interested in what was going to happen to him after
death. What he wanted was some guide and comfort in his present problems. No, religion and the
Church as it was now constituted wasn't the answer.
What was? He could not give it.

"Here I am," he soliloquized, "with the best education money can buy. And yet Roy Ewing, who
hasn't been any further than high school, tells me
I'd better submit to all this without protest. Yet he
stands for the best there is here in Central City, and
I suppose he represents the most liberal thought of
the South. How's it all going to end? Even a rat
will fight when he's cornered, and these coloured people aren't going to stand for these things all the
time. What can I do? God, there isn't anything
—anything I can do? Bob is right! Something

must be done—but what is it? I reckon these white folks must be blind—or else they figure on leaving whatever solution there may be to their children, hoping the storm doesn't break while they are living. No! That isn't it. They think because they've been able to get away with it thus far, they'll always be able to get away with it. Oh, God, I'm helpless! I'm helpless!"

Kenneth had begun to comprehend the delicate position a Negro always occupies in places like Central City—in fact, throughout the South. So little had he come into contact with the perplexities of the race question before he went away to school, he had seen little of the windings and turnings, the tortuous paths the Negro must follow to avoid giving offence to the dominant white sentiment. As he saw each day more and more of the evasions, the repressions, the choking back of natural impulses the Negro practised to avoid trouble, Kenneth often thought of the coloured man as a chip of wood floating on the surface of a choppy sea, tossed this way and that by every wind that blew upon the waters. He must of necessity be constantly on his guard when talking with his white neighbours, or with any white men in the South, to keep from uttering some word, some phrase which, like a seed dropped and forgotten, lies fallow for a time in the brain of the one to whom he talks, but later blossoms forth into that noxious death-dealing plant which is the mob. Innocent enough of guile or malice that word may be, yet he must be careful lest it be distorted and magnified until it can be the cause of violence to himself and his people. Often—very often—it is true that no evil follows. Yet the possibility that it may come must always be considered. But one factor is fixed and immutable—the more intelligent and prosperous the Negro and the more ignorant and poor the white man, the graver the danger, for in the mind of the latter are jealousy and ignorance and stupidity and abject fear of the educated and successful Negro.

His talk with Ewing had crystallized the thoughts, half developed, which his observations since his return had planted in his mind. Kenneth began to see how involved the whole question really was; he was seeing dim paths of expediency and opportunism he would be forced to tread if he expected to reach the goal he had set for himself. Already he found one of his pet ideas to be of doubtful value—the theory he had had that success would give a Negro immunity from persecution. Like a scroll slowly unwinding before his eyes, Kenneth saw, as yet only partially, that instead of freeing him from danger of the mob, too great prosperity would make him and every other Negro outstanding targets of the wrath and envy of the poorer whites—that jealousy which "is cruel as the grave." Oh, well, he reflected, others had avoided trouble and so could he. He would have to be exceedingly careful to avoid too great display, and at the same time cultivate the goodwill of those men like Roy Ewing and Judge Stevenson who would stand by him if there was need.

CHAPTER V

ENNETH was roused by a light tap upon the door. Opening it, Mamie stood on the threshold. Inquiring whether Kenneth had finished his work, and on being told he had, she entered.

"Kenneth, why do you spend all your time here in the office? Don't you think mamma and I want to talk with you occasionally?"

Mamie seated herself on the arm of Kenneth's chair.

"Seems like you're becoming a regular hermit since you've been back. Come on in the parlour—Jane Phillips is in there and she wants to see you. Remember her?"

Kenneth smiled. "Remember Jane Phillips? Of course I do. Scrawny little thing—running all to legs and arms. She was a homely little brat, wasn't she?"

It was now Mamie's turn to smile.

"I'm going to tell her what you said," she threatened. "She's lots different from the girl you remember."

They went into the parlour.

Jane Phillips stood by the piano. She turned as Kenneth and Mamie entered the room, and came towards them, a smile on her face. Kenneth, as he advanced towards her, was frankly amazed at the transformation in the girl whom he had not seen for nine years. Jane laughed.

"Don't you know me, Kenneth? Or must I call you Dr. Harper now?"

"No, my name is still Kenneth——" he answered.

"Tell Jane what you called her a few minutes ago, or I will," interrupted Mamie. Kenneth looked embarrassed. Jane insisted on being told, whereupon Mamie repeated Kenneth's description of Jane as a child.

Caught between the upper and nether millstones of the raillery of the two girls, Kenneth tried to explain away his embarrassment, but they gave him no peace.

"Let me explain," he begged. "When I went away you *were* a scrawny little thing, a regular tomboy and as mischievous as they make them. And now you're a—you're—you're——" Jane laughed at his attempt, somewhat lacking in fullness, to say what she had become with the passage of the years.

"Whatever it is you are trying to say, I hope it's something all right you are calling me—though from your tone I'm not at all sure," she ended, letting a note of mock concern creep in her voice.

By this time Kenneth had somewhat recovered his composure. He entered into the spirit of play himself by telling her his surprise had been due to his finding her *unchanged* from the little girl he had once known, but Jane laughed at his ineffectual efforts to answer Mamie's and her teasing. To change the conversation, he demanded that she tell him all that she had been doing since he saw her last.

"There isn't much to tell," she declared. "I went away soon after you did, going to Fisk University, graduated last June, got a position teaching in North Carolina, and am home for the holidays. Next year I want to have enough money to go to Oberlin and finish my music. That's all there is to my little story. You are the one who has been having all sorts of experiences. I want to hear *your* story."

"Mine isn't much longer," answered Kenneth. "Four years of medical school. A year's interneship in New York at Bellevue. Three months in training-camps. A year and a half in France. Six months at the Sorbonne. Then New York. Then exams at Atlanta for my licence. Home. And here I am."

"Don't you believe him, Jane," said Mamie. "That's just his way of telling it. Ken has had all sorts of exciting experiences, yet he has come home and we can't get him to talk about a thing except building a practice and a hospital."

"What do you want me to talk about?" asked Kenneth.

"Paris—school—army life—what did you see?— how do you like New York?—is New York as good a place to live in as Paris?"

Kenneth threw up his hands in mock defence at the barrage of questions Jane and Mamie fired at him.

[77]

"Just a minute—just a minute," he begged them. "I could talk all night on any one of the questions you've asked and then not finish with it or tell you more than half. If you two will only be quiet, I'll tell you as much as I can."

Mrs. Harper, hearing the voices, came into the room. The three women sat in silence as Kenneth told of his years at school, of his stay in New York, his experiences in the army, of the beauties of Paris even in war time, of study at a French university. He gave to the narrative a vividness and air of reality that made his auditors see through his eyes the scenes and experiences he was describing. Though none of them had been in France, he made them feel as though they too were walking through the Place de la Concorde viewing the statues to the eight great cities of France or shopping in the Rue de la Paix or attempting to order dinner in a restaurant with an all-too-inadequate French vocabulary. He finished.

"Now you've got to sing for me, Jane, as a reward for all the talking I've been doing."

With the usual feminine protests that she had no music with her, Jane went to the open piano. She inquired what he would like to have her sing.

"Anything except the 'Memphis Blues,' which is all I've heard since I came back to Central City," he answered.

Jane ran over the keys experimentally, improvising. A floor lamp stood near the piano casting a soft light over her. Her long, delicately pointed fingers lingered lovingly on the ivory keys, and then she played the opening bars of Saint-Saën's "My Heart at Thy Sweet Voice." Her voice, a rounded, rich contralto, showing considerable training, gave to the song a tender pathos, a yearning, a promise of deep and understanding love. She sang with a grace and clear phrasing that bespoke the simple charm of the singer. Kenneth gazed at her in wonder at the amazing metamorphosis of the shy, gawky child Jane whom he had only rarely noticed, and then with the condescending air of twenty looking at twelve. In her stead had come a woman, rounded, attractive—even beautiful, intelligent, and altogether desirable. The chrysalis had changed to the gorgeously coloured butterfly. Her skin was a soft brown—almost bronze. He thought of velvety pansies richly coloured—of the warmth of rubies of great price—of the lustrous beauty of the sky on a spring evening. Her eyes shone with a sparkling and provocative clearness, looking straight at one from their brown depths. Little tendrils of her black hair at the back of her neck were disturbed every now and then by the breeze from the open windows, while above were piled masses of coiled blackness that shone in the dim light with a glossy lustre. To Kenneth came visions of a soft-eyed *señorita* in an old Spanish town leaning from her balcony while below, to the accompaniment of a muted guitar, her lover sang to her of his ardent love. Kenneth blushed when he realized that in every picture he had cast himself for the rôle of gallant troubadour.

His mother had quietly slipped from the room to

[79]

retire for the evening. Mamie had gone to prepare something cool for them to drink. Kenneth had not heard them go. In fact, lost in the momentary forgetfulness created by Jane and the song, he had completely forgotten them. He did not, however, fail to realize that the dreams he was having were in large measure due to the soft light, to surprise at the great changes in Jane, to the lulling seductiveness of the music. He was sure that his feeling was due in largest measure to a reaction from his unpleasant conversation with Roy Ewing. He vaguely realized that when on the morrow he saw Jane by daylight, she would not seem half so charming and attractive. Yet he was of such a temperament that he could give himself up to the spell of the moment and extract from it all the pleasure in it. It was in that manner he put aside the things which were unpleasant, enabling him to shake off memories like mists of the morning ascending from the depths of a valley.

The song was ended. Herself caught in its spell, Jane swung into that most beautiful of the Negro spirituals, "Deep River." Into it she poured her soul. She filled the room with the pathos of that song born in the dark days of slavery of a people torn from their home and thrust into the thraldom of human bondage.

And then Jane sang "Nobody Knows the Trouble I've Seen." The song ended, her fingers yet clung to the keys but her hands hung listless. Kenneth knew not how or when he had risen from his chair and gone to the piano where he stood behind Jane.

Something deep within them had been touched by the music—a strange thrill filled them, making them oblivious to everything except the presence of each other. Kenneth lightly placed his hands on her shoulders. Without speaking or turning, she placed her hands for a moment on his. He bent over her while she raised her face to his, her eyes misty with tears born of the emotion aroused by the song. Though often laughed at in real life and often distorted in fiction, love almost at first sight had been born within them. Kenneth slowly brought her face nearer his while Jane, with parted lips, let the back of her head rest against his breast. Love, with its strange retroactive effects, brought to both of them in that moment the sudden realization, though neither of them had known it, that they had always loved each other. Not a word had been spoken—each was busy constructing his love in silence. A great emptiness in their lives had been suddenly, miraculously filled.

Their lips were almost touching when a noise brought them to themselves with a shock. It was Mamie. She entered the room bearing a tray on which were sandwiches, cakes, and tall glasses in which cracked ice clinked coolingly. Kenneth hid his annoyance and, with as nonchalant an air as possible, went back to his chair.

When they had eaten, Jane rose to go. Kenneth walked home with her. Neither spoke until they had reached her gate. Jane entered as Kenneth held it open for her. He would have followed her in but she turned, extended her hand to him as a sign of dismissal, and asked him to leave her there. Kenneth said nothing, but his face showed his disappointment at being hastened away by the same girl who less than half an hour before had almost been in his arms.

"Please don't say anything, Ken," she pleaded. "It was my fault—I shouldn't have done what I did. I used to worship you when I was little, but I thought I had gotten over that—until to-night."

Her voice sank almost to a whisper. In it was a note of trouble and perplexity. She went on:

"I—oh, Kenneth—what happened to-night must not be repeated."

Puzzled and a bit hurt, he asked her what she meant.

"Don't get the wrong idea, Ken. I wouldn't do anything to hurt you for the world."

"But what is it, Jane?" begged Kenneth. "I love you, Jane, have always loved you. I was blind— until to-night——"

Kenneth poured forth the words in a torrent of emotion. Whirling thoughts tore through his brain. He sought to seize Jane's hand and draw her to him, but she eluded him.

"No—no—Kenneth, you mustn't. I can't let you make love to me. Let's be friends, Ken, and enjoy these few days and forget all we've said to-night, won't you, please?" she ended pleadingly.

Kenneth said nothing. He turned abruptly and strode away without even saying good night. Hands thrust deep into his pockets, his head hanging in dis-

appointment and wounded pride, he hurried home
without once turning to look back. . . .

Her ten days of vacation passed all too soon for
Jane. She and Kenneth saw each other frequently,
but never alone until the night before she returned
to North Carolina. It was at a dance given in her
honour. All evening he had been seeking a dance
with her, but met with no success until the party was
almost over. They danced in silence. Jane
seemed suddenly sad. All evening she had been
happy, gay, even flirtatious, but now that she was
with Kenneth, her gaiety had been dropped like a
mask. Half-way through the dance they came near
a door that opened on a balcony overlooking a flower
garden. Saying nothing to Jane, Kenneth danced
her through the door and on to the balcony, where
they sat on a bench that stood in the semi-darkness.
Though it was December, the air was warm. No
sound disturbed the silence of the night save the
music and voices which floated through the open
door.

"Haven't you anything to say?" Kenneth anxiously
inquired, taking one of Jane's hands in his.

"Nothing except this—I don't know whether I care
for you or not," said Jane as she freed her hand
and drew herself away. Her voice was firm and determined. Kenneth, ignorant of the ways of a maid
with a man, said nothing, but his shoulders drooped
dejectedly.

"What happened the other night was madness—I
was very foolish for allowing it." She paused, and

then went on. "Kenneth, I don't know—I want my music—I want to see something of life—I want to live! I just can't tie myself down by marrying— I don't know whether I'll ever want to. You'll have to wait—if you care to——"

It was half command, half question. He said nothing.

He did not know how she longed for him to argue with her, override her objections, convince her against her will. She waited a full minute. Still he sat there silent. She rose and re-entered the house, leaving him there alone.

CHAPTER VI

Life moved along evenly with Kenneth, busied with the multitude of duties with which the physician in the half-rural, half-urban towns of the South must deal. His days were filled with his work and he was usually to be found in his office until ten or eleven o'clock every evening. Often he was roused in the middle of the night to attend some one of his patients. He did not mind this except when calls came to him from the outlying country districts. Not infrequently he made long trips of seven, eight, or ten miles into the country to treat some person who might just as well have called him during the previous day. He had purchased a Ford runabout in which he made these trips.

On a Sunday morning soon after his return to Central City, Kenneth with his mother, Mamie, and Bob attended the Mount Zion Baptist Church, but this he did without much eagerness, solely as a duty. Though years had passed since last he entered the church, Kenneth noticed that it stood as it always had, save that it looked more down-at-heel than formerly. Before the door stood the same little groups, eagerly snatching a few words of conversation before entering. Near the door were ranged the young men, garbed in raiment of varied and brilliant hue, ogling the girls as they passed in with their parents. There was much good-natured *badinage* and scuffling among the youths, with an occasional burst of ribald laughter at the momentary discomfiture of one of their number. As he passed them, Kenneth smiled to himself as he remembered how he but a few years since had been one of that crowd around the same door. That is, one of the crowd until his father, with a stern' word or perhaps only a meaningful glance, had been wont to summon him within the church. Often had he been teased unmercifully by the other boys when one of these summonses had come. Though the jests had been hard to bear, the likelihood of paternal wrath had been too unpleasant an alternative for him to dare disregard his father's commands.

Kenneth noticed the vestibule had survived the passage of years without apparent change, if one disregarded the increased dinginess of the carpet. There was the same glass-covered bulletin board with its list of the sick and of those who were delinquent in the payment of their dues. There was the same dangling rope with a loop at the end of it, and the same sexton was about to ring the bell above, announcing the beginning of the morning service. There were the same yellowed walls, the same leather-covered swinging doors with the same greasy spots where countless hands had pushed them to enter the auditorium of the church. Kenneth smiled to himself as he remembered how he once had declared in a dispute with a boy whose parents attended the Methodist church near by that the Mount Zion Baptist Church was "the biggest and finest church in the whole world." He thought of the Notre Dame Cathedral in Paris, of St. Paul's in London, as he recalled the boast of his youth.

Inside, the same air of unchanging permanence seemed also to have ruled. As he followed the officious usher and his mother and sister to their pew, Kenneth noted the same rows of hard seats worn shiny by years of use, the same choir loft to the left of the pulpit with its faded red curtains. The same worn Bible lay open on the pulpit kept open by a hymn-book. Beside it was the same ornately carved silver pitcher and goblet. Kenneth felt as though he had never left Central City when he looked for and found the patches of calcimine hanging from the ceiling and the yellowed marks on the walls made by water dripping from leaks in the roof. As a boy he had amused himself during seemingly interminable sermons by constructing all sorts of fanciful stories around these same marks, seeing in them weirdly shaped animals. Once he had laughed aloud when, after gazing at one of them, it had suddenly dawned upon him that the shadow cast by a pendent flake of calcimine resembled the lean and hungry-looking preacher who was pastoring Mount Zion at the time. Kenneth would never forget the commotion his sudden laughter had caused, nor the whipping he received when he and his father reached home that Sunday.

The hum of conversation ceased. The pastor, the

Reverend Ezekiel Wilson, entered the pulpit from a little door back of it. The choir sang lustily the Doxology. All the familiar services came back to Kenneth as he sat and looked at the dusky faces around him.

Preliminaries ended, the Reverend Wilson began to preach. He was a fat, pompous, oily man—with a smooth and unctuous manner. His voice sank at times to a whisper—at others, roared until the rafters of the building seemed to ring with its echoes. He played on it as consciously as the dried-up little organist in the gaily coloured bonnet did on the keys of the asthmatic little organ. His text was taken from the 13th chapter of First Corinthians, first verse— that familiar text, "Though I speak with the tongues of men and of angels, and have not charity, I am become as sounding brass, or a tinkling cymbal."

Slowly, softly, he began to speak.

"Breddern and sisters, they's a lot of you folks right here this mawnin' what thinks you is Christ'uns. You think jus' 'cause you comes here ev'ry Sunday and sings and shouts and rants around dat you is got the sperit of Jesus in you. Well, I'm tellin' you this mawnin' dat you'd better wake up and get yo'self right with God, 'cause you ain't no mo Christ'un dan if you neveh been to chu'ch a-tall. De Good Book says you got to have char'ty, and de Good Book don't lie."

There came from the Amen corner a fervently shouted "Amen!" From another came as equally

fervid a shout: "Ain't it the truth!" The preacher
paused for effect. He mopped his brow and glared
around the congregation. His auditors sat in ex-
pectant silence. Suddenly he lashed out in scath-
ing arraignment of the sins of his flock. Each and
every one of its faults he pilloried with words of fire
and brimstone. He painted a vivid and uncomfort-
ably realistic picture of a burning Hell into which
all sinners would inevitably be cast. Almost with
the air of a hypnotist, he gradually advanced the
tempo of his speech. Like a wind playing over a
field of corn, swaying the tops of the stalks as it wills,
so did he play on the emotions and fears and passions
of his congregation. Only a master of human psy-
chology could have done it. It was a living, breathing, vengeful God he preached, and his auditors fear-
fully swayed and rocked to and fro as he lashed
them unmercifully. Lips compressed, there came
from them a nasal confirmation of the preacher's
words that ranged from deep, guttural grunts of approval as he scored a point to a high-pitched rising
and falling moan that sounded like nothing so much
as a child blowing through tissue paper stretched
over a comb. Frequently the preacher would without perceptible pause swing into a rolling, swinging, half-moaning song which the congregation took
up with fervour. The beat was steadily advanced
by the leader until he and his audience were worked
up to an emotional ecstasy bordering on hysteria.
His jeremiad ended, the preacher painted a glowing

[89]

picture of the ineffable peace and joy that came to those who rested their faith in Him who died for the remission of their sins.

A tumultuous thunderous climax—a dramatic pause—and then he swung into a fervent prayer in which the preacher talked as though his God were an intimate friend and confidant. The entire drama lasting more than an hour was thrilling and enervating and theatric. Yet beneath it lay a devout sincerity that removed the scene from the absurd to that which bordered on the magnificent. To these humble folk their religion was the most important thing in their lives, and, after all, what matters it what a man does? It is the spirit in which he performs an act that makes it dignified or pathetic or ludicrous —not the act itself.

In spite of his sophistication, Kenneth never was able entirely to ward off the chills of excitement that ran down his spine at these weird religious ceremonies. He saw through the whole theatric performance and yet way down beneath it all there was a sincerity and genuineness that never failed to impress him. This was not a mere animalism nor was it the joke that white people sometimes tried to make of it. Fundamentally, it was rooted and grounded in an immutable and unfailing belief in the supreme power of a tangible God—a God that personally directed the most minute of the affairs of the most lowly of creatures. It had been the guide and refuge of the fathers and mothers of these same people through the dark days of slavery. In the same manner it was almost the only refuge for these children and grandchildren of the slaves in withstanding the trials of a latter-day slavery in many respects more oppressive than the pre-Civil War variety.

Kenneth walked home from church running over these things in his mind. Was this religious fervour the best thing for his people? Why did not the Church attract more intelligent and able young men of his race instead of men like Reverend Wilson? Why didn't some twentieth-century Moses arise to lead them out of the thraldom of this primitive religion? Would that Moses, when he came, be able to offer a solace as effective to enable these people of his to bear the burdens that lay so heavily upon them?

He thought again of his conversation with Roy Ewing. What was the elusive solution to this problem of race in America? Why couldn't the white people of the South see where their course was leading them? Ewing was right. No white man of the South had ever come out in complete defiance of the present regime which was so surely damning the South and America. Kenneth saw his people kept in the bondage of ignorance. Why? Because it was to the economic advantage of the white South to have it so. Why was a man like Reverend Wilson patted on the back and every Negro told that men of his kind were "safe and sane leaders"? Why was every Negro who too audibly or visibly resented the brutalities and proscriptions of race prejudice instantly labelled as a radical—a dangerous character

—as one seeking "social equality"? What was this thing called "social equality" anyhow? That was an easy question to answer. It was about the only one he could answer with any completeness. White folks didn't really believe that Negroes sought to force themselves in places where they weren't wanted, any more than decent white people wanted to force themselves where they were not invited. No, that was the smoke-screen to hide something more sinister. Social equality would lead to intermarriage, they thought, and the legitimatizing of the countless half-coloured sons and daughters of these white people. Why, if every child in the South were a legitimate one, more than half of the land and property in the South would belong to coloured owners.

Did the white people who were always talking about "social equality" think they really were fooling anybody with their constant denunciation of it? Twenty-nine States of America had laws against intermarriage. All these laws were passed by white legislators. Were these laws passed to keep Negroes from seizing some white woman and forcing her to marry him against her will? Or were these laws unconscious admissions by these white men that they didn't trust their women or their men to keep from marrying Negroes? Any fool knew that if two people didn't want to marry each other, there was no law of God or man to make them marry. No, the laws were passed because white men wanted to have their own women and use coloured women too without any law interfering with their affairs or making them responsible for the consequences.

Kenneth usually ended these arguments with himself with a feeling of complete impotence, of travelling around like a squirrel in a circular cage. No matter where he started or how fast or how far he travelled, he always wound up at the same point and with the same sense of blind defeat. Oh, well, better men than he had tried to answer the same questions and failed. He'd stay to himself and attend to his own business and let such problems go hang. But in spite of himself he often found himself enmeshed in this endless maze of reasoning. Just as frequently he determined to put from himself again the perplexing and seemingly insoluble problems.

It was after one of these soliloquies on his way from church one bright Sunday in April that Kenneth reached home and found a call for him to come at once to a house down on Butler Street, in the heart of the Negro district in the bottoms. Telling his mother to keep dinner for him as he would be back shortly, he hurried down State Street. Turning suddenly into Harris Street, which crossed State, which in turn would lead him to the house he sought on Butler Street, he caught a fleeting glimpse of a white man who looked like George Parker, cashier of the Bank of Central City. Parker, if it was he, turned hastily at Kenneth's approach and went up a narrow alley which ran off Harris Street. Kenneth thought nothing of the incident other than a vague and quickly passing wonder at Parker's presence in that part of town.

Kenneth hurried on, instinctively stepping over or around the numerous children whose complexions ranged in colour from a deep black to a yellow that was almost white, and mangy-looking dogs that seemed to infest the street. Approaching the house he sought, he found a group of excitedly talking Negroes gathered around the gate. The group separated to let him pass, and from it came one or two greetings to Kenneth in the form of "Hello, Doc." He paid little attention to them, but proceeded up the path to the house.

Entering, he was surprised to find it furnished more ornately and comfortably than usual in that section. He knew the place of old, remembering that his father had always warned him against going into this section. Here it was reported that strange things went on, that a raid by the police was not uncommon. He had upon one occasion seen the patrol wagon, better known as the "Black Maria," drive away loaded with bottles of whisky and with a nondescript lot of coloured men and women. Most of the property in this section was owned by white people, which they held on to jealously. They charged and received rentals two or three times as high as in other sections of "Darktown."

Kenneth found in the front room another excited and chattering lot of men and women. The men seemed rather furtive and were dressed in "peg-top" trousers with wide cuffs, and gaudily coloured shirts.

The women were clad in red and pink kimonos and boudoir caps. With an inclusive "Hello, folks," Kenneth followed a woman who seemed to be in charge of the house into the next room. In the centre of the darkened room there stood the bed, dishevelled, the sheets stained with blood. On them lay a man fully clothed, his eyes closed as though in great pain, and breathing heavily, with sharp gasps every few seconds. By the bed, bathing the man's brow, stood a woman in a rumpled night-dress and kimono. Kenneth recognized the man as Bud Ware, sometimes a Pullman porter, who used his occupation, it was rumoured, to bring liquor from Atlanta, which his wife sold. It was his wife Nancy who bathed his brow and who moved away from the bed when Kenneth approached. She informed him that he had come home unexpectedly from his run, and had been shot. Kenneth said nothing but went immediately to work. He found Bud with two bullet holes in his abdomen and one through his right leg. It was evident that he had but a few hours, at most, to live. Kenneth did what he could to relieve Bud's suffering. Turning to Nancy, he told her what he had discovered. She stared at Kenneth wide-eyed for a minute and then burst forth in an agony of weeping.

"Oh, Lawdy, why didn't I do what Bud tol' me to do? Bud tol' me to let dat man alone! Why didn't I do it? Why didn't I do it?"

Her screams mounted higher and higher until they reached ear-piercing shrieks. A head or two were

stuck interrogatively through the opened door at the
sound of Nancy's woe, and as quickly withdrawn.
Kenneth administered an opiate to Bud to relieve his
pain and sat by the bed to do what he could in the
short while that life remained. The sordidness of
the whole affair sickened him and he longed to get
away where he could breathe freely.

Strengthened by the opiate, Bud's eyes flickered
and then opened for a fraction of a minute. He
smiled faintly when he recognized Kenneth. He
made several ineffectual attempts to speak, but each
effort resulted only in a gasp of pain. Kenneth
ordered him to lie still. Bud, however, kept trying
to speak. Roused by Nancy's shrieks, he finally
managed to gasp out a few words, interrupted by
spasms of pain that shook his whole body.

"I knows I ain't got long, Doc. Dat's a' right,
Nancy, I ain't blamin' you none. I knows you
couldn't he'p it."

He fell back on the pillow, coughing and writh-
ing in pain.

"Lif' me a li'l—hiar—on the—pillar, Doc. Dat's
mo' like—it! Doc—I ain't been—much 'count. I
tol' dat man Parker—to stop foolin' with my 'oman
—but—he keep on—comin' here—when I'm gone.
He knew I wuz sellin' liquor—an' he tol' Nancy he
wuz gwine—hav' his brudder—She'f Parker put me
on—chain gang—if she tell me he come here—w'en
I wuz gone."

He had another paroxysm of coughing and lay for
a minute as though already dead. Kenneth adminis-

tered restoratives, meanwhile telling Nancy to keep quiet, which only made her weep the louder. After a few minutes Bud began speaking again.

"I come home to-day—an' kotched him here. W'en I got mad an' tol' him—to get out—and stahted towards him—he grabbed his gun an'—shot me." After a pause: "Doc, whyn't dese white fo'ks —leave our women alone?—I ain't nevah bothered none—of their women.—An' now—I's done got— killed jus' 'cause—I—I——"

He half raised himself on the pillow, looking at Nancy.

"Doan cry, Nancy gal—doan cry——"

He fell back dead. Kenneth, of no further assistance, left Nancy to her grief after promising to send the undertaker in to prepare Bud's body for burial, and made his way out through the crowd, now greatly increased in numbers, gathered around the door. He wondered if anything would be done about the murder, at the same time knowing that nothing would. The South says it believes in purity. What was that phrase the Ku Kluxers used so much —"preservation of the sanctity of the home, protection of the purity of womanhood"? Yes, that was it. Suppose the races of the two principals had been reversed—that Bud Ware had been caught with George Parker's wife. Why, the whole town would have turned out to burn Bud at the stake. Weren't coloured women considered human—wasn't their virtue as dear to them as to white women? Nancy and Bud weren't of much good to the community—

but if Bud wanted his wife kept inviolate, hadn't he as much right to guard her person as George Parker to protect his wife and two daughters? Again he felt himself up against a blind wall in which there was no gate, and which was too high to climb. He had determined to stay out of reach of the long arms of the octopus they called the race problem— but he felt himself slowly being drawn into its insidious embrace.

CHAPTER VII

CENTRAL CITY was the county seat of Smith
County. The morning after the murder of
Bud Ware, Kenneth went down to the County
Court House to file his report on the death. It was
a two-story building, originally of red brick but now
of a faded brownish red through the rains and sun
of many years. It sat back from the street about
fifty feet and was surrounded by a yard covered here
and there with bits of grass but for the most part
clear of all vegetation, its red soil trampled by many
feet on "co't day." The steps were worn thin
through much wear of heavy boots. On either side
of the small landing at the top, there hung a bulletin
board on which were pasted or tacked yellow notices
of sheriff's sales, rewards for the arrest of criminals,
and other court documents. The floor of the dark
and narrow hallway was stained a reddish colour by
the mud and dust from the feet of those who had
entered the building. Just inside the doorway, on
either side, were rectangular boxes filled with sawdust for the convenience of those of a tobacco-
chewing disposition, which included most of the
male population. The condition of the floor around
the boxes seemed to indicate that only a few of these
had realized for what purpose the boxes had been

placed there. Over all was a liberal coating of the dust that had blown in the door and windows.

Entering the office of the County Health Commissioner, Kenneth found that dignitary in his shirt-sleeves, feet comfortably placed on top of his desk.

"Good morning, Mr. Lane. I've come to make a report of a death."

At the sound of Kenneth's voice, County Commissioner of Health Henry Lane turned in his chair without moving his feet to see who it was that had entered. Long, lanky, a two days' growth of red beard on his face, Mr. Lane removed the corn-cob pipe from his mouth with a rising and falling of a prominent Adam's apple. Seeing that his visitor was only a Negro, he replaced his pipe in his mouth and, between several jerky puffs to get it going again, querulously replied:

"Can't you see I'm busy? Why don't you save up them repo'ts till you git a passel of them, and then bring 'em in? Got no time t' be writin' up niggers' deaths, anyhow. Ev'ry time I turn 'round, some nigger's gittin' carved up or shot or somepin'."

"I understand it's the law, Mr. Lane, that deaths of anybody, white or coloured, must be reported by the physician at once."

"Drat the law. That's fo' white folks."

He drew himself out of his chair with great reluctance and ambled over to the counter, drawing to him a pad and pencil as he turned towards Kenneth.

"What nigger's dead now?" he inquired.

"Bud Ware, who lived at 79 Butler Street," replied Kenneth.

"How'd he die?" was the next question.

"Shot through the abdomen."

"Know who shot him?"

"Yes. George Parker."

"Th' hell you say! And you come in here to repo't it?"

Kenneth was somewhat startled at the ferocity of the Commissioner's expression, which had replaced that of laziness and resentment at being disturbed.

"I thought it my duty . . ." he began.

Lane spat disgustedly.

"Duty, Hell! You're a God-damned fool and one of these damned niggers that's always causin' trouble 'round here. I always said eddication spoiled a nigger and, by God, you prove it. Lemme tell you somepin'—you'd better remember s'long's you stay 'round these parts. When you hear anything 'bout a white man havin' trouble with a nigger, you'd better keep your mouth shet. They's lots of niggers been lynched for less'n you said this mornin'. Ain't you got sense enough t' know you hadn't any business comin' in here t' tell me 'bout Mr. Parker? Don't you know his brother's sheriff? If y' aint, goin' up No'th tuk away what li'l' sense you might've had befo' you went."

Kenneth stood silent, a deep red flush suffusing his face, while the official continued his vituperative tirade. His fists, thrust deep into his pockets, were clenched until they hurt, but he did not feel the pain.

He longed to take that long, yellow, unshaven neck in his hands and twist it until Lane's eyes popped out and his face turned black. He knew it would be suicide if he did it. He realized now that he had done an unwise thing in telling Lane who had killed Bud Ware—he should have remembered and said that he did not know. If he was going to stay in the South, he would have to remember these things.

When Lane had paused for breath, Kenneth bade him good morning and left the room. As he went down the steps, he heard Lane shouting after him:

"You'd better not lemme hear o' you doin' any talkin' 'bout this. If y' do, you'll fin' yo'self bein' paid a visit one o' these nights by the Kluxers!"

Hardly had Kenneth left the court house before Lane rushed as fast as his natural indolence would permit him into the office of Sheriff Robert Parker—known throughout the county as "She'f Bob." Lane was so indignant he spluttered in trying to speak. The sheriff looked at him amusedly and counselled:

"Ca'm yo'self, Henry. What's eatin' you?"

"Bob, d'you know George shot and killed a nigger buck over in 'Darktown' yestiddy mornin' named Ware?" Lane finally managed to get out.

"Yeh. What about it? George tol' me about it las' night," was the sheriff's easy reply.

"Well, that nigger doctor Harper who's been up No'th studyin' and come back here las' fall, come into my office this mornin' to repo't it, and he had the gall t' tell me George done it."

"Th' black bastard! What th' hell's he got to do with it?"

"Said it was his duty. You bet I tol' him good an' plenty where he got off at. Guess he won't come in here repo'tin' no more 'accidents' like George run into."

Sheriff Parker's face had assumed the colour of an overripe tomato as he jumped to his feet and banged his right fist on the table with a resounding thwack.

"I'll keep my eye on that nigger," he promised. "His daddy was as good a nigger as ever I did see, but they ain't no way o' tellin' what these young bucks'll do. Roy Ewing was saying only this mornin' that Bob, that nigger doctor's kid brother, was tellin' him the other day that he'd have to stop them boys 'roun' the sto' from botherin' with th' nigger gals when they pass by. Humph! They ain't no nigger gal that's pure after she's reached fo'teen years ol'. Yep, I'll jus' keep my eye on those boys, and the first chance I git, I'll——!"

His eyes narrowed in malevolent fashion as he left his threat unuttered.

In the meantime, Kenneth had gone home. He hesitated to talk the matter over with Bob or tell him what had happened to Bud Ware or what had taken place at the court house that morning. Bob was so hot-headed and insults made him angry so easily, he was afraid of what might be the outcome if Bob knew what had occurred. He would breathe a deep sigh of relief when Bob left in the fall to go back to

[103]

school. Up in Atlanta there wouldn't be so many chances for Bob to run up against these white people and, besides, Bob's studies would keep him busy, leaving little time to brood over the indignities he had suffered. Kenneth determined that when Bob had finished his course at Atlanta University, he would urge him to go to Columbia University or Harvard and study law, and then settle down in some Northern city. It wouldn't do for Bob to come back as he had done to Central City. Sooner or later Bob's fiery temper would give way.

He wondered to whom he could turn to talk this thing out. He felt that if he didn't have a chance soon to unburden his soul to somebody, he would go insane. He thought of his mother. No, that wouldn't do. His mother had enough to worry about without taking his burdens on her shoulders.

Mamie? No, she wouldn't do either. She had no business knowing about the sordidness of the affair of Bud Ware and Nancy and George Parker. All her life she had been sheltered and kept away, as much as is possible in a Southern town, from the viciousness and filth and brutality of the race relations of the town.

Mr. Wilson, the clergyman? He was ignorant and coarse, but he had lived in South Georgia all his life and he would know better what to do than anybody else. He determined to go and talk with Mr. Wilson that evening as soon as he was free.

He had hardly made the decision when Mr. Wilson

himself entered the reception room and called out to Kenneth as he sat in his office:

"Good mawnin', Brudder Harper. It certainly has done my heart good to see you attendin' chu'ch ev'ry Sunday with your folks. Mos' of these young men and women, as soon's they get some learning, thinks they's too good to 'tend chu'ch. But, as I says to them all th' time, th' Lawd ain't goin' t' bless none of them, even if they is educated, if they don't keep close to Him."

Kenneth rose and showed his visitor to a seat. He did so with an inward repugnance as the coarseness of the man repelled him. Mr. Wilson seemed always overheated even in the coldest weather, and his face shone with a greasiness that seemed to indicate that his body excreted oil instead of perspiration. Yet, perhaps this man could give him some ray of light, if there was any to be had.

He told Mr. Wilson of his experiences of the past two days. The preacher's eyes widened with a mild surprise and the unctuous, benevolent mask which he wore most of his waking hours seemed to drop rapidly as he heard Kenneth through to the end without comment. At the same time he dropped his illiterate speech much to Kenneth's surprise, when he finally spoke.

"Dr. Harper, I've been watching you since you came back here. I knew that you were trying to keep away from this trouble that's always going on around here. That's just why I came here to-day.

Your case is a hard one, but it's small to what a lot of these others are feeling. I have asked a number of the more sensible coloured men to meet at my house to-night. I think it would be a good thing to talk over these things and try to find a way to avoid any trouble."

Kenneth looked at him in surprise, not at the idea of holding a meeting, but at the language the man was using.

"I hope you'll pardon me for asking so personal a question, Reverend Wilson, but you don't talk now as I've always heard you before. Why, your language now is that of an educated man, and before you—you—talked like a—like a——"

Mr. Wilson laughed easily.

"There's a reason—in fact, there are two reasons why I talk like that. The first is because of my own folks. Outside of you and your folks, the Phillips family, and one or two more, all of my congregation is made up of folks with little or no education. They've all got good hard common sense, it's true. They'd have to have that in order just to live in the South with things as they are. But they don't want a preacher that's too far above them—they'll feel that they can't come to him and tell him their troubles if he's too highfalutin. I try to get right down to my folks, feel as they feel, suffer when they suffer, laugh with them when they laugh, and talk with them in language they can understand."

Mr. Wilson smiled, almost to himself, as memories of contacts with his lowly flock came to him.

"I remember when I first started preaching over at Valdosta. I was just out of school and was filled up with the ambition to raise my people out of their ignorance. I was determined I would free them from a religion that didn't do anything for them but make them shout and holler on Sunday. I was going to give them some modern religion based on intelligence instead of just on feeling and emotion." He chuckled throatily in recollecting the spiritual and religious crusade on which he had based such exalted hopes.

"I preached to them and told them of Aristotle and Shakespeare and Socrates. One Sunday, after I'd preached what I thought was a mighty fine sermon, one old woman came up after the services and said to me: 'Brer Wilson, dat's a' right tellin' us 'bout Shakespeare and Homer and all dem other boys. But what we want is for you t' tell us somethin' 'bout Jesus!'"

Kenneth laughed with the preacher at the old woman's insistence on his not straying from the religion to which they were used.

"I had to discard my high-flown theories and come down to my folks if I wanted to do any good at all."

He continued:

"These same folks, however, don't want you to come down too close. Like all people with little education, whether they're black, white, or any other colour, they like to look up to their leaders. So I use a few big words now and then which have a grand and rolling sound, and they feel that I am even more wonderful because I do know how to use big words but don't use them often."

He paused while Kenneth looked at this man and saw him in a new light. He had known that Mr. Wilson, many years before coming to Central City, had attended a theological seminary in Atlanta, and he had wondered how a man could attend a school of theology of any standing and yet use such poor English. It had never occurred to him that it might be deliberate.

"And then there's another reason," continued Reverend Wilson. "The white folks here are mighty suspicious of any Negro who has too much learning, according to their standards. They figure he'll be stirring up the Negroes to fighting back when any trouble arises. I had to make a decision many years ago. I decided that somebody had to help these poor coloured folks bear their burdens, and to comfort and cheer them. I knew that if I came out and said the things I thought and felt, I would either be taken out of my house some night and lynched, or else I'd be run out of town. So I decided that I'd smile and bear it and be what the white folks think they want —what the coloured folks call a 'white man's nigger.' It's been mighty hard, but the Lord has given me the strength somehow or other to stand it this far."

With his deliberately imperfect English, there had gone from the preacher's face the subservient smile. Kenneth felt his heart warming to this man. He found his feeling of distaste and repulsion dissipating, now that the shell had been removed and he saw beneath the surface. The simile of the protective device of the chameleon came to his mind. Yes, the Negro in the South had many things in common with the chameleon—he had to be able to change his colour figuratively to suit the environment of the South in order to be allowed to stay alive. His own trouble with the Parkers and Lane seemed much more trivial now than before. He looked at Mr. Wilson and asked:

"What's the purpose of this meeting to-night? How can I help, Reverend Wilson?"

"It's like this. A good part of my congregation is made up of folks who live out in the country. They've had a lot of trouble for years getting honest settlements from the landlords on whose land they work. Within the last five years, two of my members have been lynched when they wouldn't stand for being cheated any longer. The folks out there are in a pretty bad way, and they want us to advise with them as to the best way to act. I haven't time to go into the details now, but it'll all be taken up to-night. Can I count on your being there? We need a man like you, with your education."

Kenneth deliberated several minutes before giving his answer. What Mr. Wilson wanted him to do was just exactly what he had determined not to do. But what harm could come from attending the meeting? If he didn't want to take any part in the plans, he didn't have to. Anyhow, it seemed that the more a man tried to keep away from the race question, the

more deeply involved he became in it. Might as
well do what little he could to help, if he didn't have
to take too prominent a part. He'd go anyway. He
told Reverend Wilson they could look for him that
night.

CHAPTER VIII

ENNETH was late in reaching the meeting-place that night. When he arrived he found all there waiting for him. Besides himself and Mr. Wilson were the Reverend Richard Young, pastor of Bethel African Methodist Episcopal Church, and Herbert Phillips, Jane's father. There were also three men from the farming district whom Kenneth did not know, but who were introduced as Tom Tracy, Hiram Tucker, and James Swann.

Mr. Wilson opened the meeting after the introductions had been completed.

"Brothers, we've met here this evenin' to talk over some way we can he'p these brothers who live out in the country and who ain't been able to get an honest settlement from the folks they's been farmin' for. I'm going to ask Brother Tucker to tell us just how things are with the folks out his way. Brother Tucker."

"Brother" Tucker rose and stood by the table around which they were seated and on which flickered an oil lamp. He was a man between fifty and sixty years of age, of medium height and thick-set. His black skin was wrinkled with age and toil. His hands, as they rested on the table in front of him, were gnarled and hardened through a lifetime of

[111]

ploughing and hoeing and the other hard work of farm life. It was Mr. Tucker's face, however, which attracted interest. Out of the rolls of skin there shone two kindly, docile eyes. One gained the impression that these eyes had seen tragedies on top of tragedies, as indeed they had, and their owner had been taught by dire necessity to look upon them in a philosophic and pacifist manner. One remembered a biblical description: "He was a man of sorrows and acquainted with grief." Kenneth, as he looked at him, felt that Socrates and Aristotle and Jesus Christ must have had eyes like Brother Tucker's. His impression was heightened by Mr. Tucker's hair. Of a snowy whiteness, his head bald on top, his hair formed a circle around his head that reminded Kenneth of the picture-cards used at Sunday school when he was a boy, where the saints had crowns of light hovering over their heads. The only difference was that Mr. Tucker's halo seemed to be a bit more firmly and closely attached than those of the saints, which he remembered always seemed to be poised perilously in mid-air. He had often wondered, as he gazed intently at the pictures, what would have happened had a strong gust of wind come suddenly upon the saints, and blown their haloes away.

Mr. Tucker began speaking slowly, in the manner of one of few words and as one unused to talking in public.

"Brudders, me 'n' Brudder Tracy and Brudder Swann ast Reverend Wilson here to let us come t' town some time and talk over with you gent'men a li'l' trouble we's been havin'. Y' see, all of us folks out dat way wuks on shares like dis. We makes a 'greement wif de landlord to wuk one year or mo'. He fu'nishes de lan' and we puts de crap in de soil, wuks it, and den gathers it. We's sposed to 'vide it share and share alike wif de landlord but it doan wuk out dat way. If us cullud folks ain't got money enough to buy our seed and fert'lizer and food and the clo'es we needs du'in' de year, we is allowed t' take up dese things at de sto'. Den when we goes to settle up after de cott'n and cawn's done laid by, de sto' man who wuks in wif de landlord won't giv' us no bill for whut we done bought but jes' gives us a li'l' piece of paper wif de words on it: 'Balance Due.' "

He paused to wipe the perspiration from his face caused by the unusual experience of speaking at such length. He continued:

"An' dat ain't all. W'en we starts to pickin' our cotton, dey doan let us ca'y it to de gin and weigh it ourself. De lan'lord send his wagons down in de fiel' and as fas' as we picks it, dey loads it on de wagons and takes it away. Dey doan let us know how much it weighs or how much dey sells it for. Dey jus' tells us it weighs any 'mount de lan'lord wants to tell us, and dey says dey sol' it at any price dey set. W'en we comes to settle up for de year, dey 'ducts de 'balance due' from what we's got comin' t'us from our share of de craps. I's been wukin' for nigh on to six years for Mr. Taylor out near

Ashland and ev'y year I goes deeper in debt dan de year befo'. Las' year I raised mo' dan twenty-fo' bales of cott'n dat weighed mo' dan five hundred poun's each. My boy Tom whut's been t' school figgered out dat at eighten cents a poun'—and dat's de price de paper said cott'n sol' at las' year—I oughter got mo' dan a thousan' dollars for my share. An' dat ain't all neither. Dey was nearly twelve tons of cott'n seed dat was wuth 'bout two hundred and fo'ty dollars. An' den dey was mo' dan three hundred bush'ls of cawn at a dollar'n a ha'f a bush'l dat makes fo' hundred and fifty dollars mo'. All dat t'gether makes nearly three thousan' dollars an' I oughter got 'bout fifteen hundred dollars fo' my share."

Tucker stopped again and shifted his feet while Tracy and Swann nodded agreement with his statements.

"Las' year me 'n' my wife said we wuz gwine t' get along without spendin' no mo' money at de sto' dan we had to, so's we could get out of debt. We wukked ha'd and all our chillen we made wuk in de fiel's too. My boy Tom kept account of ev'ything we bought at de sto', and when de year ended he figgered it up an' he foun' we'd done spent jus' even fo' hundred dollars. But when we goes to make a settlement at de end of de year, Mr. Taylor said he sol' our cott'n at eight cent a poun' and didn' have but sev'n hundred and thutty-five dollars comin' to us. An' den he claim we tuk up 'leven hundred dollars wuth of stuff at de sto' which he done paid for,

so that leave me owin' him three hundred 'n' sixty-
five dollars dat I got to wuk out next year."

His face took on a dejected look as though the load
had become almost too heavy to bear. His voice
took on at the same time a plaintive and discouraged
tone.

"An' when you adds on dat three hundred dollars
dat Mr. Taylor says I owed him from las' year, dat
makes neah'ly sev'n hundred dollars I owes, and it
doan look like I's evah goin' t' git out of debt. An'
I thought we wuz goin' to be able to sen' Tom and
Sally and Mirandy t' Tuskegee dis year off de 'leven
hundred dollars I thought I wuz gwine t' make."

The discouraged air changed to one of greater
courage and determination. His voice rose in his
resentment and excitement.

"Now I's tiahed of all dis cheatin' an' lyin'! Mr.
Taylor mus' take me for a fool if he thinks I'm
gwine stan' for dis way of doin' things all de time.
I stahted to tell him dat I knew he wuz cheatin' me
in Janua'y w'en he give me dat statemen', but den I
'membered whut happen t' Joe Todd two years ago
w'en he tol' dat ol' man Stanton dat he wukked for,
de same thing. W'en ol' man stahted t' hit Joe, Joe
hit him fust and run. Dey came one night and call
Joe to his do' and tuk him down in de swamp an'
de nex' mawnin' dey foun' Joe full of bullets, hangin'
to a tree. De paper say Joe done spoke insultin' to
a white 'oman, but all de cullud folks, an' de white
too, know dat Joe ain't nevah even seen no white
'oman dat day. Dey knew dat if dey say he 'sulted

a white 'oman, de folks up Nawth won't crit'cize dem
for lynchin' a nigger down here in Georgy. So I
jus' kep' my mouth close'. Now we wants t' know
if dey ain't somethin' we c'n do t' make dese white
folks we wuks for stop cheatin' an' robbin' us po'
cullud folks."

He sat down, evidently greatly relieved at finishing a task so arduous. Kenneth had listened in
amazement to the story of exploitation, crudely told,
yet with a simplicity that was convincing and eloquent. Having lived in the South all his life, he
naturally was not unaware of the abuses under the
"share-cropping" or "tenant-farming" system in the
South, but it had never been brought home to him so
forcefully how close at hand and how oppressive and
dishonest the system really was. No wonder the
South lynched, disfranchised, Jim-Crowed the Negro,
he reflected. If the Negro had a vote and a voice
in the local government of affairs, most of these
bankers and merchants and landowners would have
to go to work for the first time in their lives instead
of waxing fat on the toil of humble Negroes like Hiram Tucker. He turned to Tucker to get further information on the system.

"Mr. Tucker, have you and the other folks like
you ever thought of trying to get loans from the
Federal Government through the banks they have established to aid farmers in buying land and raising
their crops?"

"Oh, yes, Doc. Soon's they started lendin' money
to farmers, I 'plied for a loan to buy me a li'l' place

dat I wuz gwine t' wuk an' pay for off whut I raised. But dey tol' me dey didn' have no funds t' len' to niggers an' dat dey already done loaned all dey had to de white farmers. W'en I ast dem to put my name down on de lis' to get a loan when some mo' money came in, dey tol' me dat it wa'n't no use 'cause dey already had so many white folks' names down on de lis' dat dey nevah would come to de cullud folks."

"Did you think about writing to Washington and telling them that they were discriminating against Negro farmers?" questioned Kenneth.

"Yas, suh, we done dat too. But dey wrote us back dat de onliest way any loan could be made was th'u' de local agents, so dat didn't come to nuthin'."

"But, good Lord, they can't discriminate in that way against you without something being done about it!" was Kenneth's indignant comment.

Tucker looked at him with a wan smile that was almost pitying at the ignorance of the younger man. His voice became paternal.

"Son, dat's jes' zactly like de man whut wuz in jail and his frien' come by and ast him whut dey put him in jail for. When de man in jail tol' him whut he wuz 'cused of, de man on de outside said: 'Dey can't put you in jail for dat!' De man dat was lookin' out at him th'u' de bars laughed and said: 'But I'se *in jail!*' An' dat's de way 'tis wif de cullud folks in de Souf. Dey's lots of things dey *can't* do to 'em but dese white folks does it jes' de same. I reckon you got a lot of things t' learn yet, Doc, spite of goin' up Nawth t' study."

Kenneth felt properly rebuked by this humble man who, though illiterate, was far from being ignorant. He joined in, but not very heartily, at the general laughter at Tucker's homely sally.

Mr. Wilson, as acting chairman, ended the discussion by calling on Tom Tracy. Tracy was a much younger man than Tucker and was about Kenneth's age. Tall, well built, intelligent looking, his dark brown face had worn a scowl of discontent and resentment while Tucker had been talking. He began talking in a clear voice that but poorly masked the bitterness he felt but which he tried to keep out of his voice. Older men like Mr. Tucker were always quick to rebuke any sign of "uppishness" in the younger generation.

"I graduated from Tuskegee three years ago. My old mother worked herself almost to death to keep me in school, and I came back here determined to earn enough money to let her rest the balance of her life. But she and my father had been living all their lives just like Mr. Tucker here, and they didn't have anything to give me a start. So I went to work on shares, taking that thirty acres that joins on to Mr. Tucker's farm on the South. I took this land that wasn't thought to be any good, because it had been exhausted through overworking it year after year. I bought some new ploughs and fixed it up fine. I thought I could put the things I learned at Tuskegee into practice and in a couple of years pay off all I owed. But instead of doing that, I'm getting deeper in debt every year. I rent my place from Ed Stewart and he knows that I know he's cheating and robbing and lying to me, but when I try to show him where he is wrong in his figures, all he does is to get mad and start to cussing me and telling me that if I don't keep a civil tongue in my head, the Ku Klux Klan will be hearing about this 'sassy young nigger Tracy' and I'll wish I had kept my mouth shut. I'm getting sick of the whole thing, too. If it wasn't for the old folks, I expect I'd 'a' started something long ago. They are all talking about me being a dangerous character out my way already. Say I'm too 'uppity' and I need to be taught a lesson to show me that 'niggers must stay in their places.' "

Tracy finished speaking in a tone that was almost a shout. It could be seen that he was very near the breaking-point from brooding over the wrongs he had suffered.

Mr. Phillips, who had said nothing, broke in with a question.

"Tom, why don't you move away from Ed Stewart's place if he doesn't treat you right?"

Tracy replied bitterly:

"Yes, suppose I tried to leave, what would happen? The same day I left, Sheriff Parker would come and get me. They'd put me on trial for jumping my contract and fine me. Old Stewart would be in court to testify against me. He'd pay my fine and then I'd have to go back to Stewart's place and work a year or two for nothing, paying off the fine. A fat chance I've got with the cards all stacked against me!"

Mr. Young, of the Bethel African Methodist Episcopal Church, nodded assent to Tracy's statement.

"Brother Tracy's right. Look at what happened to Jeff Anderson down near Valdosta last spring. He ran away and got to Detroit where he had a good job working in an automobile plant. They swore out a warrant against him for stealing, brought him back, and the last I heard of him he was back down there working out a three-hundred-dollar fine. No, Brother Phillips, you've been reading the law that applies to white folks—not to us coloured people."

James Swann's story was along the same lines as the others. The seven men entered into a discussion of ways and means of taking some action which would alleviate conditions before the harvesting of the crop which was now in the ground. One suggestion after another was offered, only to be as quickly discarded because of local difficulties. Midnight came, with no decision reached. When it became apparent that nothing would be settled, Kenneth was chosen with Mr. Wilson and Mr. Phillips to work out some plan to be reported at the meeting to be held one week later.

CHAPTER IX

THERE was being held another meeting the same night. Two miles from Central City, to the North, was a natural auditorium, an amphitheatre formed by three hills. In this place a meeting alfresco was in progress. Though the place was far enough from the road to be reasonably free from prying intruders, sentinels paced the narrow roads that led to the place of assemblage. Skeleton-like pine-trees formed an additional barrier to the lonely spot, making as they did a natural fringe atop the three hills.

There was no moon. Light was furnished by pine torches fastened in some instances to trees, in others borne aloft by members of the gathering. About three hundred men were ranged in a circle around a rudely carved cross stuck in the ground. Each man was garbed in a long white robe reaching to his feet. On the left breast of each hood was a cross with other strange figures. Over the head of each man was a cowl with holes for eyelets. It was a meeting of Central City Klan, Knights of the Ku Klux Klan, Realm of Georgia. The Exalted Cyclops, whose voice bore a remarkable likeness to that of Sheriff Parker, was initiating new members into the mysteries of the order. He held in his hand a sheet from which he was reading the oath which the "aliens" repeated after him with their right hands upraised. Whether through fright or excitement or because the night air was chilly, the voices of the embryo "knights" had a strange quaver in them. Around them, rank on rank, stood the Klansmen, who followed the ceremony closely.

" . . . will willingly conform—to all regulations, usages, and requirements—of the Knights—of the Ku Klux Klan—which do now exist—or which may hereafter—be enacted—and will render—at all times—loyal respect— and steadfast support—to the Imperial Authority of same. . . ."

The droning voices ended the monotonous recital. The flickering torches gave forth a weird light that was lost in the darkness cast by the trees. The pungent odour of burning resin and the thick stifling smoke were blown by vagrant breezes into the faces of the hooded figures, causing a constant accompaniment of coughs, sneezes, and curses to the mumbled words. A recent rain-storm had left the low-lying ground soggy and damp and mightily uncomfortable underfoot. The crowd shifted uneasily as their feet grew cold with the dampness. Moths, mosquitoes, and other flying insects, attracted by the flaring lights, swarmed, getting beneath the cowls and robes and adding to the discomfort of the wearers. Even the imperfect illumination showed the cheap material of which the disguises were made, exhibited the wrinkles and dirt around the hems, revealed every aspect of the ill-fitting garments. Once from a spluttering torch there fell a bit of blazing resin on the hand of the man holding the light. With a yell he dropped the torch, danced and howled with pain, a ludicrous figure, until the agony had subsided. The torch, flung hastily away, set fire to the underbrush into which it had been cast. An unlooked-for intermission in the ceremonies followed as a score of the figures, holding the skirts of their robes aloft like old maids frightened at the appearance of a mouse, stamped out the fire, circling and yelling like a band of whirling dervishes.

Stodgy, phlegmatic, stupid citizens by day, these by night went through the discomforts of so unprepared a meeting-place, and through the absurdities of the rites imposed upon them by clever rogues who extracted from them fees and donations for the privilege of being made to appear more silly than is usually apparent. Add to that gullibility a natural love of the mysterious and adventurous and an instinct towards brute action restrained only by fear of punishment, by a conjuring of bogies and other malevolent dangers, and one understands, at least in part, the presence of these three hundred "white, Gentile, Protestant" citizens of Central City at this meeting.

The initiation ended, the Exalted Cyclops ordered the Kligrapp or secretary to read several communications from the Imperial Klan Palace at Atlanta. This he did, struggling manfully through the weird and absurd verbiage that would have made any of the men present howl with laughter had he heard his children using it in their play. Instead it was listened to attentively, seriously, and solemnly.

Then followed a recital of the work to be done by the local Klan. The Kligrapp consulted a sheet of paper in his hand.

"The eye that never sleeps has been seeking out those in our city who have acted in a manner displeasing to the Invisible Empire. There is in Central City a nigger wench named Nancy Ware who has been saying evil things against our brother, George Parker. In the name of our sacred order, and in the furtherance of our supreme duty of preservation of white supremacy, she is being watched and will be treated so as to end her dangerous utterances."

At this statement a robed figure that, even under the disguise, seemed to resemble him who had been "defamed" by Nancy Ware's tongue nodded approvingly. The Kligrapp continued after a pause:

"Word has also come to us from Brothers Ed Stewart and Taylor that there's a young nigger named Tom Tracy out this way who's going around among the niggers saying that they have got to stop white people from robbing them on their crops. Tracy hasn't done anything but talk thus far, but we will keep our eye on him and stop him if he talks too much." Cowled heads nodded approvingly.

"And then there's a nigger doctor who came in my office—I mean, he went into the office of Health Commissioner Lane—and had the gall to repo't the death of a nigger bootlegger and say that a white man had killed him for fooling around with the nigger's wife. This nigger's daddy was one of the best niggers that ever lived here in this town, and this boy's keeping away from the other trouble-making niggers, but we've got to watch all these niggers that's been spoiled by goin' to school." He added, as an afterthought: ". . . up Nawth."

And so he droned on. Negroes, two Jews, three men suspected of Catholic leanings—all were condemned by the self-appointed arbiters of morals and manners. One or two men were singled out as violating the code of morals by consorting with Negro women. There was not much to report on this score, as those who were violating this rule in Central City had rushed, on formation of a Klan there, to join the order, that they might gain immunity from attack and yet continue their extra-legal activities without check or interference. With the conclusion of the Kligrapp's report, the meeting dispersed, the members silently entered the woods and there disrobing, and scattering to their various homes. Some went towards "Factoryville," some towards the country districts, others climbed into automobiles parked near the road and drove towards the residential section of Central City where lived the more affluent merchants and other upper-class whites of the town.

The place was soon deserted. The ceremony had been a strange mixture of the impressive and the absurd. There was, underneath the ridiculously

[125]

worded language, the amusing childlike observance of the empty ceremonies, the queer appearance of the robes all designed alike with little regard for fatness or thinness of the prospective wearers, a seriousness which betokened a belief in the urgent need of their organizing in such a manner. They had been duped so long by demagogues, deluded generation after generation into believing their sole hope of existence depended on oppression and suppression of the Negro, that the chains of the ignorance and suppression they sought to fasten on their Negro neighbours had subtly bound them in unbreakable fashion. They opposed every move for better educational facilities for their children, for improvement of their health or economic status or welfare in general, if such improvement meant better advantages for Negroes. Creatures of the fear they sought to inspire in others, their lives are lived in constant dread of the things of evil and terror they preached. It is a system based on stark, abject fear—fear that he whom they termed inferior might, with opportunity, prove himself not inferior. This unenlightened viewpoint rules men throughout the South like those who formed the Central City Klan—dominates their every action or thought—keeps the whites back while the Negro—in spite of what he suffers—always keeps his face towards the sun of achievement. . . .

In spite of the secrecy surrounding the meeting, next morning all Central City talked of what had taken place on the previous evening. In such a town, where little diversion exists, the inhabitants seize with avidity upon every morsel of news that promises entertainment. Though they had taken fearful oaths of secrecy, it was asking too much of human frailty to expect three hundred men to refrain even from mysterious hints of their doings. With the love that simple minds have of the clandestine, the midnight secrecy, the elaborately arranged peregrinations to the place of meeting, the safeguards adopted by the leaders not so much to prevent interference as to impress their followers, the "inviolable oath," the grips and passwords—all these added to the human desire to be considered important in the eyes of family and friends and neighbours. Thus many of the three hundred dropped hints to their wives of what had been said and done. Over back fences, at the stores on Lee Street, in the numerous places where women contrived to meet and gossip, the one topic discussed was the meeting of the night before. One told her bit of information to another, who in turn contributed her mite. Each in turn told a third and a fourth. With each telling, the ball of gossip grew, and each repetition bore artistic additions of fact or fancy designed to add to the drama of the story. By noon the compounded result assumed the proportions of a feat bordering on the heroic.

At the noonday meal, known as dinner, the men found themselves viewed in a new and admiring light by their spouses and offspring. They basked in the temporary glamour and sought to add to the fame of their midnight prowling by elaborate hints of deeds of dark and magnificent proportions.

In turn, to the Negro section of Central City were borne the tales by cooks and laundresses and maids, servants, with acutely developed ears, in the houses of the whites. Everywhere in the Negro section, in homes, on street corners, over back fences, the news was discussed by the dusky inhabitants of the town. In the eyes of a few, fear could be discerned. Most of the Negroes, however, discussed the news as they would have talked about the coming of the circus to town. Some talked loudly and in braggart fashion of what they would do if the "Kluxers" bothered them. Others examined for the hundredth time well-oiled revolvers. Most generally the feeling was a hope the Klan would not bother any coloured person —but if it did——! . . .

It was natural that the news should eventually reach Nancy Ware and Tom Tracy and, last of all, Kenneth. Mrs. Amos, bustling with importance, hastened as fast as her rheumatism would allow to tell Mrs. Harper what the Klansmen had said or, to be more accurate, what Dame Rumour said the Klansmen had said, about Kenneth and Bob. It was obvious the two men had taken on a new importance in her eyes in being singled out for the attention of the clandestine organization.

That night in Kenneth's office the brothers talked over the news. Kenneth scoffed at what seemed to him a fantastic and improbable tale. He looked searchingly at his brother.

"Well, Bob, what do you make of it?"

"Trouble for somebody," said Bob positively.

[128]

"And I have a sort of feeling that that somebody is us," he added after a pause.

"I'm not so sure," was Kenneth's doubtful rejoinder. "Some of these Crackers are just mean enough to start something, but I'm pretty sure there are enough decent white people in Central City to check any trouble that might start."

Bob said nothing, though his face showed plainly he did not share his brother's confidence. Kenneth went on:

"Besides, they must have sense enough to know that a sheet and pillow-case won't scare coloured folks to-day as they did fifty years ago. It wasn't hard to scare Negroes then—they'd just come out of slavery, and believed in ghosts and spooks and all those other silly things. But to-day——"

"I think white people are right sometimes," broke in Bob with conviction, "when they say education ruins a Negro. One of those times is when you talk like that."

The irony in his voice was but thinly veiled. He continued:

"The Southern white man boasts he knows the Negro better than anybody else, but he knows less what the coloured man is really thinking than the man in the moon. I'll bet anything you say, that seven out of every ten men in town believe that you and I and all the rest of us coloured folks are scared to death every time we hear the word 'Ku Klux.' They believe the sight of one of those fool robes'll make us run and hide under a bed——"

"Oh, I don't go quite that far," interrupted Kenneth. "I only said I thought some of the good white people——"

"You can name all your 'good white folks' on one hand," replied Bob irritably. "A lot they could do if these poor white trash decide to raise hell. Why, they'd lynch Judge Stevenson or Roy Ewing or anybody else if they tried to stop 'em. Look what they did to Governor Slaton at Atlanta just because he commuted the sentence of that Jew, Leo Frank!" he added triumphantly. "A mob even went out to his house to lynch *him—the governor!*"

"But that was an extraordinary case," replied Kenneth.

"Call it what you will, it just shows you how far they will go when they are all stirred up. And with this Ku Klux outfit to stir them up, there's no telling what'll happen."

"Bob, do you really believe what you said just now about most of them really believing Negroes will be scared by the Klan? That seems so far-fetched."

"Believe it? Of course I do. Just use your eyes and see how Negroes fool white folks all the time. Take, for instance, old Will Hutchinson who works for Mr. Baird. Will cuts all sorts of monkey-shines around Baird, laughs like an idiot, and wheedles old Baird out of anything he's got. Baird gives it to him and then tells his friends about 'his good nigger Will' and boasts that Will is one 'darky' he really knows. Then Will goes home and laughs at the fool he's made of Baird by acting like a fool." Bob laughed at the memory of many occasions on which Will had bamboozled his employer. "And there are Negroes all over the South doing the same thing every day!" he ended.

"That's true," admitted Kenneth, "but what ought we to do about this meeting last night?"

"Do?" echoed Bob. A determined look came to his face, his teeth clenched, his eyes narrowed until they became thin slits. "Do?" he repeated. "If they ever bother me, I'm going to fight—and fight like hell!"

Long into the night Kenneth sat alone in his office, wondering how it was all going to turn out.

CHAPTER X

THE next day Kenneth received a letter from Jane Phillips. In it she announced that she would arrive in Central City on Monday morning. Kenneth's face took on a satisfied smile and deep down in his heart there was happiness and contentment. Jane had occupied an increasingly large portion of his thoughts ever since those wonderful ten days they had spent together last December. Kenneth's life had been singularly free from feminine influence, other than that of his mother. It was not that he was averse to such influence, but his life had been so busy that he had had no time to spend in wandering through the Elysian fields of love-making.

There had been one girl in New York. He had met her at a dance in Harlem. Together they had spent their Sundays and the evenings when he was free from his duties at the hospital in wandering through Central and Bronx Parks. Occasionally they had attended the theatre. One night their hands had touched as they sat in the semi-darkness and watched the tender love scene on the stage. She had not withdrawn her hand. He sat there thrilled at the touch and had lived the character of the make-believe hero as he made ardent love on the stage. Naturally, the heroine was none other than the girl

who sat beside him. Afterwards, they had ridden
home atop a Fifth Avenue bus, and the whole city
seemed filled with romance. He had imagined himself at the time deeply in love. But that tender episode had soon ended when he told her he was planning to return to Georgia. "Kenneth!" she had exclaimed. "How can you think of living down South
again? It's silly of you even to think of it! I could
never think of living down there where they are likely
to lynch you at a moment's notice! It's too bar-
baric, too horrible an existence to consider even for
a minute!" Kenneth had tried to show her that it
wasn't as bad as it had been painted, that coloured
people who minded their own business never had
any trouble. But she had been obdurate. Kenneth
left the house in a huff, and had never gone back
again. What silly notions women have, he had
thought to himself. The reason they talked about
the South that way was because of sheer ignorance.
As if he couldn't manage his own affairs and keep
away from trouble! Humph! Well rid of the silly
creature, and he felt glad he had found out before
going in too deep.

But now this was different. Jane had no such
absurd notions as those girls up North had. She
wasn't the sort that couldn't leave promenading down
Seventh Avenue in New York or State Street in
Chicago or U Street in Washington. It wasn't that
she didn't know what it meant to live in the North.
Hadn't she been to Atlantic City and New York and
Washington with her mother? No, Jane was just

the sort of girl who would make the right sort of
companion for him in a place like Central City.
Intelligent, with a good education, talented musically
—she would make an ideal wife. Kenneth found
himself musing along in this fashion until aroused
by his mother as she called him to supper.

It was darned silly of him, he thought as he arose
to comply, to go along thinking like this. He and
Jane had spoken no word of love when she had been
at home at Christmas. Nor had their letters been
other than those of good friends. But hadn't she
written him almost every week since she left? She
must think something of him to have done that. He
determined that as soon as he could he would skil-
fully direct the conversation to the point where he
could find out just where he stood. It was time that
he was thinking about settling down, anyhow. He
would be twenty-nine his next birthday—he was making money—if he acted wisely his future was assured. Yes, he would find out how Jane felt. Both
his mother and Mamie liked Jane—and Mr. Phillips
had called him "my boy" several times lately and had
repeated to him snatches of the letters that Jane
had written home. The only doubtful quantity was
the attitude of Jane herself.

On Monday morning Kenneth reached the railroad
station long before the train arrived. He tried to
sit in the filthy little waiting-room with the sign over
the door, "FOR COLOURED," but the air was so
oppressive that he chose rather to walk up and down
the road outside the station. At last the train came.

He walked down towards the engine where the Jim Crow car was. It was half baggage car and half coach. A motley crowd of laughing, shouting Negroes descended, calling out to friends and relatives in the group of Negroes on the ground. Standing on tiptoe, Kenneth strained his eyes to get glimpse of Jane. The windows of the coach were too dirty to see inside. At last she appeared on the platform, dainty, neat, and looking as though she had just emerged from her own room, in spite of the filth and cindery foulness of the coach. Kenneth thought of the simile of a rose springing up from a bed of noisome and unlovely weeds as he hurried forward to help Jane with her bags through the crowd of coloured people that flocked around the steps.

Jane greeted him cordially enough, her eyes shining with pleasure at seeing him again. Kenneth, however, felt a vague disappointment. He had let his thoughts run riot while she had been away. So far as he was concerned, the only things necessary were the actual asking of the all-important question and the choosing of a wedding-day. As he followed her to his car, he turned over in his mind just what it was that disappointed him so in her greeting. He couldn't put his finger on it exactly, but she would have greeted Bob or any other man just as warmly and he would not have felt jealous at all. Maybe she's tired from the ride in that dirty and noisy car? She'll be quite different when I go over to see her to-night, he thought.

He inquired regarding her trip—was it pleasant?

"Ugh, it was horrible!" she replied, shuddering at the memory of it. "I had a Pullman as far as Atlanta, but there I had to change to that dirty old Jim Crow car. There was a crowd of Negroes who had three or four quarts of cheap liquor. They were horrible. Why, they even had the nerve to offer me a drink! And the conductor must have told everybody on the train that I was up front, because all night long there was a constant procession of white men passing up and down the coach looking at me in a way that made my blood boil. I didn't dare go to sleep, because I didn't know what might happen. It was awful!"

She sat silent as she lived over again the horror of the ride. Then, shaking off her mood, she turned to him with a cheerful smile. "Thank Goodness, it's over now, and I don't want to think of it any more than I can help. Tell me all about yourself and what you've been doing and everything," she finished all in a breath.

He told her briefly what had been going on, of his plans for the hospital, of the meeting at Reverend Wilson's, and other items of interest about life in Central City, until they had arrived at her home. He waited for an invitation to come in, but in the excitement of seeing her mother and father again, she forgot all about Kenneth. Placing her bags on the porch, he turned and left after promising to run over for a while that evening.

The time seemed to go by on dragging feet that day. It seemed as though evening never would come.

It did at last, however, and as soon as he finished with the last patient, he went over to Jane's home. Refreshed by a long rest, she greeted him clad in a dress of some filmy blue material. They seated themselves on the porch, shaded by vines from the eyes of passers-by. Over Kenneth there came a feeling of contentment—life had not been easy for him and he had been denied a confidante with whom he could discuss the perplexities he had experienced in Central City. The talk for a time drifted from one topic to another. Before he knew it, Kenneth was telling Jane of his ambitions, of the plans he had made before coming back to Central City, of the successes and failures he had met with, of his hopes for the future. Jane listened without speaking for some time. Life among coloured people is so intense, so earnest, so serious a problem in the South, that never do two intelligent Negroes talk very long before the race problem in some form is under discussion. Jane interrupted Kenneth in the midst of his recital.

"Kenneth, did you really believe that you could come back here to Central City and keep entirely away from the race problem?"

"I don't know that I thought it out as carefully as that, but I hoped to do something like that," was his uneasy reply. He had the feeling that she didn't altogether approve of him. Her next words proved that she didn't.

"Well, you can't do it. Just because your father got along all right is no reason why you should do the same things he did. You are living in a time

that is as different from his as his was from his
great-grandfather's."

"But——" he attempted to defend himself.

"Wait a minute until I've had my say," she
checked him. "Only a few years ago they said that
as soon as Negroes got property and made themselves
good citizens the race problem would be solved.
They said that only bad Negroes were ever lynched
and they alone caused all the trouble. But you just
think back over the list of coloured people right here
in Central City who've had the most trouble during
the past two years. What do you find? That it is
the Negro who has acquired more property than the
average white man, they are always picking on.
Poor whites resent seeing a Negro more prosperous
than they, and they satisfy their resentment by making it hard on that Negro. Am I right—or am I
wrong?"

"I suppose there is something in what you say—
but what's the answer? You're damned if you do—
and you're damned if you don't!"

"I don't know what the answer is—if I did, I'd
certainly try to put it into use, instead of sitting
around and trying to dodge trouble. If one of your
patients had a cancer, you wouldn't advise him to
use Christian Science in treating it, would you?"

Without pausing for a reply, she went on, her
words pouring out in a flood that made Kenneth feel
as he did as a boy when spanked by his mother.
"No, you wouldn't! You'd operate! And that's
just what the coloured people and the white people of

the South have got to do. That is, those who've got any sense and backbone. If they don't, then this thing they call the race problem is going to grow so big it's going to consume the South and America. It's almost that big now."

She paused for breath. Kenneth started to speak but she checked him with her hand.

"I'm not through yet! I've been thinking over this thing for a long time, just as every other Negro has done who's got brains enough to do any thinking at all. I am sick and tired of hearing all this prating about the 'superior race.' Superior—humph! Kenneth, what you and all the rest of Negroes need is to learn that you belong to a race that was centuries old when the first white man came into the world. You've got to learn that a large part of this thing they call 'white civilization' was made by black hands, as well as by yellow and brown and red hands, too, besides what white hands have created. You've got to learn that the Negro to-day is contributing as much of the work that makes this civilization possible as the white race, if not more. Be proud of your race and quit whining and cringing! You'll never get anywhere until you do! There, I've wanted to get that out of my system for a long time— ever since we talked together last Christmas. Now it's out and I'm through!"

Kenneth sat quiet. While she had been pouring forth her tirade, he had thought of several logical arguments he could have advanced. But she had given him no chance to utter them. Now they seemed weak and useless. He was resentful—what did women know about the practical problems and difficulties of life, anyway? His anger was not abated by the realization that Jane felt that he had been trying to avoid his responsibility to himself and to his people—that he had been a coward. And yet she was right in a general way in what she had said. Masking as well as he could the chagrin he felt at her words, he told her of the trouble Tucker and Tracy and Swann and the other share-croppers were having, and gave her further details of the meeting at Reverend Wilson's.

She sensed the wound to his pride that she had inflicted. She did not regret doing what she had done —on the long ride home she had determined that she would tell him those very things as soon as she could find opportunity—but, with a woman's natural tenderness, she regretted the necessity of hurting him. She put her hand over his for an instant, touched at his dejected manner.

"I'm sorry, Ken, if I hurt you, but I did it because you are too fine a man, and you've got too good an education, to try to dodge an issue as plain as yours. Why, Kenneth, you've had it mighty soft—just think of the thousands of coloured boys all over the South who are too poor to get even a high-school training. You've never had to get down and dig for what you've got—perhaps it would have been better if you had. It's men with your brains and education that have got to take the leadership. You've got to make good! That's just the reason they try to make it hard for men like you—they know that if you ever get going, their treating the Negro as they have has got to stop! They're darned scared of educated Negroes with brains—that's why they make it hard for you!"

Kenneth threw out his hands, palms upward, and shrugged his shoulders.

"I suppose I agree with you in theory, Jane, but what are the practical ways of doing the things you say I ought to do? How, for example, can I help Tracy and Tucker and all the rest of the farmers who're being robbed of all they earn every year?"

"Don't get angry now just because I touched your masculine vanity. I know about the share-cropping system in a general way. Tell me the facts that were brought out at the meeting."

Kenneth told her in detail the things Hiram Tucker and the others had said. She sat in thought for a minute, her chin cupped in the palm of her hand, her elbow resting on the arm of the chair, as she rocked back and forth. Kenneth sat watching her in what was almost sardonic amusement. He had been wrestling with this same problem ever since Thursday night and was no nearer a solution than he had been then. It would be amusing in a few minutes, after all her high-flown thoughts and elaborate generalities about bucking the race question, when she would be forced to admit that when it came to solving one of the practical problems of the whole question her generalizing would be of no avail. He was aroused by a question thrown at him suddenly by Jane.

"Do these folks have to buy their supplies from the landlord?"

"Not that I know of," he replied. "They buy from the landlord, or the merchant designated by the landlord, because they haven't the money or the credit to trade anywhere else."

There followed another pause while the rocking began again.

"Do you remember any of the economics you learned at school?" was the next query. He replied that he supposed he did.

"Have you got any books on co-operative societies?" He doubted whether he had.

"Well, never mind." She swung her chair around, facing Kenneth, and leaned forward intently, the light from the arc-lamp in the corner illumining her face and revealing the eager, enthusiastic look upon it.

"Kenneth, why can't those coloured people pool their money and buy their goods wholesale and then distribute them at cost?"

Kenneth laughed, it must be confessed a little cheerfully, that she had gone from one problem into the mazes of another that was just as difficult.

"For the very same reason that they are in the predicament they are in to-day. They haven't got the money. Perhaps you can tell me where the money to start this co-operative scheme is coming from?"

"That's an easy one to answer. It's going to come from you and papa and three or four more of these folks here in town who can afford it! Oh, Ken, can't you see what a big thing you can do? There are lots of people, white people I mean, right here in Central City, who'd be glad to help these poor Negroes get out of debt. Papa was telling us to-day about a talk he had with Judge Stevenson the other day. The Judge said he wished there was some way to help without it making him unpopular with the other folks here in town. Of course, the folks who are making money off this system, the landlords and the store-keepers, won't like it, but you can go and talk with folks like Judge Stevenson and Mr. Baird down at the Bank of Central City. If this first trial succeeds—and I know it will be a suc-cess—it'll spread all over Smith County, and then all over Georgia, and then all over the South, and the coloured folks will have millions of dollars that they've been cheated out of before. That, Kenneth Harper, is one way you can lead, and it won't get you in bad with the white people—at least the decent ones—either."

Kenneth began to be infected by her enthusiasm. He saw that her idea had possibilities. But, man-like, he didn't want to give in too soon or too readily.

"There is something in what you say, Jane, but the details will have to be worked out first before we can tell if it is a practicable idea. I'll think it——"

Jane interrupted him, showing that she hadn't even been listening to him.

"When are you to meet again at Reverend Wilson's?" she asked.

He told her.

"Well, I tell you what we'll do. You go home and think over all the ways we can put this idea into practice. I'll do the same thing. And then we'll talk it over again to-morrow night. On Wednesday you go down to see Judge Stevenson and see if he will draw up the papers so it'll be legal and binding and everything else. Then on Thursday night you can present this as your own idea, and I'll bet you anything you say, they'll take it up and you'll be the one chosen to lead the whole movement."

After some discussion of details, Kenneth left. The more he thought of Jane's idea, the more it appealed to him. At any rate, she had suggested more in half an hour than he had been able to think of in four days. Hadn't the co-operative societies been the backbone of the movement to get rid of the Czar in Russia? If the Russian peasants, who certainly weren't as educated as the Negro in America, had made a success of the idea, the Negro in the South ought to do it. By Jove, they could do it! Idea after idea sprang to his mind, after the seed had been sown by Jane, until he had visions of a vast co-operative society not only buying but selling the millions of dollars' worth of products raised by the nine million Negroes of the South. And that wasn't all! These societies would be formed with each member paying monthly dues, like the fraternal organizations. When enough money was in the treasury, they would employ the very best lawyers money could get to take one of those cases where a Negro had not been able to get a fair settlement with his landlord, and make a test case of it. What if they did lose in the local court? They'd take it to the State Supreme Court! What if they did lose even there? They'd take it clear up to the United States Supreme Court! They were sure to win there. Kenneth walked home with his head whirling with the project's possibilities. He saw a new day coming when a man in the South would no longer be exploited and robbed just because he was black. And when that came, lynching and everything else like it would go too. He felt already like Matthew and Andrew and Peter and John and the other disciples when they started out to bring the good news to the whole world. For wasn't he a latter-day disciple bringing a new solution and a new hope to his people?

It was not until Kenneth had gone to bed that he realized that though he had been with Jane all the evening, he had had not one minute when he could have spoken of love to her. Musing thus, he fell asleep.

CHAPTER XI

EARLY the next morning Kenneth rose and rummaged through his books until he found his old and battered text-books on economics. Into these he dipped during the intervals between patients, making notes of ideas which seemed useful in the organization of the co-operative society. The more he read, the more feasible the plan seemed. Properly guided and carefully managed, there was no reason, so far as he could see, why the society should not be a success. Eighty per cent of the farmers of the South, white and coloured, he estimated, suffered directly or indirectly from the present economic system. Though his interest was in the Negro tillers of the soil, success in their case would inevitably react favourably on the white—just as oppression and exploitation of the Negro had done more harm to white people in the South than to Negroes. Kenneth felt the warm glow of the crusader in a righteous cause. Already he saw a new day in the South with white and coloured people free from oppression and hatred and prejudice—prosperous and contented because of that prosperity. He could see a lifting of the clouds of ignorance which hung over all the South, an awakening of the best in all the people of the South. Thus has youth dreamed since the beginning of time. Thus will youth ever dream. And in those dreams rests the hope of the world, for without them this world with all its defects would sink into the black abyss of despair, never to rise again.

His work finished for the day, he went as soon as he decently could to talk with Jane. She, too, had been at work. Eagerly they planned between them the infinite details of so ambitious a scheme. Confidently they discounted possible difficulties they might expect to encounter—the opposition of the whites who were profiting from the present system, the petty jealousies and suspicions of those who would gain most from the success of their scheme. They realized that the Negro had been robbed so much, both by his own people and by the whites, that he was chary of new plans and projects. They knew he was contentious and quarrelsome. These things seemed trivial, however, for with the natural expansiveness of the young they felt that difficulties like these were but trifles to be airily brushed aside.

Jane was not too much engrossed in their plans to notice the change in Kenneth's manner. She had watched him closely during the times she had seen him since his return. He had been almost morose, his mind divided between his work and the effort to keep to a "middle-of-the-road" course in his relations with the whites. The inevitable conflict within himself, the lack of decisiveness in his daily life that he consciously developed and which was so diametrically opposite to that he used in his profession, had begun to create a complex personality that was far from pleasing. In a freer atmosphere Kenneth would have been a direct, straightforward character, swift to decision and quick of action. One cannot, however, compromise principle constantly and consciously without bearing the marks of such conflicts.

His compromises were not all conscious ones, though. He believed honestly it was wisest that he observe some sort of half-way ground between rank cowardice and uncompromising opposition to the conditions which existed. In doing so, he had no sense of physical or moral timidity. He knew no Negro could yet safely advocate complete freedom for the Negro in the South. He felt there had been improvement during the past half-century in those conditions. He believed that in time all of the Negro's present problems would be solved satisfactorily. If, by not trying to rush things, he could help in that solution, he was content. In believing thus, Kenneth was different in no way from the majority of intelligent Negroes in the South: temporizing with the truth, it may be, yet of such temporizations and compromises is the life of the Negro all over the South.

With the evolving of a plan which enabled him to be of help and, at the same time, involved him in no danger of trouble with his white neighbours, Kenneth took on an eagerness which was at marked var-

iance with his former manner. His eyes shone with
the desire to make their plan a success. Of a tender
and sympathetic nature, almost with the gentleness
of a woman, he realized now that the burdens of his
race had lain heavy upon him. He had suffered in
their suffering, had felt almost as though he had been
the victim when he read or heard of a lynching, had
chafed under the bonds which bound the hands and
feet and heart and soul of his people. But launched
as he now was on a plan to furnish relief from one
of the worst of those bonds, he had changed over-
night into a determined and purposeful and ardent
worker towards the goal he and Jane had set for
themselves. Jane rejoiced at the changed air of Kenneth—he seemed to have emerged from the shell in
which he had encased himself and, womanlike,
she rejoiced that he had done so through her own
work.

So absorbed had they been in discussion of their
plans that the time had flown by as though on wings.
Ten o'clock was announced by Mr. Phillips in the
room above by the dropping of his shoes, one after
the other, on the floor. Kenneth needed no second
signal, he rose to go. Jane went to the door with
him.

"Kenneth, you're entirely different from the way
you were yesterday. I'm so glad. . . ."

The next morning he called on Judge Stevenson.
The Judge's office was above the Bon Ton Store in a
two-story brick building on Lee Street. Kenneth

climbed the flight of dingy, dusty stairs which bore alternately on the vertical portions tin signs inscribed:

RICHARD P. STEVENSON, ATTORNEY-AT-LAW

and

DR. J. C. CARPENTER, DENTIST.

The judge's office was at the head of the stairs and in it Kenneth found the old lawyer seated near the window, his coat off, and in his mouth the long, thin, villainous-looking cigar without which few persons in Central City ever remembered seeing him, though none had ever seen one of them lighted. He chewed on it ruminatively when in repose. When engaged in an argument, either in or out of a courtroom, and especially when opposition caused his choleric temper to be aroused, he chewed furiously as though he would have enjoyed treating his enemy of the moment in similar fashion. He was tall and thickset, his snow-white hair brushed straight back from his forehead like the mane of a lion. Skin reddened by exposure to sun and wind, bushy eyebrows from under which gleamed fiery eyes that could shift in an instant from twinkling good humour to flashing indignation or anger, thin nose and ample mouth, his face was one that would command respect or at least attention in almost any gathering. He wore loosely fitting, baggy clothes that draped his ample figure with a gracefulness that added to his distinguished appearance. Many thought he resembled at first glance that famous Kentuckian,

Henry Watterson, and indeed he did bear an unmistakable likeness to "Marse Henry."

The judge's life had been a curious combination of contradictions. He had fought valiantly in the Confederate army as a major, serving under "Stonewall" Jackson, whose memory he worshipped second only to that of his wife, who had died some ten years before. He bore a long scar, reminder of the wound that had laid him low during the battle of Atlanta. His mode of brushing his hair back was adopted to cover the mark, but when he talked, as he loved to do, of his martial experiences, he would always, at the same time in the narrative, brush, with one sweep of his hand, the hair down over his forehead and reveal the jagged scar of which he was inordinately proud.

With the end of the Civil War, he had reconciled himself to the result though it had meant the loss of most of his wealth. He harboured little bitterness towards the North, unlike most of his comrades in arms who never were willing to forgo any opportunity to vent their venomous hatred of their conquerors. Judge Stevenson had counselled against such a spirit. So vigorously had he done it, he had alienated most of those who had been his closest friends. Following a speech he had delivered at one of the reunions of Confederate veterans in which he urged his comrades at least to meet half-way the overtures of friendliness from the North, he had been denounced from the floor of the convention as a "Yankee-lover," and threatened with violence. Judge Stevenson with flashing eye and belligerent manner had jumped to his feet, offered to fight any man, or any ten men, who thought him guilty of treachery to the cause of the Confederacy, and when none accepted the challenge, denounced them as cowards and quit the convention.

He had hoped that, with the passing on, one by one, of the unreconstructed veterans of the Confederacy, a newer and less embittered generation, with no personal memories of the gall of defeat, would right things. Instead had come the rise of the poor whites with none of the culture and refinement of the old Southern aristocracy, a nation of petty minds and morals, vindictive, vicious, dishonest, and stupid. Lacking in nearly all the things that made the old South, at least the upper crust of it, the most civilized section of America at that time, he saw his friends and all they stood for inundated by this flood of crudeness and viciousness, until only a few remained left high and dry like bits of wreckage from a foundered ship cast up on the shore to rot away, while all around them raged this new regime, no longer poor in purse but eternally impoverished in culture and civilizing influences. On these the judge spat his contempt and he poured upon their unconcerned heads the vials of his venom and wrath.

The second devastating blow he suffered was the succumbing, one by one, of his children to the new order. Nancy, his eldest daughter, had run away from home and married a merchant whose wealth had been gained through the petty thievery of padding accounts and other sharp practices on poorer whites and Negroes. Mary Ann, his other daughter, whom he loved above all others of his children, had fallen victim to an unfortunate love affair with a dashing but worthless son of their next-door neighbour. She had died in giving birth to her child, which, fortunately, the judge thought, had been born dead. His son had "gone in for politics." He had been successful, as success was measured by the present-day South, but in his father's eyes, judged by the uncompromising standards of that member of an older and nobler generation, he had sunk to levels of infamy from which he could never recover.

The crowning misfortune dealt the judge by an unkind fate was the loss of his gentle, kindly wife. She had uncomplainingly borne their misfortunes one after another, had calmed and soothed her husband's irascible tantrums, had been a haven to which he could come and find repose when buffeted by a world which he did not and could not understand. As long as she lived, he had been able to bear up despite the bitter disappointments life had dealt him. He had gone away to try a case in a near-by county, had returned after a two days' absence and found her with a severe cold and fever. For three weeks he did not leave her bedside, drove away in anger the trained nurse Dr. Bennett brought to the house, ministered gently to his wife's every need, and held her in his arms as she breathed her last breath. Frantic at this last and most crushing blow, he cursed the doctor, though Dr. Bennett had done all he could in his bungling way, cursed God, cursed everything and everybody he could think of in his grief. He never recovered from this loss. His hair rapidly became white, he neglected his profession and sat by the hour, his eyes half closed, dreaming of his dead wife. . . .

Had he chosen to adapt himself to the new order, he could have made money. This, however, he refused to do. He boasted proudly that never had he cheated any man or been a party to any transaction from which he emerged with any stain on his honour. Friend he was to all in his gentle, kindly manner—a relic of a day that had passed.

He started, roused from one of his usual reveries, when Kenneth knocked on the open door. The gentle breezes of late spring stirred the mane of white hair as he brought his chair to the floor with a thump.

"Come in, Ken, come right in." He welcomed Kenneth heartily, though in accordance with the Southern custom he did not offer to shake hands with his visitor. "How's your maw? Heard you're doing right well since you been back. Mighty glad to hear it, because yo' daddy set a heap by you."

Kenneth assured him he was progressing fairly well, told him his mother was well, and answered the innumerable questions the judge asked him. He knew that these were inevitable and must be answered before the judge would talk on any matter of business. After a few minutes of the desultory and perfunctory questions and answers, Kenneth told, when asked, the purpose of his visit. Chair tilted back again, elbows resting on the arms of the chair, fingers placed end to end, and his chin resting on the natural bridge thus formed, the judge listened to Kenneth's recital of his plan without comment other than an occasional non-committal grunt.

". . . And what I would like from you, Judge Stevenson, is, first, do you think the plan will work, and, second, will you draw up the articles of incorporation and whatever other legal papers we need?" Kenneth ended. As an afterthought he added:

"You see, we want to do the job legally and above board, so there won't be any misunderstanding of our motives."

For a long time Judge Stevenson said nothing, nor did he give any indication that he was aware Kenneth had stopped speaking. In fact he seemed oblivious even of Kenneth's presence. Knowing better than to interrupt him, Kenneth awaited somewhat anxiously the judge's opinion. When the silence had lasted nearly five minutes, a vague alarm began to creep over Kenneth. Suppose the judge wasn't as friendly towards coloured people as he had supposed? A word from him could start serious trouble before they got started. He wondered if he had acted wisely in revealing so much of their plans. He felt sure he had done wrong when he saw a look of what appeared to be anger pass over the judge's face.

At last the old lawyer cleared his throat, his usual preliminary to speech. But when he did talk he began on another subject.

"What're the folks out your way saying about these

Kluxers? Any of you getting worried about these fools parading 'round like a bunch of damn fools?"

"To tell you the truth, Judge, I don't really know yet what the coloured people are thinking." He felt that on this subject he could speak frankly to the judge, as he was too sensible a man to take much stock in the antics of the Klan. Yet, he was not too sure—coloured people must always keep a careful watch on their tongues when talking to white people in the South.

"You ain't getting scared out there, are you?" the judge pressed the point.

"No, I wouldn't call it scared. Most of those with whom I've talked don't want any trouble with anybody—they want to attend to their own business and be let alone. But if they are attacked, I'm afraid there will be considerable trouble and somebody will get hurt." He paused, then went on: "And that somebody won't be entirely composed of Negroes, either."

"I reckon you're right, Ken. These fools don't know they're playing with dynamite." His voice took on a querulous tone. "We've been getting along all right here, 'cept when some of these po' whites out of the mill or from the tu'pentine camps or some bad nigras tank up on bad liquor or moonshine." He did not say "Negro" nor yet the opprobrious "nigger," but struck somewhere between the two—"nigra." "And now these fools are just stirring up trouble—Lord knows where it'll end."

He ran his hand through his hair—a favourite trick of his when excited, and paced up and down the room.

"I've been telling some of the boys they'd better stay away from that fool business of gallivanting around with a pillow-slip over their heads. They talk about being against bootleggers and men runing around with loose women—humph!—every blamed bootlegger and blind tiger and whoremaster in town rushed into the Klan 'cause they know'd that was the only way they could keep from getting called up on the carpet! A fine bunch they are!"

The judge spat disgustedly.

"Now about this plan you got—have you thought about the chances of your being misunderstood? Suppose some of these ornery whites get it into their heads you're trying to start trouble between the races. What're you going to do then?" he asked.

"That's just why we want to do the job right," answered Kenneth. "We want to do everything legally so there can't be any wrong ideas about the society. I know every time coloured people start forming any kind of an organization besides a church or a burial society, there are white people who begin to get suspicious and think that Negroes are organizing to start some mischief. That's why we want you and the other good white people to know all about our plans from the start."

"I ain't trying to discourage you none," replied Judge Stevenson doubtfully, "but do you think you are wise in starting coloured folks to thinking about organizing when this Klan's raising hell all over the South?"

"How else are we going to do anything?" asked Kenneth. "Farmers have been robbed so long they are getting tired of it. If something isn't done, there's going to be lots more trouble than a society like ours can possibly cause. This share-cropping business causes more trouble than any other thing that's done to Negroes. Lynching is mighty bad, but after all only a few Negroes are lynched a year, while thousands are robbed every year of their lives."

"That's so. That's so," agreed the judge, but the doubt had not been dispelled from his voice nor removed from his face. He removed his cigar from his mouth, viewed its mangled appearance through much chewing upon it, threw it with an expression of disgust out of the window, narrowly missing a man passing in the street below. He chuckled as he placed a fresh cigar in his mouth.

" 'Taint no harm in trying, though," he said, half to himself.

"Besides, our plan is to enlist the support of every white man in the county who stands for something," went on Kenneth, eager to gain the old man as a staunch ally. "We know there'll be opposition from some of the landlords and merchants and bankers who are making money off this system, but we figure there are enough decent white people here to help us through. . . ."

"Mebbe so. Mebbe so," replied the judge, though there was a distinct note of doubt in his voice now. "I wouldn't be too sure, though. I wouldn't be too sure."

"But, Judge——" interrupted Kenneth. The judge silenced him with a movement of his hand.

"Ken, have you ever thought out what a decent white man goes through with in a town like Central City? Have you thought what he has to put up with all over the South? There ain't a whole lot of them, but just figure what'd happen to a white man to-day who tried to do anything about cleaning up this rotten state of affairs we got here. Why, he'd be run out of town, if he wasn't lynched!"

"But, Judge," began Kenneth again, "take lynching, for example. You know, and I know, and everybody in the South knows that if a Negro is arrested charged with criminal assault on a white woman, if he's guilty, there isn't one chance in a million of his going free. Why don't they bring them to trial and execute them legally instead of hanging and burning them?"

"Why? Why?" The judge repeated the interrogative as though it were a word he had never heard before. "You know, and so do I and all the rest of us here in the South, that nine out of ten cases where these trifling women holler and claim they been raped, they ain't been no rape. They just got caught and they yelled rape to save their reputations. And they lynch the nigra to hush the matter up."

Kenneth was amazed at the old man. Not amazed at what he said, for that is common knowledge in the South. He was astounded that even so liberal a man as the judge should frankly admit that which is denied in public but known to be true. He hesitated to press the inquiry further, and thought it expedient to shift the conversation away from such dangerous ground.

"Why don't men like yourself speak out against the things you know are wrong, Judge?"

"What would happen to us if we did? Count me out 'cause I'm so old I couldn't do much. But take right here in Central City the men I've talked with just like I'm talking to you. How many of them could say what they really want to? I don't mean on the race question. I mean on any question—religion, politics—oh—anything at all. Suppose Roy Ewing or any other white man here said he was tired of voting the Democratic ticket and was going to vote Republican or Socialist. Suppose he decided he didn't believe in the Virgin Birth or that all bad folks were burned eternally in a lake of fire and brimstone after they died. If they didn't think he was crazy, they'd stop trading with him and all the womenfolks would run from Roy's wife and daughter like they had the smallpox. That's the hell of it, Ken. These po' white trash stopped everybody from talking against lynching nigras, and they've stopped us from talking about *anything*. And far's I can see, things're getting worse every day."

"Couldn't you organize those white people who think like you do?" asked Kenneth.

"No, that ain't much use either. It all goes back to the same root—self-interest—how much is it going to cost me? I tell you, Ken, the most tragic figure I know is the white man in the South who

wants to be decent. This here system of lynching
and covering up their lynching with lying has grown
so big that any man who tries to tackle it is beat
befo' he starts. 'Specially in the little towns. Now
in Atlanta there's some folks can speak out and say
most anything they please, but here——" The old
lawyer threw out his hands in a gesture of hopeless-
ness.

"Why can't the South see where their course is
leading them?" asked Kenneth. "Suppose there
wasn't a white man in the South who was interested
in the Negro. Suppose every white man hated every
Negro who lived. Why couldn't they see even then
that they are doing more harm to themselves than
they could ever do to the Negro? With all its rich
natural resources, with its fertile soil and its wonderful climate, the South is farther behind in civilization
than any other part of the United States—or the
world, for that matter. Aren't they ever going to
see how they're hurting themselves by trying to keep
the Negro down?"

"That's just it," replied the judge. "A man starts
out practising cheating in a petty way, and before he
knows it he's crooked all the way through. He
starts being mean part of the time, and soon he's mean
all over. Or he tries being kind and decent, and
he turns out to be pretty decent. It's just like a man
drinking liquor—first thing he knows, he's liable to
be drunk all the time."

The judge shifted his cigar to a corner of his
mouth and let fly a stream of tobacco juice from the

other corner, every drop landing squarely in the box of sawdust some ten feet away. He went on:

"That's just what's the matter with the South. She's been brutal and tricky and deceitful so long in trying to keep the nigras down, she couldn't be decent if she tried. If acting like this was going to get them anywhere, there might be some reason in it all, but they've shut their eyes, they refuse to see that nigras like you ain't going to be handled like yo' daddy and folks like him were."

"What are we going to do—what can we do?" asked Kenneth. Never had he suspected that even so fine a man as Judge Stevenson had thought things through as their conversation had indicated. He felt the situation was not entirely hopeless when men like the judge felt and talked as he did. Perhaps they were the leaven that would affect the lump of ignorance and viciousness that was the South.

"What are we going to do?" echoed the elder man. "God knows—I don't! Mebbe the lid will blow off some day—then there would be hell to pay! One thing's going to help, and that's nigras pulling up stakes and going North. When some of these white folks begin to see their fields going to seed, they'll begin to realize how much they need the nigra— just like some of 'em are seeing already."

"But are they seeing it in the right way?" asked Kenneth. "Instead of trying to make things better so Negroes are willing to stay in the South, they're trying more oppressive methods than ever before. They're beating up labour agents, charging them a thousand dollars for licences, lynching more Negroes, and robbing them more than ever."

"Oh, they'll be fools enough until the real pinch comes. Far's I can see, instead of stopping nigras from going North, them things are hurrying them up. Wait till it hits their pocket-books hard. Then the white people'll get some sense."

"Let's hope so," was Kenneth's rejoinder as he rose to go. "It's been mighty comforting to talk like this with you, Judge. Things don't seem so hopeless when we've got friends like you."

" 'Tain't nothing. Nothing at all," replied the judge. "Just like to talk with somebody's got some sense. It's a pity you're coloured, Ken, you got too much sense to be a nigra."

Kenneth laughed.

"From all we've been saying, a coloured man's got to have some sense or else he's in a mighty poor fix nowadays."

He did not resent the old man's remark, for he knew the judge could not understand that he was much more contented as a member of a race that was struggling upward than he would have been as one of that race that expended most of its time and thought and energy in exploiting and oppressing others. The judge followed him to the door promising to draw up the necessary legal documents for the co-operative society. When Kenneth broached the subject of payment, the old man waved his hand again in protest.

"Ain't got long to live, so's I got to do what little

I can to help. 'Tain't much I can do, but I'll help all I can."

Thanking him, Kenneth started to leave, but the judge recalled him after he had reached the hallway.

"Ken, just consider all I said as between us. Can't tell what folks'd say if they knew I been running on like this."

There was almost a note of pleading in his voice. Kenneth assured the judge their conversation would be treated as confidential. As he walked home, he reflected on the anomalous position the judge and men like him occupied, hemmed in, oppressed, afraid to call their souls their own, creatures of the Frankenstein monster their own people had created which seemed about to rise up and destroy its creators. No, he said to himself, he would much rather be a Negro with all his problems than be made a moral coward as the race problem had made the white people of the South.

The judge stood at the window, dim with the dust of many months, and gazed at Kenneth's broad back as he swung down Lee Street. Long after he had disappeared, the old man stood there, chewing on the cigar which by now was a mangled mass of wet tobacco. At last he turned away and resumed his seat in the comfortable old chair where Kenneth had found him. He shook his head slowly, doubtfully, and murmured, half to himself, half to the dusty, empty room:

"Hope this thing turns out all right. Hope he don't get in no trouble. But even if he does, there'll be more like him coming on—and they got too much sense to stand for what nigras been made to suffer. Lord, if we only had a few white folks who had some sense . . ."

It was almost a prayer.

CHAPTER XII

FROM Judge Stevenson's office Kenneth went directly to tell Jane of the interview. So absorbed was he in contemplation of the wider vision of the problem he was attacking which the judge's words had given him, he forgot to telephone her to ask if it was agreeable for him to call at so unconventional an hour. He found her clad in a bungalow apron busily cleaning house and singing as she worked.

They sat on the steps of the back porch while he told her all that had been said. Taken out of his preoccupation with his own affairs, Kenneth had shaken off his negative air and now he talked convincingly of their plans. Jane said nothing until he had finished.

"That's fine!" she exclaimed when he had ended. "Even if Judge Stevenson is doubtful of how much we can accomplish, we can do something. Now all that remains is for you to present your plan——"

"Not mine, yours," he corrected.

"No, it will have to be yours," she answered. "You know how folks are in the South—they think all that women can do is cook and keep house and bear children. If you want the thing to go, it'll be best to make them think it's your scheme."

Kenneth demurred, but in vain. She would have it no other way. She felt no jealousy. She knew of the peculiar Southern prejudice which relegated women to a position of eternal inferiority. Though she felt the injustice of such arbitrary assumptions, she did not resent it. Like all women, coloured women, she realized that most of the spirit of revolt against the wrongs inflicted on her race had been born in the breasts of coloured women. She knew, and in that knowledge was content, that most of the work of the churches and societies and other organizations which had done so much towards welding the Negro into a racial unit had been done by women. It was amusing to see men, vain creatures that they are, preen themselves on what they had done. It was not so amusing when they, in their pride, sought to belittle what the women had done and take all the credit to themselves. Oh, well, what did it matter? The end was the all-important thing—not the means. Jane appreciated Kenneth's thoughtfulness and felt no tinge of jealousy if her idea—their idea—should be a success in forming societies to help poor, helpless Negroes out of the morass in which they were bogged. Of such material has the coloured woman been made by adversity.

She watched Kenneth as he told her the developments of which he had thought, the details he had worked out. Each day, it seemed to her, Kenneth became more keenly alive—each day saw a brighter sparkle in his eyes, a springiness in his step that had not been there before. There are many men who

could willingly have followed—and do follow—
without revolt or much inward conflict a course of
self-abnegation such as he had mapped out for himself. Not so, however, with Kenneth. He was almost puritanical in his devotion to the fixed moral
code he had worked out for his own guidance. It
was not a superimposed one, but an integral part of
his very being. Nothing could have induced him to
surrender to deliberate malice or guile or what he
considered dishonesty or cowardice. His was a simple nature, free from the barnacles of pettiness which
encumber the average man. He was not essentially
religious in the accepted meaning of the word. He
believed, though he had not thought much on the subject of religion, so immersed had he been in his beloved profession, in some sort of a God. Of what
form or shape this being was, he did not know. He
had more or less accepted the beliefs his environment had forced upon him. He doubted the malig-
nity of the God described by most of the ministers
he had heard. As a matter of fact, he was rather
repelled and nauseated by the religion of the modern
Church. Narrow, intolerant of contrary opinion,
prying into the lives and affairs of its communicants
with which it had no concern, its energies concen-
trated on raising money and not on saving souls, of
little real help to intelligent people to enable them
to live more useful lives here on earth, and centering
instead on a mysterious and problematical life after
death, he felt the Church of Jesus Christ had so little
of the spirit of the Christ that he had little

patience with it. He went to services more as a perfunctory duty than through any deep-rooted belief that he could get any real help from them in meeting the problems of life he faced. He bore the Church no grudge or ill will—it simply was not a factor in the life of to-day as he saw it.

Nevertheless he had a deep religious or, better, an ethical sense. When he was about to return to Central City, that ethical code had been adapted to conditions he expected to find there. It was galling to him to accept a position of subserviency to things he knew were unjust and wrong, tacitly to admit his inferiority to men to whom he knew he was superior in morals and training and in all the decencies of life, solely because of the mere accident that they had been born with skins which were white and he with one which was not white. When doubts had assailed him, he had quieted or salved his conscience by the constant reminder that he was following such a course for greater eventual good. On his return, when he had found a course such as he had charted for himself was becoming increasingly difficult, he had refused to face the facts his mind told him were true and had plunged more deeply into his work, seeking in it an opiate. Only when Jane had confronted him with the utter futility of his course and had, in effect, accused him of being a moral quitter in considering only himself and blinding himself to the far greater problems of those so closely bound to him by race, did his eyes begin to be opened. Wearied of illusory hopes of peace through compromise, he had grasped the tangible reality of work towards a definite end, through means which he had created and which he would guide and develop as far as he could. With the buoyant hopes and ambitions of the young, especially of the very young, he felt that he had already created that which he was hoping to create. Like a traveller who has lost his way in a dense forest, an indefinable restlessness had pervaded his being and made him sorely discontented. Now that he had found what seemed the path which would lead him into the clear, open air, the clouds of doubt and perplexity were cleared away just as the bright sun, as it bursts forth after a shower in spring, drives away the moisture in the air.

They sat there in the warm sunlight of early summer, dreaming and planning all the great things they were going to accomplish. It had rained earlier in the morning and from the ground rose a misty vapour. The odour of warm wet earth mingled with the aroma of the flowers. Hens scratched industriously for food to feed the cluster of tiny chicks around them. A cat sneaking along the fence slyly crept near. With a great fluttering of wings and raucous cackling, the hens drove him away. From afar off came the voices of two women, resting for a minute from their morning toil, gossiping with much loud laughter. It was a peaceful, restful scene. To Kenneth as he sat there, problems seemed remote and out of place in that place where all was so calm.

He looked at the girl by his side. It seemed

Jane had never looked more charming clad in her
bungalow apron, dust-cloth in hand. He was glad
she had made no silly, conventional excuses because
of her dress. The usual girl would have tried to
rush indoors and change her dress. Most women,
he reflected, looked like angels at night, but in the
harsh glare of morning looked terrible. Jane
seemed to him to be even prettier without powder
or the soft light of evening. He felt a thrill of
pleasure as he saw her dusting furniture in *their*
home.

They rose as Kenneth started to leave. Jane was
telling him of some trivial incident, but Kenneth
heard nothing of what she said. He turned towards
her suddenly.

She divined his intentions—she could almost feel
the words that were on his lips. Quickly wishing
him success in the meeting to be held that next evening, she bade him good-bye.

After Kenneth had gone, Jane sat for some time
struggling with the problem she was facing. What
was she to do? As a little girl she had loved Kenneth with a simple, childlike love though he, with
the infinite difference of eight years of age, had paid
no attention to her. She was not at all sure now of
the nature of her feelings towards him. She liked
him, it is true, but when it came to anything deeper
than that, she was not so certain. She had been told,
and had always believed, that love came as a blinding, searing, devastating passion which swept everything before it. She felt none of this passion and

experienced no bit of that complete surrender which she had believed was a part of the thing called love. Jane was much in the position of the sinner on the mourner's bench who had been told that when he became a Christian, angels and all sorts of heavenly apparitions would miraculously appear before him, and, seeing none, feels that he is being cheated.

Jane had seen in Kenneth's eyes that soon he would make some sort of declaration of his love. What was she going to say? She did not know. . . .

So pleasant had it been sitting there in the warm sunlight talking with Jane, Kenneth had forgotten the time. Entering his office, he found half a dozen patients waiting somewhat impatiently for him. As he entered his private office, he heard old Mrs. Amos, in her chronic quarrelsomeness, mutter:

"Dat's just what I allus say. Soon's a nigger begin to get up in the world, he thinks hisself better'n us po' folks. Thinks he can treat us any way he please."

Kenneth laughed and, with a few bantering words, mollified the irascible old woman. The coloured doctor has to be a diplomat as well as a physician—he must never allow the humblest of his patients to gain the impression that he thinks himself better than they. Of all races that make up the heterogenous populace of America, none is more self-critical than the Negro—its often unjust and carping criticism of those who stand out from the mass serves as an excellent antidote for undue pride and conceit. . . .

The next evening the seven men met again at Mr.

Wilson's. Kenneth stopped by for Mr. Phillips, but he did not see Jane. The Reverend Stewart, Tucker, Tracy, Swann, and Mr. Wilson sat awaiting them. Tom Tracy was exhibiting, somewhat proudly it seemed, a note he had found tacked to his door that morning. It was crudely lettered in red ink on a cheap-quality paper. It read:

NIGGER! YOU'VE BEN TALKING TOO DAM MUCH! IF YOU DON'T SHUT YOUR MOUTH WE WILL SHUT IT FOR YOU AND FOR GOOD! LET THIS BE A WARNING TO YOU. NEXT TIME WE WILL ACT!

K. K. K.

Beneath the three initials was a crude skull and cross-bones. Though all seven of the men knew that the warning was not to be disregarded, that it might possibly portend a serious attempt on the life of Tracy, that any or all of them present might receive a similar grim reminder of the ill will of the hooded band, there was a complete absence of fear as they sat around the table and conjectured as to the possible result of the warning. The calmness with which they accepted the omen of trouble would probably have amazed the senders of the warning. Perhaps the clearest indication of how little the South realizes the changes that have taken place in the Negro is this recrudescence of the Klan. Where stark terror followed in the wake of the Klan rides of the seventies, the net result of similar rides to-day is a more de-

termined union of Negroes against all that the Klan
stands for, tinctured with a mild amusement at the
Klan's grotesque antics. It was fortunate for Kenneth, in a measure, that Tracy had received the
threat on the day it came. With such a reminder before them, the seven felt there was greater need than
ever before for organization for mutual protection.

They discussed means of protecting Tracy, but he
assured them he was amply able to take care of himself. He had sent his parents that day to stay with
friends until the trouble had blown over, telling them
nothing of the warning, as he did not want them to
be worried by it. Two of his friends had agreed to
stay with him at night. He was well supplied with
ammunition and was sure the three of them could
successfully repel any attack that might be made
upon him. Such trying periods have happened to
Negroes so frequently in the South that they have
become inured to them. The subject was soon
dropped.

Then Kenneth presented his plan. He outlined in
detail how the society should be organized. He
proposed that the first lodge be formed at Ashland,
then gradually spread until there was a branch in
every section of the county. They left until later
the problem of extending the society's activities to
other parts of Georgia and the neighbouring States.

Each member would be required to pay an initiation fee of one dollar. Men would pay monthly dues
of fifty cents each, women twenty-five. The sums
thus secured were to be pooled. Half of the amount

was to purchase supplies like sugar, flour, shoes, clothing, fertilizer, seeds, farm implements, and the other things needed to satisfy the simple wants of the members. To make up any deficit, Kenneth and Mr. Phillips agreed to lend money that the supplies might be purchased for cash, effecting thereby a considerable saving. The other half was to be used as the nucleus of a defence fund with which a test case might be made in the courts when any member was unable to secure a fair settlement with his landlord.

Similarly were other details presented and discussed and adopted or modified. A name had to be chosen. Kenneth would have preferred a short, simple one, but here he was overruled. That it might appeal to the simple, illiterate class to which most of the prospective members belonged, a sonorous, impressive name was necessary. They decided on "The National Negro Farmers' Co-operative and Protective League."

At first the plan was considered a bit too ambitious, but as Kenneth warmed up to it in presenting it as simply and forcefully as he could, the objections, one by one, were overcome. One change, however, had to be made. It came from Hiram Tucker.

"Ain't you figgerin' on havin' no signs and passwords and a grip like dey have with de Odd Fellers and de Masons and de Knights of Pythias?" he asked.

"I didn't think that was necessary," replied Kenneth.

"Well, lemme tell you somethin', son. Ef you figgers on gettin' a big passel of these cullud folks 'round here to jine in with us, you'll have t' have some 'ficials with scrumptious names, and passwords and grips. Dese here ign'ant folks needs somethin' like dat to catch their 'magination. If you put dat in, they'll jine like flies 'round molasses."

Kenneth had hoped that the society would be run on a dignified and intelligent basis, but he realized that Hiram Tucker might be right after all. Most of the share-croppers were ignorant—at least, illiterate. Mere show and pomp and colourful uniforms and high-sounding names played a large part in their lives, which, after all, wasn't so much a racial as a human trait. Hadn't the Ku Klux Klan outdone, in absurdity of name and ceremony and dress, anything that Negroes had ever even thought of?

This question was disposed of, after more discussion, by the adoption of Hiram Tucker's suggestion. Kenneth was appointed to work out the details of organization, and the meeting adjourned. The National Negro Farmer's Co-operative and Protective League had been born.

CHAPTER XIII

THE days that followed were full of interest for Kenneth and Jane. The constitution and by-laws were drafted and approved and sent to Atlanta to be printed by a coloured printing firm. Judge Stevenson prepared the articles of incorporation and did the necessary legal work, still refusing any pay for his services. Kenneth had offered to pay him out of his own pocket, but the judge told him: "Keep your money, Ken, I c'n wait. I'm gettin' along in years now and I've been hopin' that this problem that's cursin' the South would be settled befo' I passed on. But what with these damn fool Kluxers kickin' up hell 'round here, I don't know whether I'll see it or not. Your idea may do some good—I don't know whether it will or not—but if I c'n help, let me know." Kenneth thanked him and had been immeasurably encouraged by the old man's attitude.

As soon as the literature they had ordered was received, the first meeting was called by Tucker and Tracy at Ashland. Jane and her father drove out with Kenneth, who was to present the plan to the group gathered. The meeting was held at a little wooden church, whitewashed on the outside, and furnished within only with rude benches. On the walls were one or two highly coloured lithographs of religious subjects. The hall seated not more than two hundred and was crowded to capacity. Even the windows were comfortably filled by those unable to obtain a seat on the floor. The illumination was furnished by four kerosene lamps attached to the walls, two on each side.

Hiram Tucker acted as chairman, while Tom Tracy took minutes of the meeting. After a preliminary announcement of the purpose of the gathering by the chairman, Kenneth was called upon to outline the plan that had been proposed. At the outset, having had no experience as a public speaker, he stumbled and faltered and knew not what to do with his hands. After a few minutes he jammed them into the side pockets of his coat and, warming to his subject, swung into a clear, forceful, and convincing recital of the purpose and possibilities of the co-operative societies. His enthusiasm became infectious. His audience began to share his zeal. Humble and lowly folks, their vision limited by the life they led, they had the feeling, as Kenneth talked on, of having been face to face with a blank wall of immeasurable height and impenetrable thickness. Under the spell of his words they seemed to see the miraculous opening of a door in this wall. Hope, which had been crushed to earth year after year by disappointing settlements for their labour, began to mount.

As for Kenneth, he had forgotten his self-imposed inhibitions and prohibitions. Gone was the hesitation and doubt. He had seen a light where he had thought there was no light. His voice rang true and

THE FIRE IN THE FLINT

firm, and there was a look of eager earnestness on his face as the pale, flickering light from the oil lamps illumined it.

He finished with a flourish so dear to the hearts of coloured audiences. It was what the old-style coloured preacher used to call "de 'rousements."

"You husbands and sons and brothers, three years ago you were called on to fight for liberty and justice and democracy! Are you getting it?" He was answered by a rousing "No!" "What are you going to do about it?" he demanded. "Single-handed, you can do nothing! Organized, you can strike a blow for freedom, not only for yourselves but for countless generations of coloured children yet unborn! No race in all history has ever had its liberties and rights handed to it on a silver platter—such rights can come only when men are willing to struggle and sacrifice and work and die, if need be, to obtain them! I call on you here to-night to join in this movement which shall in time strike from our hands and feet the shackles which bind them, that we may move on as a race together to that greater freedom which we have so long desired and which so long has been denied us! Only slaves and cowards whine and beg! Men and women stand true and firm and struggle onwards and upwards until they reach their goal!" He paused impressively while the audience sat mute. He looked over the assemblage for a full minute and then demanded in a ringing voice: "What do you choose to be—slaves or men?"

He sat down. A salvo of applause greeted him.

A Daniel had arisen to lead them! Kenneth took on a new importance and affection in the eyes and minds of his hearers. He had heard their Macedonian cry and answered it.

As he mopped his brow, Kenneth felt that he had made a good beginning, although he was a bit ashamed of having made so direct an appeal at the end to emotion instead of to reason. At the same time he knew that it had been necessary. " 'Rousements" were absolutely essential to awaken the response needed to get the co-operative societies under way. Without them his humble audience might not have been aroused to the point of action that was so necessary.

Following Kenneth, Mr. Wilson made a stirring appeal to the crowd to come forward and give their names if they wanted to join the newly formed society. Those who had the money were urged to join at once. At first, only a few came forward. Then they came in numbers until around the table at which sat Secretary Tracy there was an excited, chattering, milling throng.

After the meeting Mr. Phillips accepted Mr. Wilson's invitation to ride home in his car. Kenneth did not object—it enabled him to be alone with Jane. They talked of the meeting as they walked to the car. Jane gave Kenneth's hand a faint squeeze. "Oh, Kenneth, you were splendid!" she declared.

It was a perfect night—one created for making love. A soft light filtered through the leaves of the trees, casting a lace-like shadow on the earth. The air was soft and languorous, as it can be only on a spring evening in the South, as soft and caressing as the touch of a baby's hands. From near at hand came the mingled odour of honeysuckle and cape jasmine and magnolia blossoms and roses. The world seemed at peace. No sound disturbed the air save the chattering and singing of a mockingbird, as lovely as the sob of velvety, full-throated violins, and the voices, growing fainter and fainter, of the crowd leaving the now deserted church. It would have taken a much stronger man than Kenneth to resist the spell of so perfect an evening. He was not mawkishly sentimental—rather he detested the mooncalfish type of man who rolled his eyes and whispered empty, silly compliments in the ear of whatever girl he met. On the other hand, he was amazingly ignorant of women. As a youngster he had been exceedingly chary of the little girls of the neighbourhood, preferring to spend his time playing baseball or shooting marbles. This shyness had never entirely left him. From his youth on he had had but one strong passion in his life—that passion had possessed his every thought and in it was centred his every ambition—his desire and determination to become a great surgeon. His one serious venture into the realm of love-making had been the affair with the girl in New York, but that had not taken a strong enough hold upon him to leave much of a mark. So rapidly had it begun and ended that he had had in it little experience in the great American sport of "petting." It was thus easy for him to fall head over heels in love with Jane, for she was, in fact, the first girl in his life outside of his sister who had come into his life in more than a casual way.

Jane, on the other hand, had, innocently enough, flirted as every pretty girl (and many who are not pretty) will do. She appreciated Kenneth's fine qualities: he was capable, industrious, and handsome in a way. He annoyed her at times by his almost bovine stupidity in expressing his love. She naturally liked the idea of having the love of a man who is naïve, who has not run the whole gamut of emotions in affairs with other girls; yet, also naturally enough, she did expect him to have at least some *savoir faire*, to be able to win her with some degree of the finesse that every girl wants and expects. She resented his business-like matter-of-factness in seeking her—as coldly calculating, it seemed to her, as though he were operating on one of his patients. In this she was doing him an injustice. Underneath his surface placidity Kenneth's love had become a raging flame—he cursed the shell of professional dignity which had crossed over and become a part of himself.

Thus they walked through the soft spring air, she wishing he would do that which he in his ignorance felt would be the unwisest thing he could attempt. Thus is life made up of paradoxical situations where a word, a look, an otherwise insignificant gesture, would clear away at one fell swoop mountainous clouds of doubt and misunderstanding.

Jane stood, one foot on the ground, the other on
the step, her hand resting on the opened door of the
car. A faintly provocative smile flitted over her
face. Kenneth longed to seize this elusive, seductive
girl in his arms, press her close to him, and tell her
of his love. She wanted him to. Instead he steeled
himself against yielding to the impulse that almost
overcame him, and helped her with complete decorum
into the car. . . .

They did not say much on the way home. Jane
bade him good night, he thought somewhat coldly—
as though she were vexed. He told her he was leaving the next morning for Atlanta to operate on Mrs.
Tucker. She made no comment. He wondered as
he drove home what he had done to offend her. . . .

As he neared the house, he suddenly remembered
that he had promised to look in on old Mrs. Amos,
whose "rheumatics" had been giving her considerable
pain. It was charity work, as she would never be
able to pay him. She had sent for him several times
during the day, but he had been kept so busy he
had had no time to go. He was annoyed at himself
for promising to call to see the quarrelsome old
woman who was far more dictatorial and exacting
than most of the patients who paid him promptly.
With a muttered imprecation at being bothered with
her just after his annoying experience with Jane and
her inexplicable behaviour, he drove through the
darkened streets to Mrs. Amos' home. He found her
sitting in a creaky rocking-chair. She began immediately to pour maledictions on his head for neglect-

ing her all day. He answered her shortly, gave her her medicine, and left.

Carefully guiding the car through the gullies and holes in the unpaved street, he set out for home. Nearing the corner of Harris and State Streets, he heard a sound as of several automobiles. He looked down Harris Street just in time to see three closed cars stop suddenly at the corner. From one of them two white-robed figures descended, lifting a large, black bundle that seemed exceedingly heavy. This done, the figures jumped hurriedly into the car, and it with the other two speeded away in the direction from which they had come.

Kenneth, his curiosity aroused, turned his car around and drove to the spot to see what was going on. As he slowed his car at the corner, a muffled groan came from the object lying there in the street. Hastily getting down, he turned it over and in the half-light found it to be the body of a human being. His hands felt sticky. Holding them close to his face, he found them smeared with tar.

He got from his car a small flashlight. Going back to the inert mass, he turned the ray of light on the body and found it to be that of a naked woman, covered with tar yet warm to the touch. Between the dabs of the sticky mess on the woman's back were long welts, some of them bleeding, as though a heavy-thonged whip had been applied with great force. The hair was dishevelled and in its strands were bits of the melted tar. Kenneth experienced a feeling of nausea at the revolting sight. The woman lay on her face. From her mouth and nose there ran a stream of blood which already was forming a little pool beneath her face that became bloody mud as it mixed with the dust in the road. Seizing her by her left shoulder, Kenneth half raised the body and turned his flashlight on the woman's face. It was Nancy Ware, the wife of the Negro killed by George Parker.

Half carrying, half dragging the limp form, Kenneth managed in some fashion to get Nancy to her own home a few doors away. The door stood open as though Nancy had left it for a minute to call on one of her neighbours. On the table in the front room, there stood a lamp yet burning, the chimney blackened with the soot caused by the wind blowing upon it. Beside the lamp lay a garment on which Nancy had been sewing.

Kenneth placed her on the bed and hurried next door to summon help. His efforts were unsuccessful. He pounded on the door with both fists, calling out in his excitement to the occupants to open up. After what seemed an infinite delay, a window to the left of the door cautiously opened and an inquiring voice wanted to know what was the matter. Seeing who it was, the owner of the voice disappeared and a minute later opened the door. Kenneth hastily told what had happened, brushing aside a muttered excuse that the delay in answering was due to the fact that "I didn' know but whut you might 'a' been the p'lice."

On going back to Nancy's cottage, Kenneth gave her a restorative and endeavoured to relieve her suffering. She began to revive after a few minutes. In the meantime the neighbours called by Kenneth arrived, and they removed as much as they could of the tar from Nancy's body. Kenneth then examined her back, finding it covered with long and ugly gashes that bled profusely. He dressed them and Nancy was arranged as comfortably as possible. He found himself so tired after the hard work and excitement of the day and evening that he was almost ready to drop in his tracks. At the same time he had an uncontrollable desire to find out just what had happened to Nancy Ware. He was almost certain the Ku Klux Klan had done it, but he wanted to hear the story from Nancy's own lips. The neighbours had gone, with the exception of an evil-looking, elderly woman who had volunteered to remain with Nancy until morning.

After the application of restoratives regularly for an hour, she began to show signs of returning consciousness. Kenneth watched her eagerly. Five minutes later her eyelids fluttered. She gave a low moan—almost a whimper. Suddenly she cried out in the terror of delirium: "Doan let 'em whip me no mo'! Doan let 'em whip me no mo'!" and writhed in her agony. She struggled to arise but Kenneth, sitting by the side of the bed, managed with the aid of the other woman to restrain Nancy and calm her. Afterwards she became more rational. Her eyes opened. In them was a gleam of recognition of Kenneth and he knew she was regaining consciousness.

Another wait. Then, at Kenneth's questioning, she began to tell what had happened. For weeks he had thought but little of her and the tragedy that had taken place in this same house, other events having crowded it out of his mind.

"Doc, you won't let 'em get me again, will you?" she pleaded with a whimper like a child's. Kenneth assured her he wouldn't.

"Doc, I ain't done nuthin' t' them Kluxers. Hones' t' Gawd, I ain't." Kenneth told her soothingly that he knew she hadn't.

"I was jes' sittin' here tendin' to my own business when dey come a rap on de do'. W'en I open de do', dere wuz two o' dem Kluxers standin' dere—befo' I could holler dey grab me and put a rag in my mouf." A shudder passed through her body as the terror came back to her at the memory of what she had been through.

"Dey put me in a automobile and ca'ied me way out yonder in de woods by de fact'ry. Dey pull all my clo'es off me and den dey whip me till I couldn' stan' up no mo'. Den dey tell me I been talkin' too much. Doc, I ain't said a word t' nobdy 'cept dat dey oughter do somethin' t' that man George Parker for killin' my man Bud. . . . Den dey po'ed tar all over me and kick me and spit on me some mo'. . . . Said I oughter had mo' sense dan t' talk 'bout no white gemmen. Oh—oh—oh—ain't dey nothin' to he'p us po' cullud fo'ks—ain't dey nobody—ain't dey nobody?"

It was just as Kenneth had suspected. Good God,

and these were the self-elected defenders of morals in the South! What if Nancy wasn't all that she should have been?—whose was the greater fault—hers or George Parker's? He could see him now in the bank—smug, a hypocritical smile on his face, talking about what the white people have got to do to stop these troublesome "niggers" from getting too cheeky—about protecting "pure" Southern woman-hood from attacks by "black, burly brutes." And the Klan with all its boasted and advertised chivalry —twenty or thirty strong men to beat up and maltreat one lone woman, because she "talked too much" about the brutal, cold-blooded murder of her husband! Kenneth's optimism over the organization of the co-operative societies began to cool—in its stead there came a blind, unreasoning hatred and furious rage against the men who had done this deed to Nancy Ware. God, but he would have given anything he owned to get them all together and kill them one by one—slowly, with all the tortures he could devise! The damned, cowardly devils! The filthy, smug-faced hypocrites!

Nancy was resting easily. Kenneth, shaken by the fury of his anger, more devastating because he knew that he could do nothing but hurl silent imprecations on the heads of those who had done this deed—impotent because his skin was black and he lived in the South—went home to roll and toss during the few hours of the night which remained before he took the train to Atlanta.

CHAPTER XIV

I T seemed to Kenneth he had just fallen into a troubled slumber when he was aroused by the tinkling of the telephone bell at the side of his bed. It was Hiram Tucker.

"Doc, I reck'n you won't have to go t' Atlanty today, after all. My wife, she tol' me to tell you she's changed her min' 'bout that op'ration. . . . What's dat? . . . Naw, suh, she's kinder skeered she won' wake up from dat chlo'form. . . . Yas, suh, yas, suh, I knows 'rangements been made but, Doc, you ain't married, so you don't know nuthin' 'tall 'bout wimmenfolks. . . . Some day you'll learn dat when dey says dey ain't gwine do somethin' dey's done sot dere minds on not doing, dey ain't gwine t' do it. . . . Hello. . . . Hello. . . . Hello!"

But Kenneth had hung up. He telephoned the local telegraph office to send a wire to the hospital in Atlanta to cancel the arrangements he had made for the operation on the following day, and tumbled back in bed to sleep like a log until late in the morning.

He was awakened by Bob, who informed him that the reception room was half filled with patients who were no longer patient at being kept waiting so long. He arose reluctantly, his eyes still filled with sleep. Bob leaned against the wall, hands in pockets, and looked at his brother with a smile of amusement. Kenneth, not thoroughly awakened as yet, paid no attention to him for a time, but at last noticed Bob's smile.

"Why this early morning humour? I've seen many 'possums with a more engaging smile then the one that distorts your face now!" he half-grumblingly, half-cheerfully observed.

Bob but grinned the more at Kenneth's remark.

"I was just thinking that if Jane could only get one glimpse of you in the morning before breakfast, your chances would be mighty slim with her."

"Jane? What have my looks to do with her?" Kenneth retorted with some heat, in a vain attempt to spar for time.

Bob addressed the world in general, calling on it for some aid in understanding this brother of his.

"Jane?" he mimicked Kenneth's tone of surprise. "You talk like a ten-year-old boy with his first love affair. Isn't he the innocent one, though? Why, you poor maligned creature, everybody in Central City who isn't blind knows that you are head over heels in love with Jane Phillips. And," he added as an afterthought, "those who are blind have been told it. But to return to my original observation, if there was some means by which, with all propriety, all the girls in the world who are in love could see, and be seen by, the poor boobs with whom they are so infatuated, marriage-licence bureaus would be closed that day, never to open again." This last with an omniscient air of worldly wisdom that caused

Kenneth to burst into a roar of laughter, while Bob
watched him, somewhat discomfited.

"What're you laughing at?" he demanded in an
aggrieved tone. Kenneth laughed all the harder.
"Why, you poor little innocent, you haven't gotten
rid of your pin feathers, and yet you are talking as
though you were a philosopher like Schopenhauer.
You'd better wait until you finish school and see
something of the world. Then you can talk a little
—though only a little—as you did just now. By the
way, it's about time for you to be planning for school
this fall. Still thinking about going back to
Atlanta?"

"I don't know what I want to do," was Bob's troubled rejoinder. "I've seen too much of what's going on around this town since papa died to be satisfied with school again. I've probably seen more of
the real sordidness and meanness and deviltry of
this place since I've been settling up papa's affairs
than you'll see in five years. At any rate, I hope you
don't," he finished somewhat doubtfully.

"Bob"—Kenneth walked over and put his arm
around his brother's shoulders—"the trouble with
you is that you're too darned sensitive. I know
things aren't all they ought to be around here, but
we've got to buckle down and make them that way.
And perhaps I've seen more of this deviltry than you
think."

He told Bob of what had happened to Nancy Ware
the night before. A long whistle of surprise escaped from Bob's lips.

"And this happened right here in the coloured section?" he asked in surprise. Kenneth nodded in assent.

"I felt they were planning some mischief but I didn't think they would have the nerve to come right here in 'Darktown' and do it. I wonder," he said musingly, "if that dirty little Jim Archer who said those filthy things to Minnie Baxter that day is a member of the Klan. I passed him on Lee Street this morning and he grinned at me like a cat that has just eaten a fat mouse."

"He may be," Kenneth replied. "Nancy Ware told me last night she recognized the voices of Sheriff Parker and Henry Lane and George Parker and two or three other prominent white people here."

"That settles it," Bob answered determinedly. "When you first came back here I thought you were foolish to do so after having been in France. I said I was going to get out of this country as soon as I could and live in France or Brazil or any old place where a man isn't judged by the colour of his skin. But I've decided that I'd be a coward if I did run away like that. Ken," he said in voice that showed he had passed in spite of his years from childhood into the more serious things of manhood, "I'm going to Harvard this fall. I'm going to take whatever course I need to get into the law school. I'm going to make myself the best lawyer they can turn out. And then I'm coming back here to the South like you did and give my time to fighting for my people!"

Bob's eyes flashed. In them was a light of

high resolve—such a look as might have shone in the eyes of Garibaldi or of Joan of Arc.

Kenneth said nothing, but he gripped Bob's hand in his and there passed between the two brothers a look of mutual understanding and sympathy that was more potent and meaningful than words.

Kenneth went down to attend to his patients and nothing more was said of the incident between them. Bob took on a new interest in life. His moodiness, his brooding over the constant irritations and insults he had to suffer in his dealings as a coloured man with the whites of the town, his resentment at the attitude of condescension on the part of the poor and ignorant whites who had neither his intelligence, his education, nor his wealth—all these disappeared in his eager preparations for the new life he had mapped out for himself. He already saw himself a powerful champion of his race and he gloried in that vision with all of the impetuosity and idealistic fervour of youth.

As for Kenneth, he divided his time between his practice, Jane, and the formation of more branches of the N. N. F. C. P. L.

Kenneth knew there was nothing to be done towards the punishment of the men who had so brutally beaten Nancy Ware. He knew that it would even be unwise for him to talk too much about it. If Sheriff Parker was himself a member of the Klan, reporting the outrage to him would be in effect a serving of notice that he was meddling in the affairs of the Klan which might bring disastrous results at a time when Kenneth was most anxious to avoid such a complication, certainly until the co-operative societies were well under way and actively functioning. Much as he chafed under the restraint and at his own impotence in the situation, Kenneth knew that his interference would be a useless and foolhardy butting of his head against a stone wall.

It occurred to him to tell what had happened to Judge Stevenson. He could be trusted and was as much opposed to the outlawry of the Klan as Kenneth himself. The judge listened gravely to the end without comment other than a question here and there. "That looks worse than I thought," he said half to himself. "A few mo' cracks like that and there'll be hell to pay 'round here. But 'twon't do no good for you t' meddle in it," he observed in answer to Kenneth's question as to what he could do. "If Nancy's right about Bob Parker being in it, your sayin' anything will only set them on you. You'd better go ahead and get your societies on their feet and then you'll have somethin' behin' you. Then you won't be playin' a lone hand."

As for the coloured people, there were several days of excited gossip over what had happened to Nancy Ware. There was not much to go on, as she had been so frightened by her terrible experience that she refused for once to talk. The only tangible effect was that mysterious parcels marked with the names of household implements began to arrive at the homes of the coloured people, but which contained fire-arms and ammunition. There was also a noticeable tightening of the lips and the development of a less cordial relationship between white and black. Negroes, feeling that there was no help they could expect from the law, felt that their backs were being slowly pressed against the wall. Within a few hours the old *esprit cordial* between white and black had been wiped out. Negroes who had been happy-go-lucky, care-free, and kindly in manner began to talk among themselves of "dying fighting" if forced to the limit.

July came with all its heat. August passed with yet more heat. With the coming of September there had been formed in Smith County alone seven branch societies of the Co-operative and Protective League with a membership of more than twelve hundred. Kenneth worked as one inspired, one who knew neither heat nor cold, fatigue nor hunger. During the day he was busy with his practice, but it mattered not how busy he had been, he was always ready and willing to drive five, ten, fifteen miles at night to aid in establishing new branches or directing and guiding and advising those already established.

The Ashland Branch, through the hard work of Hiram Tucker and Tom Tracy, had enrolled three hundred and fifteen members. In its treasury it had $657.85, to which it was constantly adding as new members were enrolled. At a meeting held during the latter part of August the members decided that they would forgo the purchasing of their supplies in bulk that year but would use the money raised towards prosecuting one of the cases of dishonest settlements when the time came for such settlements, usually in December or January. This step was decided upon after due and lengthy deliberation, as it was felt that if they could end the cheating of the farmers through court action, then these same farmers would have more money through the settlement of their accounts for the present season and could then begin the co-operative buying and distribution the following year.

News of the new society that was going to end the unsatisfactory relations share-croppers had with their landlords spread rapidly throughout the surrounding counties. Letters, crudely and cumbersomely worded and with atrocious spelling, came to Kenneth and often individuals came in person to ask that he come to their counties to organize societies there. Kenneth was elated at this sign of interest. He had expected a great deal of opposition from the coloured farmers. Bickering and carping criticism there was aplenty, but most of them regarded him as a new Moses to lead them into the promised land of economic independence. Minor disputes over authority in the local societies there were in abundance. But none of them was hard to settle, for the members themselves were too eager to get out of bondage to tolerate much petty politics and selfishness on the part of their officers.

As a loyal ally Kenneth learned to rely on Jane more and more. Often she went with him to attend meetings and to talk to groups not yet organized. While Kenneth talked to the men, Jane circulated

among the women, who were subtly flattered that one
so daintily clad and well educated should spend so
much of her time and energy talking to lowly ones
like themselves.

Her mother's health had not been of the best during the summer. That had been throughout the summer her only worry. In August her mother had
suffered an attack of paralysis, her second one.
Jane decided to remain at home instead of going to
Oberlin to resume her music. Dr. Bennett had been
dismissed and Kenneth was now treating Mrs. Phillips. During her more serious illness in August,
Jane often sat on one side of her mother's bed until
late in the night while Kenneth sat on the other,
ministering to the aged woman's wants. There came
a new and stronger feeling of companionship between the two. Often Kenneth would look up suddenly and catch in Jane's eyes a new tenderness.
Without knowing what it meant, he felt a subtly con-
veyed encouragement in them.

He had, however, spoken no word of love to her,
preferring to bide his time until a propitious occasion
arose. He had told her that he loved her—had he
not done so, she would have known—he was content
to wait until she could decide what she wanted to do.
At times the task was hard not to tell her again and
again of his love. Often as she sat by his side and
talked of inconsequential things, he would again be
seized by that consuming impulse to sweep away all
her objections and demolish by the very violence of
his love the obstacles that held him back from possess-

ing her. He found himself more and more filled with a wonderment that bordered on dismay as he tried to suppress this devastating longing with less success every time this feeling came over him. He tried staying away from Jane. At first he had seen her but once a week and that on Sunday evenings. Then he began dropping by to see her on Wednesdays. Of late his visits had numbered three and four a week. On those nights when he was away, he was restless and irritable. This became so noticeable that Mamie threatened jokingly one night to go over and beg Jane to marry Kenneth or throw him down hard or anything that would make him less like a bear around the house. She and Jane had become fast friends—which pleased Kenneth not a little, as it meant that Jane would be more frequently in the house than otherwise would have been the case.

As for Jane, in spite of herself, she found herself more and more interested in Kenneth and the things he was doing. She found herself eagerly looking forward to the evenings when he called. She wondered if she were entirely honest in seeing so much of him.

Why didn't Kenneth say something now? She felt rather annoyed at him for being so considerate. With a woman's prerogative of inconsistency, she resented his obeying so implicitly her demand that he wait until she had made up her mind. Men were so silly—you told them to do a thing and they went like fools and did it. Why didn't he talk about something else besides his old co-operative societies and the Ku Klux Klan and his old hospital and what that old Judge Stevenson had said to him that day? Life is such a funny thing.

But Kenneth went along his way, not even suspecting what was going on in Jane's mind. He was like the majority of men—wise in their own minds but amazingly naïve and ignorant when they left the beaten paths of everyday affairs.

The end of the first week in September came. Bob had completed all arrangements to leave the following week for Cambridge, there to take his entrance examinations, after studying for them all summer. Kenneth had written to an old friend there who had made the necessary negotiations. Bob was an entirely new individual from the one he had been when Kenneth had returned to Central City. His air of moody resentment had been replaced by an eager earnestness to begin the course he had planned for himself. The bond had grown closer between him and Kenneth, and many hours they spent together discussing and planning for the years to come. Often the two brothers and Mamie, sometimes Mrs. Harper also, sat until far in the night talking of the future. If Mamie felt saddened by the broader and more active life her brothers were planning which she, as a woman, was denied, it never showed on her face or in her voice. She might have been married long before—in fact, there had been three or four men who wanted to marry her. None of them would she have. Decent enough men they were. But she was unwilling to settle down to the humdrum life of

[199]

marriage with a man so far beneath her in intelligence, in ideals, in education. Being a normal, warm-hearted human being, naturally she often pictured to herself what marriage in Central City would be like. But, keenly sensitive and ambitious, she shrank from marrying the type of men available, farmers, small merchants, and the like—she shuddered when she vis-ualized herself bearing children to such a man to be brought up in a place like Central City. She yearned for love—and as steadfastly put it from her. There are thousands of tragedies—for tragedy it is—like Mamie's in the South, and the world knows it not. When Kenneth or Bob teased her about marrying, she answered him with a brave and all-concealing smile—all-concealing, that is, to masculine eyes. Only her mother and Jane knew her secret, and their lips were sealed in the bond which women sel-dom, if ever, break. . . .

That night Jane looked better than Kenneth had ever seen her look before. They seldom went out except for a short ride in his car. For there was no place to which they could go. Central City boasted one place of public amusement—the Idle Hour Moving Picture Palace. And to that no Negro could go. Once they had admitted Negroes to the gallery. None of the better element ever went, as they had to go through a dark and foul-smelling alley-way to reach the entrance they had to use. The type of Negroes whose pride permitted them to go were so boisterous and laughed so loud that even they were soon barred.

As usual they sat on the vine-covered porch where a breath of cool air was more likely to be had than in the parlour. That day he had had one of his more frequently recurring spells when he felt that he could not keep his promise a day longer to wait until Jane had made up her mind. At first he had thought of telephoning her and saying that he was ill or busy— any old excuse to stay away. But he wanted to see her too much for that patent evasion. He would go over to see her but would talk of nothing but business or co-operative societies. That's it, he would keep in "safe" territory. But Jane had never looked more lovely than on that particular night. Kenneth's heart jumped as he greeted her after she had kept him waiting just the right length of time. He likened her instinctively to a flame-coloured flower of rare beauty. All of the suppressed passion surged upward in him. He felt himself slipping. He turned away to gain control of himself. Had he not done so, he would have seen the swift look of disappointment on her face at his restraint.

Keeping his eyes resolutely in front of him, he talked wearily and wearisomely of the meeting he had attended the night before, of how troublesome and irritating Mrs. Amos had been that day with her rheumatism, of his having at last persuaded Mrs. Hiram Tucker to go to Atlanta to have the operation she had so many times postponed. Jane answered him abstractedly and in monosyllables. At last she moved, almost with obvious meaning, to the canvas porch swing and there rested against the pillows piled in one corner. And yet Kenneth talked drearily on and on and on. He spoke at length of a conversation he had had with Bob that morning—of how glad he was that Bob was going away to school. Jane swung gently back and forth—and said nothing. Mr. Phillips came out on the porch and offered Kenneth a cigar, which he accepted and lighted. Mr. Phillips sat down and talked garrulously while the two men smoked. Jane felt that she could hardly keep from screaming. After what seemed an hour, Mr. Phillips, his topics of conversation exhausted, and at a sign from Jane that was not to be disregarded, rose heavily and lumbered into the house again.

Kenneth threw away the stump of his cigar. It had suddenly occurred to him that Jane hadn't said very much for the past hour. He rose to go.

Jane sat silent as though unmindful of his having risen. He looked closely at her. Tears of he knew not what stood in her eyes. He dropped to the seat beside her, wondering what he had done to hurt her so. "Jane, what's the matter?" he asked in a troubled voice. "What have I done?" She looked at him. . . . He didn't know what happened next. Suddenly he found her in his arms. He strained her to him with all the passion he had been restraining for the months that seemed like years. He kissed her hair. He mumbled incoherently, yet with perfect understanding, to Jane, tender endearments. At length she raised her face from where it had been buried on his chest, gazed straight into his eyes.

Their lips met in a long, clinging, rapturous kiss. . . .

"How long have you known?" he asked her. Men are such idiots—they are never satisfied to take what comes to them—they must ask silly and nonsensical questions.

She told him. Of her long struggle, of her decision, of her annoyance at his blindness. They talked eagerly until long past the hour of ten. He heard Mr. Phillips moving chairs and dropping his shoes —obvious hints that the time to go had long since passed. They paid no attention to these danger signals but laughed softly to themselves.

Everything must end eventually. Kenneth walked homewards through the soft light of the September moon. Amusedly, the phrase "walking on air" occurred to him. He laughed aloud. "Walking on air" was as the rheumatic stumping along of old Mrs. Amos compared to the way he felt. . . .

CHAPTER XV

IT was the next night. In the gully on the road leading from that one out of Central City which went northward, there was being held a hastily called meeting of Central City Klan, Knights of the Ku Klux Klan, Realm of Georgia. Before, there had been three hundred robed figures. To-night, three months later, the popularity of organized intolerance was attested to by the presence of fully five hundred. What had happened to Nancy Ware had acted as a powerful incentive to the recruiting of new converts. It was mighty fine to have a strong and powerful organization to shut mouths of those who talked too much about the night-time deeds of loyal Klansmen. And, by gum, if you're doing anything you don't want known or stopped, you'd better be on the inside.

A figure whose arms waved excitedly as he talked was haranguing the crowd, which paid close attention to him. Had Tom Tracy been there, he would certainly have recognized the voice of the speaker. Ed Stewart's wife, had she been there, would also have recognized it and dragged the speaker home by force had he resisted.

"White civilization in the South is tottering on its

throne!" he shouted. "We who hold in our hands the future of civilization have been asleep! While we have gone about our ways, the damn niggers are plottin' to kill us all in our beds! Right now they're bringing into our fair city great passels of guns and ammunition marked 'sewin' m'chines' and 'ploughs'! They're meetin' ev'ry night in these nigger churches all over the county and they're plottin' an' plannin' to kill ev'ry white man, woman an' chile in this county and take the lan' for themselves! They're led by a damn nigger doctor right here in Central City named Harper! I know it's so, 'cause another nigger doctor named Williams tol' me yestiddy mornin' all about it and said that this nigger Harper was leadin' this vile plot! He's been goin' all over the county stirrin' up the damn niggers and incitin' them to murder all of us! What're you men goin' to do?" he challenged in a voice that shrilled in pretended rage and terror.

A deep-throated roar answered him. Cries of "Kill the bastards!" "Lynch 'em!" "Kill every black bastard befo' mornin!" It was the age-long voice of the mob bent on murder—the pack in full cry. But it was more than the voice of the mob of the Roman Colosseum, for that ancient cry was one of pleasure at the death of a single Christian. This was the shout of those intent on a wild, murderous rampage that spared neither man, woman, nor child.

"Klansmen!"

A voice like that of a bull roared until the tumult had subsided. It was the Exalted Cyclops of the

Central City Klan. He stood in silence until the group of hooded figures was still.

"The noble order of the Ku Klux Klan don't handle situations such as this like a mob!" The figures stood expectantly, eagerly waiting to hear what would come next.

"We have listened to the story told by our fellow Klansmen. Hol' yo'se'ves ready for the call of the Invisible Empire at any minute. We have planned the way to en' this dastardly plot and to punish those responsible with death!"

"That's right! Kill 'em! Lynch 'em! Burn th' bastards!" shouted the crowd.

"That'll be done till ev'ry one is killed!" promised the Exalted Cyclops. "But it can't be done so's it can be laid to our noble order! Already our enemies are charging us with crimes! The Fed'ral Gov'-nment will be down on our heads!"

There were cries of "Damn the Gov'nment!" from some of the more hot-headed. But calmer judgment prevailed. Something was to be done, but what that ominous "something" might be, was not revealed. Each man was to be ready for instantaneous duty upon call of the Klan. Immediate action was not wise, for the Klan investigators had not completed their work. Action must wait until that had been done, for it was essential that not one of the plotters should escape.

This last point was emphasized. At last the crowd became more calm with the determination to postpone its vengeance until it was certain of being complete.

It then dispersed its several ways, dissolving into separate groups that talked excitedly of the astounding and terrifying news, the need of prompt action, the great luck the white folks had had in discovering the plot so soon, violent denunciation of the Negroes in the plot.

In one of the groups the conversation was different. One of the group was the Exalted Cyclops, in private life Sheriff Bob Parker; another was the Kligrapp, otherwise Henry Lane, Commissioner of Health; the third was the speaker who had revealed the plot, Ed Stewart, Tom Tracy's landlord.

Sheriff Parker chuckled softly. "Well, Ed, looks like somethin' is about to break loose, eh?" he observed.

"Yep, I reck'n you're right. Them damn niggers've got a hell of a nerve! Formin' sassieties to 'stop robbin' share-croppers'! When we get through with 'em, they'll be formin' coal-shov'lin' sassieties in hell!" The other two joined in the laugh at his grim joke. "We'll put in th' papers they was formin' to kill white folks and they'll never know but what that ain't true."

Parker laughed again. Waving his hand at the departing Klansmen, there came to his face a cynical sneer. "An' them damn fools really think they're sho'ly goin' to be murdered by the damn niggers!"

In another section of Central City there was being enacted at the same time another scene of poignant drama that threatened to translate itself into tragedy.

The place was a darkened bedroom in the home of Roy Ewing on Georgia Avenue, and the actors in it were four in number. Roy Ewing, owner and manager of the Ewing General Merchandise Store, whom Kenneth had seen but little since Ewing had discontinued his nocturnal visits to Kenneth's office, was one of the actors. His wife, whose face still bore evidences of a youthful beauty that was fast fading, was a second. A third was old Dr. Bennett, who sat by the bed, his hair dishevelled, his face lined with perplexity and anxiety, as he apprehensively watched the fourth actor in the drama, a girl of nineteen who was restlessly tossing in pain on the bed. Roy Ewing stood at the foot of the bed. His wife sat on the other side uttering little snatches of phrases of soothing sympathy which her daughter did not hear.

Dr. Bennett was plainly worried and at a loss what to do to relieve the torture Ewing's daughter was so clearly experiencing. He turned to Ewing.

"Roy, to tell you the truth, it don't seem like I can find out what's the matter with Mary. When she had that first attack, I thought she had appendicitis, but she ain't got no fever to speak of, so it can't be her appendix that's botherin' her. Looks like t' me she's got some sort of bleedin' inside, but I can't tell."

Ewing and his wife looked anxiously first at their daughter, then interrogatively and pleadingly at the old physician as he watched the sufferer in her con-

tortions of pain and agony. Mary, married two
months and her husband working in Atlanta, had
lived with her parents after a short honeymoon.
She had her mother's beauty—that is, the delicate,
patrician, statuesque charm that had been her mother's when Roy Ewing had courted and won her two
decades ago in Charleston, South Carolina. It was
not the harsh-lined, blonde beauty of Georgia but the
fragile old-world, French loveliness of that spot in
South Carolina where French tradition and customs
and features had not yet been barbarized by the in-
fusion of that Anglo-Saxon blood which is the boast of
the South. She lay there, a pitiful sight. Her face
was pale, covered with cold, clammy perspiration;
all blood had fled from it. She breathed with great
difficulty in short and laboured respiratory efforts.
Her pulse was failing, very rapid and thready; at
times it was barely perceptible. She had been seized
with the attack around seven o'clock, when she began vomiting. Now she appeared to be so weakened
with the pain she had endured that a state of coma
was obviously fast approaching. At least it seemed
so. Dr. Bennett tried to revive her, but with little
success. The absence of fever puzzled him. He
feared an internal hæmorrhage—all signs pointed to
such a condition—yet he did not know. Roy Ewing
and his wife were among his closest friends. He
would have tried an operation had they not been.
That he feared to risk with their daughter. Yet,
what could he do? Mary was obviously so weak that

he knew she could not be moved to Atlanta, three hundred miles away. Nor would a physician be able to get to Central City in time to operate.

"I'm puzzled, Roy, mighty puzzled," he said, turning to Ewing. "I might as well tell you the truth. Looks like t' me she c'n hardly last till mornin'."

It was gall and wormwood for him to admit his impotency, but he did it.

"Dr. Bennett, you've got to do somethin'! You've got to! You've got to!"

It was Mrs. Ewing who cried out in her agony—the piteous cry of a mother who sees her first-born dying before her eyes. Her face was as blanched as Mary's—every drop of blood seemed to have been drained from it. She looked pleadingly at him, chill terror gripping her heart as she realized from his words that her Mary, who had been so happy and well that morning, was about to die.

"If you-all wasn't such good friends of mine, I'd try it anyhow," Dr. Bennett answered her, his voice as agonized as hers. "But I'm skeered to op'rate or do anythin' that might hasten her on."

Ewing walked over to the doctor, grasped the older man's shoulders so fiercely that he winced in pain.

"By God," he shouted at Dr. Bennett, "you've got to operate! I can't see my little Mary die right here befo' my eyes! Go ahead and do what you think best. It'll be better'n seein' her die while we stand here doin' nothin'!"

"Roy," Dr. Bennett groaned, "you know there ain't anythin' I wouldn't do for you—'cept this."

He waved his hand vaguely towards the bed. As he did so, he looked with keen appraisement at Ewing in the dim light. He seemed to be debating in his mind whether or not he dared take a very long chance. If the chance would not be more disastrous. If Mary's life might not be better lost than that! Ewing almost stopped breathing as he saw the momentary indecision in the physician's face. Mrs. Ewing saw none of this by-play, for she had sunk down on the bed, where her body was shaken with the sobs she could not restrain.

"There's jus' one chance t' save her," Dr. Bennett hesitatingly began. Ewing leaned forward in his eagerness.

"There's jus' this one hope," Dr. Bennett repeated, "but I don't know if you'd be willin' to take that chance."

"I don't give a damn what it is!" Ewing shouted in his anxiety. "I'll take it! What is it, Doc? I don't care what it costs! What is it?" He quivered as with a chill in his excitement—the excitement of the drowning man who sees a possible rescuer as he is about to go down for the third time. Mrs. Ewing had stopped crying—she seemed as though she had forgotten to breathe. They both waited eagerly for the older man to speak. At last he did. He paused after each word.

"Th'only — man — I know — near enough — to op'rate—in time—is—a—nigger—doctor—here—named—Harper!"

"Oh, my God!" groaned Ewing as he sank to his

knees beside the bed and buried his face in his hands. "A nigger—seein' my Mary—operatin' on her— Good God! I'd rather see her dead than have a nigger put his hands on her! No! No! No!" He fairly screamed the last in his fury.

"I didn't think you'd do it," said Dr. Bennett miserably. "I jus' felt I oughter tell you. He's jus' out of school—studied in one of the bes' schools up No'th—and in France. He might save Mary—but I can't blame you none for not havin' him."

While he was speaking, Ewing jumped to his feet and paced up and down the room like a caged and wounded tiger. On the one hand was the life of his daughter—on the other his inherent, acquired, environmental prejudice. None but those who know intimately the depth and passion of that prejudice as it flourishes in the South can know what torture— what a hell—what agony Ewing was going through. Prejudice under almost any circumstances is hard enough to bear—in Ewing's case his very soul was tormented at such an unheard-of thing as a Negro operating on his daughter.

"Roy!"

He turned abruptly at the sound of his wife's voice, having forgotten for the time everything—wife, surroundings, all—as he struggled with the problem he faced.

"Roy!" Her voice was weak because of the ordeal through which she was passing. She ran to him, seizing his arm and looking up at him pleadingly.

"Roy! I can't see our Mary die! I can't let her die!"

"Would you have a nigger see her naked?" he demanded of her fiercely. "Would you? Would you?"

Her head went back sharply at the roughness of his tone. In her eyes flashed that brilliant, burning look of mother love that submits to no dangers, no obstacles.

"I'd do anything to save her!" she cried.

"No, no, Mary," Ewing pleaded, "we can't do that! We can't!"

She did not hear him. Brushing past him, she caught Dr. Bennett by the arm as he rose to his feet. "Get that doctor here quick!" she demanded of him. . . .

When Dr. Bennett telephoned him to come to Roy Ewing's home as quickly as he could, Kenneth was somewhat puzzled. He went at once, deciding that one of the servants was sick. When told that it was Mary Ewing he was to treat, he could not conceal his amazement. He followed Roy Ewing and the doctor to her room, the while he was trying to make himself realize that he, Kenneth Harper, a Negro doctor, had been called to treat a white person—a white woman—in the South. Reaching the bedside, though, he put aside his bewilderment and began at once the diagnosis to discover what the trouble was. He listened without speaking to Dr. Bennett as the old man told him the symptoms Mary had shown and what he thought was the matter. Ewing was sent from the room. Kenneth rapidly examined the patient—and decided that she was having severe internal hæmorrhages. It looked like an acute and dangerous case. Immediate operation seemed the only hope. And even that hope was a slim one. He informed Dr. Bennett of his diagnosis.

Ewing was summoned. Briefly Kenneth told him his theory of the trouble—that the only hope was immediate operation. Ewing faltered, hesitated, seemed about to refuse to allow it. At that moment a loud scream of pain was wrung from Mary's lips. He winced as though he had been struck. He shrugged his shoulders in assent to the operation. . . .

Kenneth telephoned Mrs. Johnson, the nurse who had helped him before, to be ready to go with him for an operation in ten minutes. He drove rapidly home, secured his instruments, ether, sterilizer, gown and other equipment, bundled them into his car, called for Mrs. Johnson, explaining briefly to her the nature of the case as he drove as rapidly as he could to the Ewing home.

Mary was carried downstairs and placed on the dining-room table. Dr. Bennett agreed to give the anæsthetic. Kenneth went rapidly, yet surely, to work. In his element now, he forgot time, place, the unusual circumstances, and everything else. Swiftly he began the delicate and perilous task as soon as Dr. Bennett had sufficiently etherized the patient.

Yet, even in the stress of the moment, he could not

keep down the ironical thoughts that crept to his
brain in spite of all efforts to bar them. The South's
a funny place, he mused. Must have been a mighty
hard thing for old Bennett to have to admit that he,
a Negro, knew more about operating in a case like
this than he did himself. Roy Ewing must have had
a bad half-hour deciding whether or not he'd let a
Negro do the operation on his daughter. Hope nothing goes wrong—if it does, might as well pick out
some other town to go to. Oh, well, won't let that
worry me. Have to make the best of it—save her if
possible.

Weakened by the severe hæmorrhages she had been
having, Mary was in a condition of extreme shock.
The least slip, Kenneth realized, and nothing could
save her. Her face wan and drawn, Mary's life hung
precariously in the balance—the odds were all
against her while the grim spectre of death crept
slowly but surely upon her.

Beads of perspiration stood upon Kenneth's brow
as he fought for her life. Though he could not have
done the operation himself, Dr. Bennett sensed the
gravity of the situation. The older man leaned forward in his anxiety—hardly daring to breathe for
fear of interrupting the deft, sure touch of the op-
erator. Ten—fifteen—twenty—thirty—forty—fifty
minutes crept by on lagging feet—to the two doctors
and the nurse each minute seemed an hour.

Despite all his efforts, Kenneth knew Mary was
rapidly sinking. The loss of blood and strength,
the severity of the shock, the enervating spasms of

pain she had suffered, had sapped her strength until all resistive power was gone. Kenneth knew that Dr. Bennett knew this too—even in the desperate struggle he wondered what the other would say and do—if the girl died. He tried to shake off the fear that seized him—fear of what would happen if it became known among the whites that Mary Ewing had died while a Negro was operating on her. No mortal could have done more. Even were that known and admitted, it would not save him, Kenneth knew.

The tense situation became too much for him. When he should have been steadiest, the double strain on his nerves caused his hand to slip. Blood spurted forth. Kenneth feverishly caught the bleeding artery with a hæmostatic and sought to repair the damage he had done.

"Tough luck," muttered Dr. Bennett. Kenneth looked up at him. The older man grunted and smiled—encouragingly. A burden seemed lifted from Kenneth's shoulders. Mrs. Johnson wiped the perspiration that streamed from Kenneth's face. She seemed endowed with a sixth sense that told her his needs almost before he was aware of them himself.

It was a strange sight. Anywhere in America. In Georgia it was amazing beyond belief. A white woman patient. A white anæsthetizer. A black nurse. A black surgeon. . . .

All things must come to an end. Kenneth rapidly sewed up the incision. He bandaged the wound tightly. She yet breathed.

Kenneth opened the door and admitted Ewing, who

had paced the hall since the operation began. Every minute of the hour he had been there, he had had to fight hard to keep himself from bursting into the room and stopping the operation. He had been restrained by the positiveness with which he had been ejected from the room by Kenneth—there was something in the physician's air that had warned him without words that he must not interfere. Something within him told him Kenneth was right—knew what he was doing. The colour and race of the surgeon had been almost forgotten in the strange circumstances.

"Will she live?" he asked, his words whispered in so hoarse a tone they could hardly be heard.

"I don't know—it'll be forty-eight hours before we can tell—if she lives that long," answered Kenneth.

The strain had been greater than he had known. Kenneth felt a strange weakening—lassitude gripped his body—he felt a nausea that came with the reaction after the mental ordeal. Ewing stood by the table on which lay his child. Tears which he forgot to wipe away stood in his eyes as he watched her laboured breathing. Dr. Bennett put his hand on Ewing's shoulder.

"He did all he could!" he declared, nodding at Kenneth. There was admiration in the old doctor's voice.

Ewing rushed off to give the news to his wife. . . .

The three men carried the unconscious form to her room. With a short "Good night" to Dr. Bennett, Kenneth left the house with Mrs. Johnson and drove away. . . .

CHAPTER XVI

THE following day Kenneth was kept busy arranging his affairs in order to leave the following morning for Atlanta for the operation on Mrs. Tucker. It had been a most difficult task for him to persuade her to have it done. He had been at last successful when he made her realize that it would mean either the operation or death. She dreaded the trip to Atlanta but Kenneth refused to perform the operation except at a hospital and there was none nearer than Atlanta at which a Negro could operate.

During the day he had been kept so busy that he had not had time to go out of the coloured section except once, and that when in the late afternoon he drove through Lee Street to see how Mary Ewing was faring. He had been so busy with his own thoughts that he had paid little attention to the whites who were standing around on the streets. He did not see the threatening and hostile looks they gave nor did he notice the excited whispering and muttering when he came into their sight.

Ed Stewart had partly told the truth at the meeting of the Klan when he said that Dr. Williams had informed him of the organization Kenneth and the others were forming. Kenneth had seen little of the pompous and intensely jealous physician since the time when he had forced Dr. Williams to assist him in the appendicitis operation on Mrs. Emma Bradley. Kenneth had felt nothing but an amused contempt for his fellow-practitioner, for he knew that Dr. Williams covered his deficiencies in medical knowledge and skill with the bombastic and self-important air he affected.

Dr. Williams, on the other hand, had never forgiven Kenneth for the incident in which Kenneth had shown him up in a manner that injured the former's pride far more than Kenneth had suspected. Dr. Williams felt that the younger man had deliberately and with malice aforethought offered a gratuitous insult to him as dean of the coloured medical profession of Central City, though that profession numbered but two members. Kenneth's success as a physician in Central City, having taken as he had some of the best of Dr. Williams' own patients whom he had considered peculiarly his own, the insult plus Kenneth's success had rankled in his breast until, being of a petty and mean disposition, he hated the younger man with a deep and vindictive hatred.

He had not, however, intended that his conversation with Ed Stewart should assume the proportions that it eventually did. On the day before the meeting of the Klan at which Kenneth had been named as the one responsible for the organization of the Negroes, Dr. Williams had met Ed Stewart driving out along a country road near Ashland. Williams was returning from making a professional call in that neighbourhood. Stewart, a big, raw-boned, and lanky "Cracker" or "Peck," as they are called by Negroes in the South, was going to inspect the cotton crops of his tenant-farmers, that he might estimate how big the crops would be and might know accordingly how large the tenants' bills should be for supplies furnished.

They had stopped to pass the time of day and for Stewart to find which of the Negroes on his place was sick. He wanted to know if that sick one was too sick to work the crop, as the loss of even one worker during cotton-picking time was serious, what with the number of Negroes who had gone North. Having gained the information, he started to question Dr. Williams in a way that he thought was exceedingly adroit and clever, but through which ruse the coloured doctor saw instantly and clearly.

"Say, Doc, you know anything 'bout these niggers 'round here holdin' these meetin's nearly ev'ry night? Seems t' me it's mighty late for them to be holdin' revival services and indo' camp-meetin's?" he queried in as casual a tone as he could manage.

An idea sprang full-grown to Williams' mind. Kenneth Harper was getting far too popular through the organization of his co-operative societies. Williams was shrewd enough to see that if they were as successful as they gave promise of being, Kenneth would be the leading Negro of the town, if not of that entire section of Georgia. And correspondingly he, Williams, would become less and less the prominent figure he had been before Kenneth had come back from France to Central City. That was it! Stewart was one of the biggest planters in Smith County. It was also rumoured he was prominent in the Ku Klux Klan. Stewart's fortunes would be the hardest hit in the county if Kenneth's societies achieved their purpose, for he, Stewart, had as many share-croppers and tenant-farmers as any other man in the county if not more. Stewart also had the reputation, a long-standing one, of being the hardest taskmaster on his Negro tenants in the county—the one who profited most through juggled accounts and fraudulent dealings. He could have cut, had he chosen, five notches in the handle of his gun, each one signifying a Negro who had dared to dispute the justness of settlements for crops raised.

All these thoughts raced through Williams' brain while Stewart waited for a reply to his questions. Williams had no intention of the exaggeration of his statements which Stewart later made. He merely intended that by telling Stewart of the societies, Kenneth's rapidly increasing prominence in the community should receive a check through obstacles which Stewart and his fellow-landlords might put— in fact, were sure to put—in the way of success of the farmers' organizations.

"No, sir, they ain't holdin' revivals, Mr. Stewart. I reckon if you white folks knew what was goin' on, you wouldn't feel so comfortable."

Williams was playing with Stewart as is done so often by Negroes in the South with the whites, though the latter, in their supreme confidence that they be-

long to an eternally ordained "superior race," seldom
realize how often and how easily they are taken in
by Negroes. Williams enjoyed the look of concern
that had come to Stewart's face at his words.

"What's goin' on, Doc?" he asked in an eager tone,
from which he tried with but little success to keep the
anxiety that he felt.

"Heh, heh, heh!" laughed Williams in a throaty
chuckle. "These Negroes are figurin' on takin' some
of these landlords to court that's been cheatin' them
on their crops. Of course," he added hastily, "that
don't need to worry you none, Mr. Stewart, but from
what I hear, there are some 'round here that the news
will worry."

Stewart flushed, for he was conscious of a vague
feeling that Williams might have been indirectly hitting at him when he had said that the court proceed-
ings wouldn't affect him. He fell back on the old
custom of flattering and praising fulsomely the Negro
from whom a white man wants information regarding
the activities of other Negroes. Williams, like every other Negro in the South, knew what value to
put on it, but he was playing a far deeper game than
Stewart suspected.

"Doc, why ain't all these niggers good, sensible
ones like you? If all the niggers in the South were
like you, there never would be any trouble."

"That's right, Mr. Stewart, that's right. As I was
sayin' to some of the folks out your way this mornin',
they'd better stop followin' after the fool ideas of
these coloured men who've been up No'th."

He looked at Stewart shrewdly and appraisingly to see if he had penetrated the subtlety of his remark. Stewart, slow of thought, had not fully done so, it seemed. Williams continued:

"You see, it's like this, Mr. Stewart. Folks like you and me could live here for a hundred years and there'd never be no trouble. There'd never be no race problem if they was only like us. But"— and his voice took on a doubtful and sorrowful sound—"the most of this trouble we're havin' is caused by fool Negroes who go up No'th to school and run around with those coloured folks in New York and Chicago who tell 'em how bad we po' coloured folks are bein' treated in the South. They get all filled up with 'social equality' ideas, and then they come back down here and talk that stuff to these ignorant Negroes and get them all stirred up——"

Stewart was seeing more clearly what Williams was driving at.

"I see," he said reflectively. "I alw'ys said too much education sp'iled niggers—that is, some niggers," he added hastily for fear Williams might take offence before he had done with him. "Co'se it don't bother sensible ones like you, Doc." The last was said conciliatingly. "Let's see, mos' this trouble's stahted since that other doctor's been back, ain't it?" he asked as casually as he could.

"I ain't sayin' who's doin' it," replied Williams as he started the engine of his car. "But you're a good guesser, Mr. Stewart," he threw back over his shoulder as he drove away. . . .

Stewart clucked to his horse and rode in deep thought down the road. His mind was busy devising schemes to circumvent the action of the societies to take into court men like himself who had been robbing Negroes. They'd lose in the local courts, he knew, but suppose they raised enough money to take a case to the United States Supreme Court. No, that would never do! He'd see Parker and talk it over with him right away! He put the whip to his horse and drove rapidly into town. Mustn't let the damn niggers organize, that *would* be hell! . . .

Kenneth was going about his business on the day following the meeting of the Klan that had been caused by Dr. Williams' talk with Stewart, in blissful ignorance of the storm rapidly gathering about his head. His mind was intent on a number of things—but trouble on account of the co-operative societies was furthest from his mind. Had he been told there was any trouble, such news would probably have been greeted with a laugh of unconcern. All the white people of the South weren't scoundrels and thieves like Stewart and Taylor and their kind! They were but a few. Besides the poor whites, the majority of whites would undoubtedly heartily approve his plan when it had been developed to the point where it could be made public.

But Kenneth thought of none of those things. His mind was too full of other events that loomed on the horizon. First, of course, he thought of Jane. He thought of his great good fortune in knowing a girl like her. There was a girl for you! He thought of

the home he would build for her—he was mighty glad
his father had been in fairly comfortable circumstances and that he had been successful in his practice. He would be able to build a mighty nice home
for Jane. They wouldn't bother with the cheap and
flashy furniture, fumed oak or mission, to be obtained in Central City. Oh, no! Soon's Mrs. Phillips was better, the three of them would go to Atlanta
and buy everything they needed there. They'd have
the best-looking home in Central City, white or coloured! His mother and Mamie wanted him to bring
Jane into the house. He might do that . . . but the
house which had seemed so comfortable before, now
seemed too ordinary to bring a girl like Jane to. . . .
He'd talk that over with her to-night. . . . And then
after a time there might be a little Jane . . . and a
Kenneth, Jr. . . . Kenneth laughed softly to himself
as he saw Jane and himself sitting by the fire of an
evening with two little rascals playing on the
floor. . . . And later they'd go off to school. He'd
see that they got the best there was in life. . . . So
his thoughts ran.

And then he thought of Roy Ewing and the operation of the night before. Must have been a mighty
terrible ordeal for them to have to call a Negro in
to operate on their daughter. Race prejudice is a
funny thing! A white man will eat food prepared
by black hands, have it served by black hands, have
his children nursed by a black nurse who most of the
time was more a mother to them than their own
mother, let his clothes be taken into a black home to

be washed, allow all the most intimate details of his life to be handled by black folks. . . . Even lots of them would consort with black women at night to whom they wouldn't raise their hats in the daytime. . . . But when it came to recognizing a Negro outside of menial service, then there came the rub. . . . Yet in a matter of life and death like Ewing's case, they forgot prejudice. . . . Maybe in time the race problem would be solved just like that . . . when some great event would wipe away the artificial lines . . . as in France. . . . He thought of the terrible days and nights in the Argonne. . . . He remembered the night he had seen a wounded black soldier and a wounded white Southern one, drink from the same canteen. . . . They didn't think about colour in those times. . . . Wouldn't the South be a happy place if this vile prejudice didn't exist? . . . He wondered why folks didn't see it as clearly as he did. . . .

At last the long, busy day ended. He went over to have supper with Jane. That dress she had on the night they had told each other of their love, that reddish-coloured one, that had been a beauty. But to-night—ah, the other one wasn't nearly so pretty! It was of white, simply made. Satin slippers, silk stockings, also of white. Her hair piled high and pierced with a large tortoise-shell comb. Always she brought pictures to Kenneth's mind. To-night it was again of the dark-eyed, seductive Spanish *señorita* on a balcony. After supper, they sat in the canvas porch swing. They talked of their plans—impetuously, enthusiastically—with all the glorious dreams of youthful love. All the little things—little, but so great when one is young and in love—they said to each other. The things they said when the Pyramids were being built. The things they will say a thousand years from now.

To-night there were no warning signals from Mr. Phillips when ten o'clock came. He had been glad, and had said so, when Kenneth asked him for Jane. "We don't feel we're losing a daughter—we're gaining a son instead!" he had said.

They talked on until there was no other sign of life discernible in the neighbourhood, save for the passage of a prowling cat, or the sound of the crickets in the grass. At last he had to go. Early the next morning he was to leave for Atlanta with Mrs. Tucker. Three days he was to be gone. He would return on Friday.

In October they were to be married. Mrs. Phillips' health was not improving as they had hoped. She was cheerful but she wanted Jane to be happily married before she died. They had decided to live at his house with his mother and Mamie. They'd refurnish it and do over all the rooms. Later on, when he had made lots of money, they'd build.

Mamie and Jane and Kenneth were to go to Atlanta the latter part of September, there to buy the furniture and all the other things they would need. Mrs. Phillips was too ill to stand the strain of the long journey and the excitement of the shopping.

Jane tiptoed into the house so as not to wake her

mother. She returned in a few minutes with a fluffy white mass in her arms. It was her wedding-gown which she was to make herself. They sat silent for a minute at the token of what it meant.

Tears stood in Jane's eyes when he went down the stairs. He saw them when he looked back to say the last soft good-bye.

"Three days is an awful long time," she said plaintively.

Of course, there was nothing else for him to do but go back up the steps and kiss her good-bye all over again. . . .

CHAPTER XVII

B OB was packing for his journey to Cambridge, whistling cheerfully the while. It was certainly great to be going away up to Boston to school. All his life he had wanted to live there for a while where he could learn the things which he knew of only at second hand now. He pictured in his mind how he would arrange his life at school. There'd be none of the kiddish pranks he had read about that college boys did. He was too old for that. He had seen too much of the seamy and sordid side of life to waste *his* time playing. He'd study every minute he could. He'd make a record in scholarship that would make his mother and Mamie and Kenneth proud of him. He'd go to summer school so as to finish the rest of his college course in two years instead of three. And then, law school. By jiminy, he'd be the best lawyer there was! Not the best *coloured* lawyer. The best *lawyer!* Never did youth have more brilliant dreams of life than Bob.

He paused at the sound which came from downstairs through the half-opened door. It couldn't be in Ken's office, for he had gone to Atlanta with Mrs. Tucker that morning. It sounded like crying—as one would cry who had suffered some great bereave-

ment or terrible misfortune. He went out in the hall
and leaned over the balustrade, the better to find
out what was the matter.

It was Mamie and his mother. He looked puzzled, for he could think of nothing to make Mamie
cry that way. His mother was trying to soothe and
calm her as Mamie told her the cause of her weeping.
Bob crept down the stairs as softly as he could to
hear.

Mamie between sobs was telling her mother of
some accident that had befallen her.

"I had been—to Ewing's Store—and that Jim
Archer—and Charley Allen—and two or three other
white boys—that hang around Ewing's Store—said
nasty things to me—when I came out—I hurried
home—they must have followed me——."

Here she broke down again while her mother
crooned softly to her, pleading with her not to cry
so hard. Mamie choked back her sobs and went on.
Bob's face became terrible to see. He hung there on
the steps almost breathless, waiting, and dreading
what he felt was coming.

"At that old field—near the railroad—they jumped
out—and grabbed me—oh, my God! My God!
Why didn't they kill me? Why didn't they kill me?"
Mamie's screams were horrible to hear. "Then—oh,
God! God help me!"

For a minute Bob stood there as one frozen to the
spot. Then a blind, unreasoning fury filled him.
He ran up the stairs to Kenneth's room and got the

revolver he knew Kenneth kept there. Without hat
or coat he ran down the stairs. Out the door and
down the street. Mamie and her mother were roused
by his action. Mamie, lying on the floor with her
head in her mother's lap, her clothes torn and bloody,
her face and body bruised, struggled to her feet.
She ran to the open door through which Bob had
disappeared. An even greater terror, if such was
possible, was on her face.

"Bob! Bob! Come back! Come back!" she
cried in ever louder cries.

"Bob! Bob!"

But Bob was too far away to hear her.

In front of Ewing's Store there sat a group of nine
or ten men and boys. They were gathered around
one who seemed to be relating a highly interesting
and humorous story. Every few minutes there'd be
a loud laugh and a slapping of each other on the
back. Suddenly, silence. A hatless and coatless
figure was running down the street toward them. The
group opened as its members started to scatter. In
the middle of it there stood Jim Archer and Charley
Allen. The former had been telling the story.

Bob walked straight up to Jim Archer, whose face
had turned even paler than its usual pasty colour.
He turned to run but it was too late. Without saying a word, his eyes burning with a deadly hatred,
Bob raised the revolver he had in his hand and fired
once—twice—into Archer's breast. Charley Allen

rushed upon Bob to overpower him. He met head-on the two bullets that came to meet him, and fell gasping and coughing on the ground at Bob's feet.

The rest of the crowd had fled.

Without hurrying, Bob stepped into a Ford delivery truck that had been left at the curb, its engine running. Before the crowd which with miraculous suddenness filled the street could stop him, he drove straight down Lee Street, turned into Oglethorpe Avenue, and headed for the country beyond the town. . . .

Three miles out of town the Ford spluttered, coughed, shook mightily, and stopped. Its gasolene tank was empty. Shoving it into the underbrush on the side of the road, far enough to be out of sight, Bob ran on. If he could only get across country as far as the railroad going North, he might be able to get to Macon, where he could hide. When the excitement died down, he could go on farther North. Perhaps he could eventually reach Canada. He fought his way through brushes, across vast fields of cotton that seemed to have no end. Near midnight he could go no farther. He had eaten nothing since breakfast—he had been too excited over his packing to eat any dinner. Bitterly he thought of the change a few hours had brought forth. Twelve hours before, he had been eagerly planning to leave for school. Now, his sister ruined, he a murderer twice over—fleeing for his life! He hoped that he had killed both of them! It would be too ironical a fate for them to live. . . . He thought for a moment

of what would happen if they caught him. He put
the thought away from him. God, that was too
terrible! Mustn't think of that! I'll lose my
nerve. . . .

What was that? Lord, he must have fallen asleep!
What is that? Dogs? Bloodhounds! Great God!
I must get away! How did they get away from
bloodhounds in books? That was it! Water!
He'd find a stream and wade in it. Then the damned
dogs would lose the scent.

The thought of water reminded him suddenly that
he was thirsty—terribly thirsty. God, but his throat
was dry! Felt like ten thousand hot needles were
sticking in it!

His legs and thighs ached. He dragged them
along like a paralysed man. He thought petulantly
of a paralysed man he had seen once in Atlanta.
What was his name? Bill? No, that wasn't it.
Jim? No, not that either. Some sort of a name
like that.

Wonder how Mamie was? Mamie? Who's
Mamie? What had happened to her? He racked
his brain to remember. At last he gave it up. No
use trying. Old—old—brain don't work right.
Wonder what's the matter with it?

His delirious brain was suddenly cleared by an
ominous baying close at hand. Those damned dogs
again. They'd never take him alive! He felt in
his pockets to see if the gun was still there. It was.
He felt in the other pocket to count the cartridges
there while he ran. One—two—three—four—five

—six—seven—eight! All there! Seven for the mob! One—for—Bob!

An old barn suddenly loomed up before him in the rapidly approaching light of dawn. He dragged himself into it and barred the door. Not much protection! But—a little! Just a little! Better'n none! He sat down on an old box by the door. There was a knot-hole farther over. He dragged the box in front of it. Reloaded the revolver. One—two—three—four cartridges! Two that hadn't been used! That left six in the gun! And four more!

Listen! The dogs sound like they're near! There they are! He wouldn't waste his precious bullets on dogs! Oh, no! He'd save them for the human dogs! God damn 'em! He'd show 'em a "damned nigger" knew how to die! Like a man!

Here they come! God, but it was tough to have to die! Just when life seemed so sweet! Wonder who'd sit in his seat at Harvard! Hope a coloured boy'd get it! Harvard seemed so far away from where he was! Looked like it was as far's the moon! Might as well be for him!

Look at 'em spreading out! Whyn't they come up like men and get him? There's Jim Archer's brother! Bang! Got him! Look at 'im squirm! That's two Archers won't run after coloured girls any more! Bang! Damn it, I missed 'im! Can't waste 'em like that! Got to be more careful! Must take better aim next time! Bang! Bang! Hell, I missed again!. Nope! Got one of 'em!

One—two—three—four gone! Six left! Five

for the "Crackers"! One for me! Bang! Bang!
Got another! Must reload! One—two—three—
four! Nearly all gone! Five—ten—fifteen minutes to live! Why did they pick on Mamie?
Whyn't they take one of those girls that live in those
houses on Butler Street? That's always running
around after men? Why'd they bother a nice girl
like Mamie?

Bang! Listen at 'im howl? That's music for
you! Listen to the damn "Peck" squalling!
What's th' matter? Looks like they've gone! Wonder if I can make a run for it? Th' damn cowards!
Fifty—one hundred—a thousand—five thousand—
to one! That's the way "Crackers" always fight
coloured folks! Never heard yet of one "Cracker"
fighting one Negro! Have to have thousan' to kill
one little fellow like Bob Harper!

Smoke? Can't be smoke! Yes, it is! Goin' t'
burn me up! Bang! Bang! Got one of 'em!

My God! Only one bullet left! Never take him
alive! Lynch him! Might burn him! Burned
coloured boy last month 'n Texas! Better not let
'em get him! Good-bye, everybody! Good-bye!
Good-bye! Good—— Bang . . .

It was some time after Bob had died before the
posse dared enter the barn which by this time was
burning rapidly. They feared the cessation of fir-
ing was only a ruse to draw them into the open. At
last, after riddling the burning structure with bullets,
a few of the more daring cautiously approached the
barn, entered, and found Bob's body. After the bul-

let from his own gun had entered his head, killing him instantly, his body had fallen backwards from the box on which he had been sitting. His legs were resting on the box, his thighs vertical, his body on the floor and his head slightly tilted forward as it rested against a cow-stall. His arms were widespread. The empty revolver lay some ten feet away, where he had flung it as he fell backwards. His face was peaceful. On it was a sardonic smile as though he laughed in death at cheating the howling pack of the satisfaction of killing him.

The mob dragged the body hastily into the open. The roof of the old barn was about to fall in. Before dragging it forth, they had taken no chances. A hundred shots were fired into the dead body. Partly in anger at being cheated of the joy of killing him themselves. They tied it to the rear axle of a Ford. Howling, shouting gleefully, the voice of the pack after the kill, they drove rapidly back to town, the dead body, riddled and torn, bumping grotesquely over the holes in the road. . . .

Back to the public square. In the open space before the Confederate Monument, wood and excelsior had been piled. Near by stood cans of kerosene. On the crude pyre they threw the body. Saturated it and the wood with oil. A match applied. In the early morning sunlight the fire leaped higher and higher. Mingled with the flames and smoke the exulting cries of those who had done their duty—they had avenged and upheld white civilization. . . .

The flames died down. Women, tiny boys and

girls, old men and young stood by, a strange light on their faces. They sniffed eagerly the odour of burning human flesh which was becoming more and more faint.

. . . Into the dying flames darted a boy of twelve. Out he came, laughing hoarsely, triumphantly exhibiting a charred bone he had secured, blackened and crisp. . . . Another rushed in. . . . Another. . . . Another. . . . Here a rib. . . . There an armbone. . . . A louder cry. . . . The skull. . . . Good boy! Johnny! . . . We'll put that on the mantelpiece at home. . . . Five dollars for it, Johnny! . . . Nothin' doin'! . . . Goin' to keep it myself! . . .

The show ended. The crowd dispersed. Home to breakfast.

CHAPTER XVIII

THREE men sat around a table that evening in the office of Sheriff Parker in the court-house. The sheriff was one. Another was Commissioner Henry Lane. The third was Ed Stewart. The latter was talking.

"Yep, after I talked to that nigger Williams, I rustled 'round among the niggers on my place. At fust, they wouldn't talk much. But I found a way to make 'em! By God, a taste of a horse-whip'll make any of 'em open up! Found they's only two niggers we got to worry 'bout. One's this nigger doctor. The other's my nigger Tom Tracy. She'ff, if you hear'n tell of an accident out to my place in the nex' few days, you needn't bother to come out to investigate. It'll be se'f-defence. Tom Tracy's goin' t' come up on me with an open knife. I'm goin' t' shoot t' save my life."

The three laughed at the good joke. The sheriff agreed not to bother. "Good riddance!" he commented. Stewart went on:

"Now 'bout this other nigger. He's the brains of the whole thing. But we've got to be mighty careful, 'cause these other niggers thinks he some sort of a tin god. Ef they think he's bumped off 'cause of these lodges he's been organizing, they might raise

[238]

hell. Ev'ry nigger out my way would go through
hell 'n' high water for him. Never seen 'em think
so much of another nigger befo'. Mos' the time
they'll come and tell me ev'rythin' that any them
other niggers doin'. This nigger Harper's got 'em
hoodooed or somethin'."

The sheriff broke into Stewart's monologue in a
complaining, reminiscent fashion:

"Don't know what's gettin' into the niggers nowadays. They ain't like they useter be. Take this
nigger's daddy, f'r example. Old man Harper was
as good a nigger's I ever seen. If he met you on
the street twenty times a day, he'd take off his hat
'n' bow almos' to the groun' ev'ry time. But these
new niggers, I can't make heads nor tails of 'em.
Take that uppity nigger they burned this mornin'.
Always goin' 'round with a face on 'im like he's swallowed a mess of crabapples. What if that Jim
Archer did have a little fun with the nigger's sister?
'Twon't hurt a nigger wench none. Oughter be proud
a white man wants her."

His voice took on at the next remark a tone of
pained and outraged surprise.

"Nigger gals gettin' so nowadays they think
they're's good as white women! And what 'chu think
that old fool Judge Stev'nson said t' me to-day?
Had the nerve t' say t' me that he don't blame that
nigger Bob for killin' Jim Archer!"

He demanded of his companions in an almost ludicrous surprise: "What's goin' t' come of the South
when *white men* like the judge say such things?

Guess he's gettin' so old he's kind of weak in the head! I tol' him he'd better not say that to nobody else. Somethin' might happen to *him!*"

"Damn Judge Stevenson!" broke in Stewart, anxious to get a chance to tell his story. "He alw'ys was a sort of 'nigger-lover' anyway!"

Henry Lane spoke for the first time.

"Reck'n the Gov'nor'd say anythin' 'bout this burnin'?" he asked in a tone that anticipated the answer.

Parker laughed ironically.

"What kin he do?" he demanded. He answered his own question. "Nothin'! Under the laws of Georgy, he can't even sen' a man down here to investigate unless he's officially asked by citizens of th' county! And who's goin' t' ask him?" He laughed again. "If anybody's fool enough to ask him, they'll be havin' a visit paid 'em one of these nights! Reck'n we don't need to bother none 'bout the Gov'nor meddlin' in our affairs," he ended assuredly.

"Le's get back to this Harper nigger 'n' quit all this foolin' 'round," Stewart demanded, irritably. "How're we goin' t' settle him?" He added, after a pause: "Without stirrin' up the niggers all over the county?"

"An' they ain't all we got to look out for," added Sheriff Parker. "They's some white folks 'round here who'll kick up a stink if we ain't careful."

"Who'll do that?" asked Stewart contemptuously. "Judge Stev'nson can't do it all by hisse'f."

"Well, there's him an' old Baird an' Fred Griswold. An' then the one's mos' likely to raise the mos' fuss is Roy Ewing. He thinks a lot of that nigger lately for some reas'n. Ain't been able t' figger it out as yet, but he sets a heap by him." He scratched his head in an abstracted manner. "Tol' me over t' the sto' yestiddy that this Harper's a fine type of nigger t' have 'round Central City 'n' that we oughter encourage other niggers to be like him."

"Another one gettin' ol' and weak-minded befo' his time!" was Stewart's comment. "But I want t' know if we're goin' to sit here all night talkin' 'bout things that's goin' t' keep us from punishin' this nigger or if we're goin' to get down to business. Fust thing we know, we'll be 'lectin' this nigger mayer the town!" His sarcasm was thinly veiled, if veiled at all. Parker and Lane showed by the sudden flush on their faces that the shot had reached its mark.

"You don't have to be so cantankerous 'bout it, Ed." Parker showed in his voice, as well as on his face, that he didn't particularly care for Stewart's brand of irony. "You know we're jus' as anxious as you to get rid of him. But we got to be careful. You live out in the country 'n' you don't know the situation here in town like me 'n' Henry."

He sat meditatively for a time. Stewart fidgeted in his chair, and Henry Lane sat lost in thought. Parker suddenly sat up eagerly.

"I got it!" he exclaimed. The others looked at him inquiringly.

"We'll fix it so's we can say that Harper insulted a white woman!"

His companions looked slightly disappointed and doubtful.

"How're you goin' t' do that?" asked Lane. "This nigger, as fur's I can see, since he been back's been stayin' out where he b'longs in the nigger section. Only time he comes over this way's when he comes to the bank or the sto' or here to th' court-house. That's one thing I can say in his fav'r! Bein' in France ain't sp'iled him none so fur's white women's concerned. If he ran around with them Frog women, he never tried any of it 'round here."

"It ain't necessary for him to bother with white women in Central City for us to put that on 'im," Parker declared defensively. "Nearly all white folks ev'n up No'th b'lieves that ev'ry time a nigger's lynched down this a way, its 'cause he's raped a white woman." His manner became triumphant. "Here's how we'll fix it."

The three men, although they were alone in the dark court-house and there was none to hear, drew their chairs together. Their heads were close for more than ten minutes, while they talked excitedly together. Occasionally there would be a low burst of laughter—again an oath. At last Stewart rose, took a paper-bound book from the desk, copied for some time from it, and left the court-house.

The next morning each of fifteen "white, Protestant, Gentile" citizens of Central City received a letter. There was no writing of any sort on the envelope save their names and addresses. They were of ordinary quality such as can be purchased at five cents a package in any cheap stationery store. In it was a letter typed on plain paper, of a quality to match the cheapness of the envelope. There was no printing of any sort on the letter, nor was it addressed other than: "Dear Sir." It read:

"DEAR SIR:

"You have been chosen, as one known to be loyal, brave, and discreet, to meet a situation affecting the welfare of the Nation, the State, and the Community. You are hereby commanded to be present at the time and place and date given on the enclosed card.

"Be wise! Be discreet! Discuss this with no one! Fail not!

"THE COMMITTEE."

There was a plain card enclosed, also of cheap and easily obtained quality, on which was typed a date, time, and place. . . .

Mirabile dictu, each of the fifteen recipients of this cryptic missive was a Ku Klux Klansman. . . .

CHAPTER XIX

MRS. TUCKER was operated on at Atlanta on Thursday morning at the Auburn Infirmary, owned and conducted by a group of coloured physicians of that city, as none of them could operate in the white hospitals. Kenneth keenly enjoyed being in a hospital again, with all its conveniences. The operation finished and Mrs. Tucker resting easily, he purchased, after much picking and choosing, Jane's engagement ring—a beautiful, blue-white diamond solitaire.

That important task performed, he telephoned Dr. Scott, to whom Judge Stevenson had given him a letter of introduction. So engrossed had he been in the operation and the purchasing of the ring, he had almost forgotten the promise made to the judge to see and talk with Dr. Scott, known to be a liberal leader of Southern public opinion and one deeply concerned with the problem of race relations.

"That's a mighty intelligent plan you've worked out," Dr. Scott boomed over the wire. "I'd like to have you talk that over with me and one or two others here. Can you do it before going home?"

Kenneth told him he had to leave early next morning for Central City. As Dr. Scott had a meeting that would keep him engaged all afternoon, it was decided that they should meet that evening at an office in a building downtown in the business section.

It was with a deal of eagerness—and with some degree of anxiety, for he did not know how he would be received by Dr. Scott and the others—that Kenneth set forth that evening for the meeting. He found three men awaiting him in the office of John Anthony, who was one of the three. His footsteps echoed in ghostlike fashion as he walked down the hallway of the deserted building. From the open window there floated from the street below the subdued clatter of automobiles, the cries of newsboys, the restless shuffling of the leisurely crowd as it moved up and down Peachtree Street. Kenneth sought to weigh the three, who were, he felt, representatives of that "new South" of which so much was heard, but signs of whose activities he had so seldom seen. He was seeking to find out their motives, their plans of accomplishing that spirit of fair play toward the Negro, to determine how far they would go towards challenging the established order that was damning the South intellectually, morally, economically. Kenneth, with too-high ideals for his environment, was almost naïve in his eager search for the great champion he had dreamed of who would brave danger and contumely and even death itself for a newer and brighter day for his people in the South. That hope had been dulled somewhat by the things he had seen since his return to Central City, for he was not of an unreflective mind. Yet he had not seen far

enough beneath the surface of that volcano of passion and hate and greed which is the South to realize
that the South had never produced a martyr to any
great moral cause—one who had possessed sufficient
courage to oppose, regardless of consequences, any
one of the set, dogmatic beliefs of the South. True
it was that there were some who had fought in the
Civil War with firm belief that the South was right—
even though it had been shown that their idealism was
a perverted one. But even then these had moved
with the tide of sectional sentiment and not against
it.

Educated in Southern schools where the text-books
of history always exalted the leaders of the Confederacy, raising Lee and Jackson and Johnston and
Gordon to heights but little lower than the heroes of
Grecian mythology, and ever tending to disparage
and revile the Union cause and its leaders, Kenneth,
like many coloured youths, had accepted the ready-
made and fallacious estimates set before him. It
was, therefore, but natural that he set his hopes for
stalwart, unafraid leadership too high and, at the
same time, failed to realize that the South had never
begotten an Abraham Lincoln, a Garrison, a Sumner,
or even a meteor-like John Brown, bursting into bril-
liance born of indignation against stupidity or ignorance or wrong and dying gloriously for that cause.
Kenneth's eyes had partially been opened by his
memorable talk with Judge Stevenson. Etched upon
his mind by the acid of bitter truths were the judge's
words that the boasted Anglo-Saxonism of the South

had curdled into moral cowardice on all subjects by the repression incident to the race problem. Nevertheless Kenneth was too inexperienced as yet in the ways of life to comprehend the full import of the older man's cynicism. He yet sought him who would fulfil his ideal of a great leader who, like a latter-day Crusader, would guide white and black together out of the impasse in which the South seemed to be. Kenneth thus anxiously examined the three before him to see if by chance any one of them bore the accolade which would stamp him the Moses that he sought.

Naturally enough, his eyes first went to Dr. Scott, as it was of him that Judge Stevenson had spoken most favourably. Minister to one of the larger Atlanta churches, he had spoken frequently and with considerable vigour for Georgia in behalf of greater kindness and fairness toward the Negro. He was very tall. His more than ordinary height with his attenuated and lanky slenderness gave him an almost cadaverous appearance which the loose suit of black mohair he wore accentuated. From beneath the folds of a low collar there sprang a white starched-linen bow tie, the four ends standing stiffly, each in a separate direction, like the arms of a windmill. His rather large head was bald on top but around the edges ran a fringe of yellowish-white hair with curling ends that made his face appear rounder than it was. Bushy eyebrows shaded pale blue eyes that twinkled in unison with the ready smile which revealed large yellow teeth. Into his conversation Dr.

Scott injected at frequent intervals ministerial phrases—"the spirit of Jesus"—"being Christians" —"our Lord and Saviour." He always addressed his white companions as "Brother Anthony" and "Brother Gordon." Kenneth he always called "Doctor."

Kenneth felt a certain doubt of Dr. Scott's sincerity. He tried to penetrate what seemed to be a mask over the minister's face that effectively hid all that revolved in the mind behind it. Something intangible but nevertheless real blocked his path—an unctuous affability that seemed too oily to be sincere. No, Kenneth reflected, Dr. Scott is not the man. All of this examination had taken but a few seconds, yet Kenneth's mind was made up. In prejudging him so hastily, Kenneth did an injustice to Dr. Scott that was unconscious but real. In his heart of hearts Dr. Scott had realized that to accomplish anything at all in the South towards enlightenment he must necessarily become, at least as discretion seemed to dictate, a mental chameleon. He had suffered because of that decision, for had circumstances placed him in a more liberal and intelligent environment, he would have been far more advanced in his religious and other beliefs. The traces of gold in the ore that was his mind had been revealed in the suffering which had come to him through his speaking out against a system that seemed to him wrong.

He had been reviled, misunderstood both deliberately and by those who were not so advanced as he. He had borne in silence whatever had come to him, even threats of tarring and of death from the Ku Klux Klan, seeking a course directed by wisdom if not by valour.

While he was being introduced by Dr. Scott, Kenneth examined critically the other two men. Mr. Anthony, who had volunteered the use of his office for the conference, as no comment would be likely if the four of them were seen in the office building, was first presented.

John Anthony might well have posed as model for a typical American business man or lawyer. Of rotund figure, well-fed appearance, hair close-cut, his face clean-shaven, clad in neatly tailored but undistinguished clothing, he sat leaning slightly forward, his fingers interlocked, his thumbs and forefingers holding his cravat while his elbows rested on the arms of his chair. He acknowledged the introduction to Kenneth with a brief "Pleased t' meetcha." He did not rise, nor extend his hand in greeting, but he at once shrewdly appraised and catalogued Kenneth. John Anthony's interest in interracial affairs had been first aroused by the war-time migration of Negroes to the North. His personal fortunes had been touched directly by this loss of labour, and the resultant decrease in profits had caused him to inquire into the problem of the labourers who had been always so plentiful. Like most Americans, and particularly those in Southern States, he had had no idea of, or interest in, what Negroes were forced to endure. Though near to this problem, he had been a living example of those in the proverb who "live so close to the trees, they cannot see the woods." His inquiry, conducted with the clear-sightedness and energy he had acquired from long business training, had revealed brutalities and vicious exploitation that had amazed and sickened him. He was too shrewd to believe that Negroes would be restrained from leaving the South by attempts to picture Negroes freezing to death in the North, or to try to beguile them by transparent falsehoods to the effect that the Southern white man is the Negro's best friend. Though he did not voice it save to his more intimate friends, he felt naught but contempt for the hypocrisy of those who too late were attempting to flatter the Negro to keep him in the South. His motives were therefore curiously mixed in his support of efforts toward interracial goodwill. Economic in part were they, because retention of Negro labour meant the continuation of his own successful business career. Equally, almost, did they proceed from a hitherto latent sense of moral indignation against the treat- ment which the South had accorded to Negroes in the past. Direct of speech, analytical of mind, he went straight to the heart of the problem with that same perspicacity that had won for him more than usual success in his business of conducting one of the South's largest department stores.

Here again did Kenneth figuratively shake his head and decide that John Anthony was not destined to be the Moses of the new South. He could not for the life of him dissociate Anthony's interest in be- half of justice from his direct financial interest in

keeping Negroes in the South, where, with the inevitable working of the law of demand and supply, a
surplusage of Negro labour would mean continued
high profits for men like Anthony. Kenneth was too
young to know that the more largely a man profits
from a liberal cause, the more loyal will be his
support of that cause and the lesser likelihood of his
defection when difficulties arise.

Of the three men, Kenneth felt greatest hope in
the third—David Gordon—younger than Kenneth,
alert, capable, and with an engaging frankness of
face and of manner to which Kenneth warmed instinctively. Gordon was a graduate of Harvard,
where he for the first time in his life had learned to
know coloured fellow-students as men and human be-
ings instead of as "niggers." At first he had re-
belled strenuously, his every instinct had revolted
against dining in the same room, however large, with
a "nigger." So indignant had he been that he had
taken it up with the president. Benign, kindly, clear-
headed, and patriarchal, the older man calmly and
dispassionately and without rancour had shown Gordon the injustice of his position—how unfair it was
to deny an education to a man for the sole offence of
having been born with a black skin. Before he quite
knew how it had happened, Gordon found himself
ashamed of what now was seen to be petty nastiness
on his part. So interested had he become after his
eyes were thus opened that he had made a special
study of the Negro problem. After finishing both
his college and law courses, he had returned to

Atlanta to practise law with his father. His interest in the race question had increased since his return. He was now one of that liberal and intelligent few who are most free from prejudice—an emancipated Southerner. Some inner voice told Kenneth instantly that greatest hope of the three lay in David Gordon —and men like him. . . .

The introductions completed, Dr. Scott opened the conversation.

"Doctor, we've heard of the society you've started in Central City. Tell us how you're getting along."

"You have heard of it?" asked Kenneth in surprise. He did not know his fame had preceded him.

"Oh, yes," answered Dr. Scott. "You see, I know a man in the Klan headquarters here. They've got, so I understand, a pretty full account of your movements."

"They honour me," laughed Kenneth, a note of irony in his voice. He was not a physical coward— threats bothered him little. He had paid little attention to the report of the Klan meeting at Central City, though it had worried his mother and Bob considerably. No more would he be perturbed by any reports of his activities the Klan might have in their files.

"Then, too, Judge Stevenson's been writing me about you," continued Dr. Scott. "We are all interested in what you're doing, Doctor, and we want you to talk frankly. You can to us," he added.

The three men were genuinely interested in the

plan on which Kenneth was working. They were too intelligent to fail to see that something would have to be done towards adjustment of race relations in the South to avert an inevitable clash. What that something was they did not know. They felt the time was not ripe for a challenge to the existing order, and they would not, in all probability, have been willing to issue such a fiat had the time been propitious. Yet they were anxious to examine the plans of this coloured man, hoping against hope that therein might lie an easy solution of the problem.

Frankly and clearly Kenneth told of the simple scheme. Occasionally one of his hearers would interrupt him with a question, but for the most part they heard him through in silence. The story ended, the three men sat in silence as each revolved in his mind the possibilities of the plan. John Anthony was the first to speak, and then he approached the whole race problem instead of Kenneth's plan for attacking one phase of it.

"Doctor," asked Mr. Anthony, "do you believe there is any solution to the race problem? Just what is the immediate way out, as you see it?"

"It would take a wiser man than I to answer that," laughed Kenneth. "You see, we're in the habit of thinking that we can find a simple A-B-C solution for any given problem, and the trouble is there are mighty few that are simple enough for that."

"Yes—yes—I know all that," interjected Mr. Anthony, rather testily. "What I want to hear is what you, as an intelligent Negro, think. I want you to tell us exactly what men like you are saying among yourselves."

"Well, we're talking about lynching—poor schools —the way Negroes are denied the ballot in the South——" began Kenneth.

"Er—that's a thing we can't discuss," hastily interrupted Dr. Scott. "Conditions in the South are too unsettled to talk about giving the Negro the vote as yet."

"As yet," echoed Kenneth. "If we can't discuss it now, when *can* we talk about it?"

"It'll be a long time," answered Dr. Scott frankly. "There are a lot of white people in the South who know disfranchisement is wrong. We know that we can't keep the ballot from the Negro always. But," he ended with a shrug of his shoulders and a thrusting-out of his hands, palms upward, in a gesture of perplexity and despair Kenneth was learning to know so well that he was associating it instinctively with the Southern white man, "we'd stir up more trouble than we could cope with."

"And while you're waiting for the opportune time, conditions are getting steadily worse, the problem is getting more complicated, and it'll be harder to solve the longer you put off trying to solve it," urged Kenneth. It was with an effort that he kept out of his voice the impatience he felt. "Why don't men like you three band together with those who think as you do, so you can speak out?" he asked.

"That's just what we are trying to do, but we have to go very cautiously," answered Dr. Scott. "We

must use discretion. How much are Negroes thinking about voting?"

"They think about it all the time," replied Kenneth. "We know the mere casting of a ballot isn't
going to solve all our problems, but we also know
we'll never be able to do much until we do vote."

"You must be patient—wait until the time is
ripe——" cautioned Dr. Scott.

"Patience can be a vice as well as a virtue." It
was David Gordon who spoke.

Kenneth looked at him gratefully.

"Your race's greatest asset," continued Dr. Scott,
addressing his remark to Kenneth, yet seeking to im-
part a gentle rebuke to Gordon, "has been its wonderful gentleness under oppression. You must continue to be sweet-tempered and patient——"

"That's all very well to advise, but how would you
or any other white man act if you had to suffer the
things the Negro has had to suffer?" demanded Kenneth. "Suppose you saw your women made the
breeding-ground of every white man who desires
them, saw your men lynched and burned at the stake,
saw your race robbed and cheated, lied to and lied
about, despised, persecuted, oppressed—how would
you feel, Dr. Scott, if somebody came to *you* and
said: 'Be patient'?"

Kenneth poured forth his words like a burning
flood of lava—indicative of the raging fires of resentment smouldering beneath. He paused, completely out of breath. Dr. Scott flushed until his face
became a dull brick-red in colour. He restrained

with an effort the anger caused by the coloured man's impetuous words.

"I know—I know," he said soothingly. "It's hard, I know, but you must remember the words of Jesus to his disciples: 'When men shall persecute and revile you——' The spirit of Jesus is growing in the hearts of the South—it will come to your rescue in due season."

"We're always hearing about this liberal white opinion," rejoined Kenneth, nettled by the unctuous suavity of the words, "but we so seldom see any signs of it—almost never in places like Central City. Sometimes I think it's like trying to put your finger on mercury—when your finger is about to touch it, it rolls away—it's somewhere else. Meanwhile lynching goes on."

"You're right, Doctor," broke in John Anthony, who had been following the conversation with deep interest though he had taken little part in it. "We've got to do something, and that soon—the only problem is how to do it. Now about your society in Smith County—tell us how we can help you make it a success. Do you need any money to get it working properly?"

Kenneth turned to the quiet man who had proposed the first tangible offer to help.

"Thanks a lot for the offer," replied Kenneth. "There are two things I can think of that'll be immediately helpful. One is that you and Dr. Scott and Mr. Gordon do what you can to help mould pub-

lic sentiment so this liberal white opinion will become
a force in the South against the Ku Klux Klan and
lynching and all the other forms of prejudice.
That's what seems to me to be most needed."

"Yes—yes—I agree with you, but tell us just exactly how we can help *you*." Anthony, in his direct
way, was impatient of theorizing. "Do you need
any money—credit—legal advice—that is, any we
can give quietly without it getting out that we gave
it?"

"Yes, there is something," answered Kenneth.
"Most of the men in our societies have been working
on shares for so many years that instead of having
any money, they owe their landlords large sums.
The big problem is credit for the things they need
until they sell their crops next fall."

Kenneth gave a detailed statement of their needs
and their plans. John Anthony took notes as he
talked and agreed to see what he could do towards
securing credit when they needed it. David Gordon
volunteered his aid as a lawyer. They rose to go.
Anthony gazed intently at Kenneth as he asked
gravely:

"Doctor, have you thought of the possibility of—er
—trouble if your motives are not understood?
That is, suppose some of the poor whites are stirred
up by the landlords and merchants you're trying to
take these coloured farmers away from—have you
figured out what might be the result?"

"Yes, I have," responded Kenneth. "I realize

there might be some who'd break up our groups——"

"No—no—I mean to you personally," interjected Anthony.

"I don't think they'll bother me," was Kenneth's confident reply. "But if something should happen —well, if I can feel I've perhaps pointed a way out for my people, I can die happy. . . . At any rate, killing or running me away wouldn't kill the spirit of revolt these coloured people have—it might stir it even higher. Not that I've any ambition for martyrdom," he ended with a laugh.

Kenneth spoke with no bravado, with none of the cant of the *poseur*. His words, rather, were uttered with the simplicity of the earnest seeker after truth— the unheroic but sincere worker in a cause that is just.

"Let's hope you'll come through," said Anthony. "I'm a Southerner with all the traditions and preju- dices of the South, but I wish you luck." He added after a pause: "You'll need it."

After Kenneth had gone, the three men looked at each other questioningly.

"What do you think of him and his plan?" asked Dr. Scott, half to himself.

It was Gordon who answered.

"It's a good scheme—if it works. I'm mighty afraid, though, he's going to run into deep water if his societies grow very large. And the pity of it is that we in Atlanta can't help him if we dared."

Anthony grunted.

"And yet the South is trying to solve the race problem and leave educated Negroes like Harper entirely out of the equation. It's about time we woke up."

CHAPTER XX

EARLY Friday morning Kenneth left for Central City, before the Atlanta *Constitution* appeared on the streets for sale. Soon after his train left Macon on the way South, the engine blew out a cylinder head. They remained there until another could be dispatched from Macon to replace it. There had come to his stopping-place in Atlanta, a few minutes after he had left, a telegram which had been sent from a town twenty miles distant from Central City, telling him to remain in Atlanta until further notice. Jane had paid a man liberally to drive through the country to get the telegram off in time. It would not have done to send such a wire from Central City. All these things had so happened as though the very fates themselves were in league against Kenneth.

In total ignorance of what had happened to Mamie and Bob and the eventful chain of happenings since he had left Central City three days before, Kenneth sat in the stuffy, odorous, and dirty Jim Crow car, busied with his thoughts. A noisy and malodorous Negro sat next to him who seemed to know some person at every one of the thousand and one stations at which they stopped. Kenneth sat next to the window. His companion leaned over him to stick his head out of the window to shout loud-mouthed and good-natured greetings to his friends on the ground. At those few stations where he knew no one, he would ask foolish, sometimes humorous questions of those he did not know. Kenneth stood it as long as he could and then requested the troublesome fellow to be less annoying. Kenneth, though vexed, was amused at the man's complaint to another of his kind behind him. "Humph!" he grunted. "Tha's whut I say 'bout a dressed-up nigger—thinks he owns the train. I paid jes' as much," he declared more aggressively, "as he did, an' ef he don't like it, he can git off and walk." At this, a long laugh at his own witty remark, but Kenneth looked out of the window and paid no attention to him. His thoughts were busy with other things.

Every few minutes he would feel the lump in the lower right-hand vest-pocket with a touch that was almost loving in its tenderness. He hoped Jane would like the ring—it had cost a little more than he had expected to pay or could afford, but the best was none too good for a girl like her. He could see Jane's eyes now when he opened the little box and she for the first time saw the glittering facets of the beautiful stone. He smiled in anticipation of her joy. And then he'd put it on her finger and she'd put her arms around his neck and he'd feel again her warm, soft, passionate, clinging lips. Lucky he didn't get too deeply tied up with that girl years ago in New York. She had kissed as though she'd had long practice at it. Too sophisticated—nothing like Jane. Jane wasn't experienced in kissing—but the thrill it gave him! It was funny about girls. Most of them didn't think a kiss meant very much. He had kissed one—two—three—four —oh, lots of them! But all of them put together couldn't begin to equal in warmth, the vividness of one kiss from Jane.

And just think of it—six weeks from now, and Jane would be Mrs. Kenneth B. Harper! My, but that sounded good! Reverend Wilson would marry them. Then they'd go to Atlantic City for their honeymoon.

Hoped the cotton crop would turn out well. Then he'd be able to collect some of those long-outstanding accounts from the farmers. That money would come in mighty handy right now. That's the devil of being a country doctor. You had to wait until the cotton crop was gathered and sold before you could collect the bulk of what's due you. And if the cotton failed or the market was so flooded the price was down, you'd have to wait on the most of them until the next year. Sometimes two or three years. Dr. Johnson over at Vidalia had some accounts that're six years old. Oh, well, they're good anyway. Couldn't expect to practise in the country districts unless you were willing to wait for your money.

Wonder why this darned train doesn't make better time. Slow as all outdoors. Like molasses in winter-time. If it only gets in on time, I'll surprise Jane by running in on her on the way home.

Due in at five-fifty. Let's see, it's four-thirty now. Where are we now? Hoopersville. Nearly ninety miles yet to go. Good Lord, won't get in until nearly eight o'clock! Hope we won't lose any more time. Don't see why so darned many people are travelling to-day anyhow. Just slows up the train, getting on and off with their ten bundles and suitcases each.

Wonder how Bob feels about going to school. Hope he'll like the shirts I bought him. Ought to. Cost four dollars apiece. Prices are certainly high. Few years ago you could get the best shirts on the market for a dollar and a half apiece—not more than two dollars.

I can see Jane now. Let's see, it's five o'clock. Probably getting supper. Glad she can cook so well. Most girls nowadays can't boil water without burning it.

He reflected on the unusual conversation he had had the night before with Dr. Scott, John Anthony, and Gordon. It was good to know there were some white men who were thinking seriously on the race problem. And trying to be fair. Most white Southerners were modern Pontius Pilates. Figuratively and literally, mentally and morally, they washed their hands of all personal responsibility for the increasing complexities of the race question.

He wondered how many more men there were in the South like those three. Broadminded but afraid to speak out. Ewing, Judge Stevenson, Scott, Anthony, Gordon—all by word or action seemed

[263]

mortally afraid lest the public know they were even thinking of justice. How soon, he wondered, would they gain sufficient courage to take a manly stand? Would that time come before the inevitable clash that continued oppression would cause?

Coloured folks weren't going to stand it much longer. They were organizing up North and even in the South to use legal means to better their lot. But some of them were getting desperate. Armed resistance would be foolish. Would be certain death. At any rate, even that would be better than what has been going on.

Good Lord, he reflected, let's forget the race problem awhile! A Negro never gets away from it. He has it night and day. Like the sword of Damocles over his head. Like a cork in a whirling vortex, it tosses him this way and that, never ceasing. Have to think about something else or it'll run him crazy.

Guess Mary Ewing's about out of danger now. Glad when she's all right again. Don't like to be going over there to those white folks' house. Neighbours might begin to talk. How much can I charge Roy Ewing? Two hundred dollars? Yes, he can stand it. Hope he'll pay me soon. Can use it when Jane and I go on our honeymoon. Just about cover our expenses. Honeymoon. Always thought it a darned silly name. But it doesn't sound so bad now. Not when it was mine and Jane's.

Thank Goodness, there's Ashland! Next stop's Central City. Be home in an hour. Guess I'll go home first and take a bath and put on some clean clothes. Feel dirty all over and there are a thousand cinders down my back. Ugh, but this is a nasty ride! Hope Bob'll be at the train with the car. . . .

Kenneth descended from the train and looked for Bob. He wasn't there. He looked around for some other coloured man to drive him home. He knew it was useless to try and get any of the white taxi-drivers to take him home—they would have considered it an insult to be asked to drive a Negro. He thought it strange that there were no Negroes to be seen. Usually there were crowds of them. It formed the biggest diversion of the day for white and coloured alike to see the train come in. It was the familiar longing for travel—adventure—contact with the larger and more interesting things of the outside world, though none of them could have given a reasonable statement of the fundamental psychological reactions they were experiencing when they went to the station. They never thought of it in that light—it was simply a pleasurable item in the day's course. That was enough.

When he found no one around, Kenneth picked up his bag and started down the platform to the street. He noticed, but paid little attention to, the silence that fell over the various groups as he passed. He heard a muttered oath but it never occurred to him that it might have any possible connection with himself. Intent on reaching home, seeing the folks, telephoning Hiram Tucker that his wife had passed safely through her operation and was resting well

[265]

—eager to get freshened up and go over to Jane's, he cut across a field that would save a half-mile walk instead of going the longer route through Lee Street and town. Swinging along in a long, free stride reminiscent of his army days, he continued the musing he had done on the train.

He thought nothing of the fact that his house was darkened. He rang the bell but no one answered. Thinking his mother and Mamie were out visiting in the neighbourhood, he dug down in his bag, got his keys, and let himself into the house. His mother was coming down the stairs, an oil lamp in her hands. As he went up to kiss her, he noticed her eyes were sunken and red. Anxiously he inquired the reason.

"Oh, Kenneth, my boy—my boy—haven't you heard?"

She burst into a torrent of weeping, her head on his shoulders. He took the lamp from her hand perplexedly and placed it on the table.

"Heard what, mamma? What's the matter? What's happened? Why are you crying like this? What's wrong?"

The questions poured out of him like a flood. For some time his mother could not speak. Her sobs racked her body. Though she tried to control herself, every effort to do so but caused her to weep the more. Kenneth, puzzled, waited until she could gain control of herself. He thought it funny she carried on this way—she'd never acted like this before. She had always been so well poised. But

his alarm and feeling of impending disaster increased to definite proportions when the flood of
tears seemed endless.

"Where's Bob?" he asked, thinking that he could
find out from his brother what had gone wrong. At
this a fresh burst of weeping greeted him. He led
her into his reception room and sat her down on the
lounge and himself beside her. At last, between
body-tearing sobs, she told him.

"Great God!" he shouted. "No! No! Mamma,
it can't be true! It can't be true!" But even as he
demanded that she tell him it was not true, he knew
it was. . . .

Mrs. Harper's lamentations were even as those
of that other Rachel who wept for her children because they were not. Kenneth sat stunned. It was
too terrible—too devastating—too cataclysmic a
tragedy to comprehend! Mamie—his own dear
little sister—torn, ravished, her life ruined! Bob
—with all his fire and ambition, his deep sensitive-
ness to all that was fine and beautiful, as well as
his violent hatred of the mean, the petty, the vicious,
the unjust, the sordid—Bob—his brother—dead at
the hands of a mob! Thank God, he had died before they laid hands on him!

He laughed—an agonized, terrible mockery that
made his mother look at him sharply. He had been
a damned fool! He thought bitterly of his thoughts
on the train a few hours before. Good God, how
petty, how trivial they seemed now! Surely that
couldn't have been just hours ago? It must have

been centuries—ages—æons since. He heard the crickets chirping outside the window. From down the street there floated a loud laugh. His wilted collar annoyed him. Cinders from the train scratched his back. He wondered how in such a circumstance he could be conscious of such mundane things.

He laughed again. His mother had ceased her loud wails of grief and sat rocking to and fro, her arms folded tightly across her breast as though she held there the babe who had grown up and met so terrible a fate. Low, convulsive sobs of anguish seemed to come from her innermost soul. . . . She anxiously touched Kenneth on the shoulder as he laughed. It had a wild, a demoniacal, an eerie ring to it that terrified her. . . .

What was the use of trying to avoid trouble in the South, he thought? Hell! Hadn't he tried? Hadn't he given up everything that might antagonize the whites? Hadn't he tried in every way he could to secure and retain their friendship? By God, he'd show them now! The white-livered curs! The damned filthy beasts! Damn trying to be a good Negro! He'd fight them to the death! He'd pay them back in kind for what they had brought on him and his!

He sprang to his feet. A fierce, unrelenting, ungovernable hatred blazed in his eyes. He had passed through the most bitter five minutes of his life. Denuded of all the superficial trappings of civilization,

[268]

he stood there—the primal man—the wild beast, cornered, wounded, determined to fight—fight— fight! The fire that lay concealed in the flint until struck, now leaped up in a devastating flame at the blows it had received! All the art of the casuist with which he had carefully built his faith and a code of conduct was cast aside and forgotten! He would demand and take the last ounce of flesh—he would exact the last drop of blood from his enemies with all the cruelty he could invent!

His mother, whom he had forgotten in the intensity of his hatred, became alarmed at the light in his eyes. He shook off the hand with which she would have restrained him.

"Oh, Ken!" she cried anxiously. "What're you going to do?"

"I'm going to kill every damned 'Cracker' I find!" She fell to her knees in an agony of supplication and clung to him, the while he tried to loose her arms from around his knees. He shook as with a chill— his face had become vengeful, ghastly. Filled with a Berseker rage, he was eager to tear with his hands a white man—any white man—limb from limb.

"Kenneth, my boy! My boy!" cried his mother. "You're all I've got left! Don't leave me! Don't leave me! My little Bob is dead! My Mamie is ruined! You're all I've got! You're all I've got! Don't leave me, lambkins! Don't leave your old mother all alone, honey!"

In her torture at the prospect of losing this, her

last child, she used again the endearing names she had called him when he was a babe in her arms—endearments she had not used since.

"Mamma, I've got to! I've got to! God, if I only can find those who killed him!" he shouted.

She, like a drowning person, clutched at the fragile straw his last words implied. Her voice was almost a prayer.

"But you don't know, Ken, you don't know who was in the mob!" she cried. "That Jim Archer and Charley Allen—they're the only ones Mamie recognized! And they're dead—they've paid! My little Bob killed them! Who're you going to get? How're you going to find out to-night who the others were? You can't, Ken, you can't!"

She realized this was her only hope. If she could only keep him in the house the rest of the night, when morning came she was sure he would be more calm. He would realize then how foolish and foolhardy his intentions of the night before had been. She pleaded—she begged—she moaned in her terror. He tried to shake her off. He did loosen her grip around his knees where she had clung like death itself. As he leaned over to pry her hands loose and was about to succeed, she grasped his arm and held on. He tried to jerk his arm loose and rush from the house. She was struggling now with that fierce, grim, relentless tenacity and courage of the mother fighting for her young. She held on. His jerks dragged her over the floor but she was conscious neither of the act nor the pain. She would have

died there gladly if by so doing she could restrain
her boy from rushing forth to certain death. Oh,
yes, he might get one or two before he died. Maybe
five or ten. But the odds were all against him.
Death would most surely overtake him before
morning.

Kenneth raged. He cursed in spite of himself.
She did not even comprehend what he said nor the
significance of his words. She did not even consciously hear them. He damned without exception
every white man living. The damned cowards!
The filthy curs! The stinking skunks, fighting a
thousand against one!

"Superior race"! "Preservers of civilization"!
"Superior," indeed! They called Africans inferior!
They, with smirking hypocrisy, reviled the Turks!
They went to war against the "Huns" because of
Belgium! None of these had ever done a thing so
bestial as these "preservers of civilization" in Georgia! Civilization! Hell! The damned hypocrites!
The liars! The fiends! "White civilization"!
Paugh! Black and brown and yellow hands had
built it! The white fed like carrion on the rotting
flesh of the darker peoples! And called *their* toil
their own! And burned those on whose bodies their
vile civilization was built!

Bob had been right! Bob had been a man! He'd
fought and died like a man! He, Kenneth, with all
his professed and vaunted wisdom, was the coward!
He cursed himself! Building a fool's paradise!
A house of cards! To hell with everything! What

was life worth anyway? Why not end it all in one glorious orgy of killing?

In his agonized fulmination against the whites and in his vow of vengeance on those who had dealt him so cruel and heart-sickening a blow, Kenneth forgot those who had been and were true friends of the black man—who had suffered and died that *he* might be free. He forgot those who, though few in number and largely inarticulate, were fighting for the Negro even in the South. Kenneth's grief, however, was too deep and the blow too crushing for him to think of these in his hour of despair.

At length his raging subsided a little. His mother was pleading with him with a fervour he had never believed she possessed. Snatches of her words penetrated his mind.

". . . and who'll protect Mamie and me? . . . all alone . . . you're all we've got! . . . need you . . . need you now as never before . . . mustn't leave us now . . . mustn't leave . . ."

He sank to the floor exhausted by the fierceness of his rage. A feeble cry came from above stairs.

"It's Mamie!" his mother whispered, frightened. She left him lying there to rush to her other child. Before she left she made Kenneth promise he wouldn't go out before she returned. He lay on the floor as in a stupor. It was his Gethsemane. He felt as though some giant hand was twisting his very soul until it bled. He thought of the hours Mamie had lain in the field after the fiends had accomplished their foul purpose on her. Bleeding, torn, ravished!

Mamie, always tender, so unselfish, so unassuming—
God, why hadn't he thought more of her and been
more considerate of her?   No, he'd been so wrapped
up in his own happiness and future he'd never given
her much attention or thought.   Why hadn't he?
Why had he been so selfish?   How could he make
up to her for all his remissness of the past?

That brought to his mind what his mother had said.
They did need him now!   More than ever before!
How could he have started on his rampage of revenge
had his mother not held him?   Where and on whom
would he have begun?

But wasn't this cowardice not to exact some kind
of revenge?   He hated himself at the mere thought
of cowardice at this time.   Good God, he had had
enough of that all along!   Wouldn't Bob in death
curse him if he failed now to play the man?   Or
wouldn't it take more courage to live?   The thought
comforted him.

As though the sounds were worlds away, he heard
his mother moving in the room above as she ministered to Mamie's wants.   He heard the noises of
the street.   Miles away a dog barked.   Nearer a
rooster crowed.   He thought of a sermon Reverend
Wilson had preached the Sunday before.   Of the
Christ in his hour of betrayal.   Of Peter denying
his Lord.   And the cock crowing thrice.   Wasn't he
denying his duty—his family—his conscience—his
all?   Back again over the same ground he had already travelled so thoroughly, his mind went. . . .
For hours he lay there.   The noises of the street

ceased. He heard no more his mother above. Exhausted with the ordeal through which she had passed, she had probably fallen asleep. . . . And yet he did not move. He heard the clock in the hall strike eleven. . . . He counted the strokes, marvelling the while that time was yet measured in hours and minutes and days. . . . His soul was even as the body of a woman in travail. . . .

CHAPTER XXI

KENNETH lay on the floor he knew not how long. At last he awakened to the realization that his telephone was ringing furiously. Subconsciously he was aware of the fact that it had been ringing for some time. He lay there and let it ring. Telephone—office—house—profession—life itself—all seemed vague and nebulous phenomena remote from his existence—far from him and as uninteresting to him as life on Mars.

The raucous dissonance continued. "R-r-r-r," the bell seemed to scream in its existence. It was like a mosquito in a darkened room when one wanted to get to sleep. "Damn the telephone!" he cried aloud. "Let the fool thing ring its head off!". . .

He thought of Jane. He wondered if she would be content to remain in Central City after the disasters to Mamie and Bob. If she didn't, then they'd part. *He* was going to stay there if all hell froze over until he found who had composed the mob that had killed Bob. Until he had wreaked the utmost in vengeance upon them. . . . But Jane would feel just as he did. She was no coward! Hadn't she been the one to awaken him to the asininity of his own course in trying to keep away from the race problem? No, she'd stick! *She* wasn't the quitting kind! . . .

The telephone bell shrilled as though it were human—it sounded like a vinegar-dispositioned virago berating her spouse. It paused only, apparently, to catch enough breath to break forth again. Its shrieking reverberations beat upon his eardrums in wave after wave of sound until it seemed as though he would go mad. "Why doesn't the fool get it through his head that there's nobody here to answer?" he exclaimed in vexation that bordered on hysteria. He pressed the heels of his palms against his ears as tightly as he could. That was better! He could hear himself think now. . . .

Mamie and her mother couldn't stay in Central City, though. Too terrible for them—especially for Mamie to stay here where she couldn't help but see, every day, things that'd remind her of her awful experience. And where fool people would come in with long faces to sympathize with her and drive her mad. People were such asses! Why didn't they have sense enough to show their sympathy by staying away? Instead of coming in and sitting around, talking empty nothings by the hour? Old Mrs. Amos would be that way. And Mrs. Bradley. They *were* such nuisances. Wonder if he hadn't better send Mamie and mamma to Philadelphia to his Uncle Will? Or would it be best to send them to Virginia to his Uncle Jim? No, that wouldn't do. Best for them to leave the South entirely. Where they could get away from everything that'd remind them of Georgia. No, they'd go to Philadelphia.

Suppose Mrs. Tucker's about able to take some slight nourishment now. Good Lord, had he performed the operation only yesterday morning? That couldn't be possible! Too much has come in between then and now. Must have operated on her in a previous existence. And died since. Reincarnation? Yes, that's the word. Never thought he'd actually experience it himself. . . .

His arms and hands became tired from pressing on his ears. His ears ached. He loosened the pressure on them a bit. The telephone was yet ringing. Lord, he moaned, the thing will drive me crazy! Won't be able to live long enough to get those damned scoundrels who murdered Bob. He decided to answer it, curse the voice on the other end, and hang up. He tried to get up from the floor. There was a terrible pain in his legs. He was sore all over. He crawled over to the desk in his office and painfully pulled himself to a seat in his office chair. He stretched his arm out to pull the telephone to him. A sharp twinge shot through his arm and he groaned. He caught the cord in his hands and slowly pulled the instrument to him and placed the receiver to his ear. At first he could not speak. He made several ineffectual efforts. At last a faint, hoarse "Hello" was wafted into the mouthpiece.

"Oh, Rachel, I'm so glad to hear your voice. This is Mrs. Ewing—Mrs. Roy Ewing over on Georgia

Avenue. I've been trying to get you for half an hour. Has your son come home from Atlanta yet?"

The voice went chattering on while Kenneth tried to moisten his parched throat sufficiently to speak. It seemed to him that his saliva-producing gland must have died along with his hope of a peaceful existence in Central City. Finally, he was able to speak. He answered Mrs. Ewing wearily:

"This isn't Mrs. Harper, Mrs. Ewing. This is Dr. Harper."

"Oh, my God! Why did you come back?" she exclaimed.

Puzzled at her tone, Kenneth abruptly answered:

"Why shouldn't I have come back?"

She laughed nervously

"Nothing—oh, nothing. But I'm awfully sorry about what's happened." At a disbelieving grunt that came to her over the wire, she hastened to add: "Really I am—I am from the very bottom of my heart!"

She went on philosophically before Kenneth could reply.

"But everything'll come out all right, don't you fear. Doctor, I'm so glad for one reason you're back. Mary's had a set-back and she's in an awful fix. Dr. Bennett can't do nothing for her. I know it's awful hard to ask you, but can't you come over and see what you——"

"No, damn it, *no!*" shouted Kenneth into the mouthpiece. His voice mounted higher and higher in the rage that possessed him. "No, I hope she'll die—I hope she'll die! And every other white beast that's living! No! No! No! *No!*" he shouted as though mad.

He started to slam the receiver down upon its hook. The voice of Mrs. Ewing came to him in an agonized moan and made him pause.

"Oh, Doctor, don't take it out on my po' little Mary. I know just how you feel, but don't blame it on her! Please, Doctor, please come over and I'll never bother you again! If you don't come, I jus' know she'll die!" she begged.

Kenneth's fit of passion had passed. In its stead there came a cold, terrifying calmness that was but another form of the raging torment and fury in his breast. He spoke with biting directness into the telephone:

"Mrs. Ewing, if by raising one finger I could save the whole white race from destruction, and by not raising it could send them all straight down to hell, I'd die before I raised it! You've murdered my brother, my sister's body, my mother's mind, and my very soul! No, I know that," he said to her interjected remark, which he repeated. "I know you didn't do it with your own hands! But you belong to the race that did! And the race that's going to pay for every murder it's committed!"

He paused for breath and then continued his vitriolic diatribe against the white race. It was relieving his brain, he found, to be able thus to vent his spleen on a white person. He went on in the same voice of deadly calm and precision of statement:

"And where's that cowardly husband of yours?"
he demanded in a voice of rising fury. "Why
didn't he come and ask me to save your daughter?
No, he's like the rest of the damned cowards—makes
his wife do it, thinking I'm fool enough not to know
he's there at the telephone telling you what to say.
No, no, wait until I'm through! . . . He's where?
Atlanta? What's he doing there? Why did he
leave his daughter when he knew she might die any
minute? Oh, no! You can't feed me any bait like
that! I'm through, I tell you—I'm through listening to the lying flattery you white folks use to fool
ignorant and blind Negroes like me! What? Why
—I don't see—don't understand! Oh, well, I suppose I might as well, then. Yes, I'll be over within
ten minutes. Tell Dr. Bennett to wait there until
I come. What? He's gone! All right, I'll come!
Good-bye!"

Slightly puzzled, he hung up the receiver and sat
for a minute gazing at the desk pad in front of him,
but seeing nothing. Why should Roy Ewing have
gone to Atlanta to see him? Ewing knew he'd be
back on Friday. He had told him so before leaving.
It was mighty strange for him to act that way.

His mother entered the room, awakened by the
sound of his shouting over the telephone. She spoke
to him apologetically for having left him so long.

"Mamie was so restless," she explained, "and
when I got her quiet at last, I must have fallen asleep
sitting there by her bed." On her face there came a

wistful smile. "You see, I haven't been to sleep for three days now."

Kenneth went to her and put his arm around her. "That's all right, mamma, that's all right. I'm glad you did get a minute's rest. You needed it. What's that? Oh, yes, I feel much better now. The storm has passed for a time, I reckon. I'm going to run over to the Ewings' for a minute—Mary's in a bad way. Oh, that's all right, you needn't worry," he hastily interjected at his mother's cry of alarm. "The streets are empty now—everybody's in bed. I'll go there and come straight back as soon as Mary's resting easily again," he promised in order to quiet her fears. "There won't be anybody for me to see on the streets, much less start any trouble with. You go to bed and I'll come in and sit with you for a few minutes when I come back."

With this promise Mrs. Harper had to be content. Her fears allayed, Kenneth kissed her and helped her up the stairs to her room. Going back to his office, he put the things in his bag he would be likely to need, went out to the garage in the rear, cranked up the Ford, and drove over to Georgia Avenue to treat a white patient less than seventy-two hours after the double catastrophe which had descended upon him and his family at the hands of those same white people.

As he drove out of the yard, he heard his mother call from her window: "Hurry back, sonny." It had been more than fifteen years since she had last

called him that. . . . He drove through the darkened
streets of Central City—down Lee Street past the
deserted business houses, past the Confederate Monument, and on across that intangible, yet vivid line
that separated the élite of the whites of Central City
from the less favoured. . . .

His mind intent on his own tragedy, Kenneth drove
on, guiding his car without conscious volition, me-
chanically. His conscious mind was too busy re-
volving the string of events and trying to find some
solid spot, it mattered not how small, on which he
could set mental foot. . . .

CHAPTER XXII

FIFTEEN men sat around a table in an office on Lee Street. There was above them a single electric-light bulb, fly-specked, without a shade over it. At eleven o'clock they had silently crept up the stairs after looking cautiously up and down the deserted expanse of Lee Street to see if they were observed. Like some silent, creeping, wolf-like denizen of the forest, each had stolen as noiselessly as possible up the stairs. The window carefully covered, no ray of light could be seen from the outside. Though unsigned, the mysterious note each of the fifteen had received that morning had brought them all together promptly.

A fat man, with tiny eyes set close together, looking from amazing convolutions of flesh which gave him the appearance of a Poland-China hog just before slaughtering-time, was giving instructions to the men as they eagerly and closely followed his words. He occasionally emphasized his points by pounding softly on the pine table before him with large, over-sized fists covered profusely with red hair. He was clad in a nondescript pair of trousers, a reddish faded colour from much wear and the red dust of his native hills, a shirt open at the neck and of the same colour as the trousers, the speaker's neck innocent of collar and tie. He was ending his instructions:

"... Now you-all mus' r'member all I said. You mus'n' fail! When the 'accident' happens"—here he laughed softly as he emphasized the word "accident," and was rewarded by an appreciative titter from his audience—"when the accident happens, you ain't t'breathe a word to anybody 'bout it! Even th' others here to-night!"

He paused impressively and allowed his eyes slowly to traverse the group, resting upon each man in turn a penetrating, malevolent stare. Measuring his words carefully, he spat them out like bullets from a Browning gun.

"Th' mos'—important—thing—you got to r'member is this! You're not—to repo't—back to me—or any off'cer—of the Invis'ble Empire!" He paused again. "After—the 'accident'—happens!" he added.

"I reck'n that's all you need to know," he said in dismissal. "He came back t'night from Atlanty! We've got the newspaper fixed! Ef any of you is arrested, I don't reck'n She'ff Parker'll hol' you long!" he concluded with a confident laugh in which his companions joined. . . .

Though there was none to hear or see, they dispersed with silent and cautious movements and voices. They crept down the unlighted stairs, hands extended, fingers touching the walls on either side to aid them in making as little noise as possible. As the foremost reached the landing at the botton, he drew back sharply as he was about to step into the street.

"Sh-h-h-h!" he cautioned the others behind him. "Somebody's comin' lickety-split down the road in a Ford!"

They all waited with bated breath. The leader peered forth cautiously to see who it was stirring about at that time of night. The others waited, poised on the stairs above him.

Lee Street was bathed alternately in moonlight and shadow as a vagrant moon wove its way in front of and behind small patches of clouds. The clattering car approached—came abreast the doorway— and passed rapidly by.

"It's that damn nigger himself!" he exclaimed to the men behind him. "What'n th' hell's he doin' out this time of night 'round here? An' headed towards Georgy Avenue, too! It's damn funny!"

There was an outburst of excited whispering. Various speculative surmises were offered. None was able to offer a sensible reason for Kenneth's nocturnal pilgrimage. One proposed that Kenneth be followed to see where he went and why he went there. Afar off could be heard the puttering of the engine. And then it stopped.

"Ain't gone far," one of them declared. They set out to trail the automobile. Before they had gone two blocks, they saw Kenneth down the street as he tinkered with the engine of the car, the hood raised. One of the wires connecting with a spark-plug had become loosened. He quickly screwed it tight again, started the engine, and drove off, as he was closely watched from the shadows of trees and fences by his trailers. They pushed forward to keep as close as they could, hoping to be guided by the sound of the engine.

He drove but a few yards more and then drew up and stopped in front of Roy Ewing's house. Getting out, he took his bag from the floor of the car and entered the house quickly as the door opened to admit him.

There was another short session of excited whispering among the watchers.

"What'n the hell's he goin' to Roy Ewing's house for?" one of them demanded. "Roy Ewing went t'Atlanty this mornin' on important business! Heard him tell George Baird down t' the bank to-day he was goin'!"

"Th' damn sneaky bastard!" another one declared venomously. "I thought he was mighty slick, but didn't know he was foolin' 'round with a woman like Roy Ewing's wife! I allus said these niggers who went to France an' ran with those damn Frenchwomen'd try some of that same stuff when they came back! Ol' Vardaman was right! Ought never t' have let niggers in th'army anyhow!"

And so it went. They had caught the "slick nigger" with the goods on him! They talked eagerly among themselves in subdued tones as to what would be the best course to pursue. Some were all for rushing into the house and catching them together. None of them entertained the opinion that Kenneth could have gone to Roy Ewing's house with Roy Ewing out of town for any other purpose than for

sexual adventure. Their convictions were strengthened when the light in the lower hall which had been
shining when the door was opened to admit Kenneth
was extinguished, and another appeared in a few
minutes in the bedroom on the second floor which
faced on the streets, and the shades lowered. . . .

The fat man who had been speaking in the office on
Lee Street a few minutes before abruptly ended the
conjecturing.

" 'Tain't no use t' stand here all night talkin'!"
he asserted. "We'll jus' stay here and see what's
goin' t' happen! Looks damn funny t' me! Tom!
You 'n' Sam 'n' Jake go 'roun to th' back do' an'
watch there! Bill! You 'n' Joe 'n' Henry watch
that side do'! Me 'n' the res'll stay here and watch
th' front do'! Then, when he sneaks out, we'll get
him any way he comes!". . .

Within the house, Kenneth, all unaware of what
was going on outside, was listening to Mrs. Ewing
as she excitedly told him of Mary's change for the
worse, and as she explained her husband's absence.
She was so worried over her daughter's condition
that Kenneth realized she would never be able to
solve the mystery of her words over the telephone
until he had done what he could for Mary. He therefore asked no questions but followed her up the
stairs to Mary's room, although his brain was whirling, it seemed to him, like the blades of an electric
fan.

Mary Ewing was in a worse condition than even
her mother knew. This Kenneth realized as soon

as he looked into her flushed face and measured her
pulse and temperature. He questioned Mrs. Ewing
as to her daughter's diet. The cause of her relapse
became clear to him when she told him with a naïve
innocence that since Mary had begged so hard that
day for something to eat, she had, with Dr. Bennett's
consent, given her a glass of milk and a small piece
of fried chicken. Kenneth set to work. He knew it
was useless to berate the mother for disregarding
his express orders that Mary should be given no solid
food for at least ten days. He knew that Dr. Bennett's word counted more than his. This in spite of
the fact that Dr. Bennett had done nothing but the
ordinary measuring-out of pills and panaceas which
he had been taught almost half a century ago in a
third or fourth-rate Southern medical school. Dr.
Bennett knew medicine no later than that of the early
eighties. But Dr. Bennett was a white man—he a
Negro!

As he laboured, he suffered again the agony of
those hours he had spent on the floor in his reception
room earlier that night. It brought to life again his
bitterness. His skin was black! Therefore, though
he had studied in the best medical school in America,
though he had been an interne for one whole year
in the city hospital at New York, though he had had
army experience, though he had spent some time in
study in the best university in France, and, save in
pre-war Germany, the best medical school in Europe,
his word and his medical knowledge and skill were
inferior to that of an ignorant, lazy country doctor

in Georgia! When, oh, when, he thought, will Americans get sense enough to know that the colour of a man's skin has nothing whatever to do with that man's ability or brain?

A fleeting, devilish temptation assailed him. He tried to put it from him. He succeeded for a time. And then back it came, leering loathsomely, grinning in impudent, demoniac fashion at him! Here, lying helpless before him, was a representative of that race which had done irreparable, irremedial harm to him and his. Why not let her serve as a vicarious sacrifice for that race? It wouldn't be murder! He did not need to do anything other than hold back the simple things needed to save her life. No one would ever know. He'd tell the Ewings that they had killed their own daughter by giving food she should not have had. Old Bennett didn't know enough to detect that he, Kenneth Harper, a Negro, a "damned nigger," had failed to do the things he could have done.

The thought charmed him. He toyed with it in his mind. He examined it from every possible angle. Yes, by God! He'd do it! It'd serve the Ewings right! The punishment would be just what they deserved! It would be a double one. They'd lose their daughter. And they'd be eaten up with remorse the rest of their days because by disobeying his orders in giving food to Mary Ewing they themselves, her parents, had killed her! Murderers! That's what they'd be! Like all the rest of their stinking brood!

He pictured the scene in which he'd play the lead-

ing rôle on the following day. The pleasurable
tingle this thought brought him caused a hard smile
to come to his lips. Mary'd be lying downstairs in
the parlour in her coffin. Roy Ewing and his
damned, snivelling wife would be howling and crying and mourning upstairs. He, Kenneth Harper, a
Negro, a "damned nigger," would be standing triumphantly over them, castigating and flaying their
very souls with his biting words of denunciation!
Tongue in cheek, he'd rage! He'd tell them they
were fools, villains, murderers, child-killers!

The words he'd use sprang to his mind. "You
murdered Mary yourselves!" he'd say. "Didn't I
tell you not to give her any food for ten days?"
he'd demand. And then they'd shiveringly admit
that he had told them those very words. "But, no,"
he'd go on, "you wouldn't listen to a 'damned nigger's' word! Old Bennett, who doesn't know as
much about medicine as a horse-doctor—probably
less—he's got a white skin! And mine's black!
Therefore—" his sarcasm would be great right there
as he bowed in mock humility—"*therefore* you listened to him instead of me! And, doing so"—here
another low bow—"you killed your own daughter!"
Here his voice would rise in violent denunciation:
"You're murderers! Yes, that's what you are!
You're murderers! *You've murdered your own
daughter! And I'm glad of it! I wish every one of
you and your dirty breed lay in the coffin with her!
You, who think you're God's own pet little race!
You, who think that all the wisdom in the world is*

wrapped in your dirty little carcasses! And all the virtue! And all the brains! Everything! Everything! EVERYTHING!"

Oh, yes, he'd finish with infinite scorn: *"And you've got nothing! Nothing! NOTHING! Nothing but lies and deceit and conceit and filthy, empty pride!"*

Lord, but he'd be magnificent! Booth and Tree and Barrymore and all the rest of the actors they called great, rolled into one, couldn't equal his scorn, his raising and lowering of voice, his tremendous climax! And then he'd walk magnificently from the room, leaving them huddled there like whipped curs!

His maniacal exultation swept him on and on. He had stopped ministering to the sick girl on the bed before him. He leaned back with a terrible leer on his face as he watched the half-unconscious form before him struggling in her pain. The strain of the horrible day which had started out so radiantly and optimistically had been too much for him. He gloried in the kindly fate that had delivered so opportunely into his hands one who should serve as a vicarious victim for those who had struck him mortal blows without cause. He felt that Bob, whatever he was, was smiling even now in approval of his actions. . . .

The minutes sped by. Half past twelve! One o'clock! Half past one! Mrs. Ewing sat anxiously by the bed, not daring to speak. She had misinterpreted Kenneth's smile. It had frightened her a little. It's because he'd been through so much to-day, she thought. I'll turn down the light so it won't be too great a glare. She did. It never occurred to her that Kenneth's smile could mean anything other than that he was gaining ground in his fight for her little girl's life. . . .

Outside, the fifteen waited. . . . Minutes, hours passed. It grew cold. The strain was getting irksome. They watched the room where shone only a faint light now. They pictured what was going on in that room. It made their blood boil and grow cold alternately. Two o'clock! They began to grumble. "Le's go in an' get the damn nigger and roast him alive!" some demanded. "We can't do that!" the fat man declared. "The damned bitch'll yell and wake up the neighbours! She, a *white* woman, with her nigger lover! Can't let it get out she consented! We'll get him outside an' say he was unsuccessful in th'attempt!". . . With that they had to be satisfied. They grumbled, but they knew he was right. Can't let the niggers know a white woman willingly went to bed with a nigger! . . . That'd never do! Must preserve the reputation of white women! . . .

Kenneth still sat by Mary's bed. His eyelids felt heavy. It was hard to keep them open. Revenge began to lose its savour. Wasn't so sweet as it had seemed. What's the use, he thought, of telling what he had planned to the Ewings? They wouldn't understand. They'd never seen great actors on the stage. All they'd seen was mushy movie actors and silly women. Like casting pearls before swine!

[292]

They'd never appreciate the wonder of his acting!
No, not acting. Irony. Sarcasm. Vials of wrath.
Beakers of gall.

Why does the air seem so heavy? Can't keep
eyes open. Feel like bathing in chloroform.

Kenneth awakened suddenly from his stupor.
Mary was coughing horribly—gasping—strangling.
Her mother cried out sharply. Kenneth rapidly re-
gained his senses. God! That had been an awful
dream. Feverishly he worked. He called to his
aid every artifice known to him. Valiantly, eagerly,
desperately he toiled. Mary had been almost gone.
After what seemed hours, she began to recover the
ground she had lost while Kenneth gloated over his
fancied revenge. My God! Just think I was about
to let her die! May the Lord forgive me! . . .

At last she passed the danger point. She sank
into a deep slumber. She was safe!

Kenneth, wearied beyond measure, rose and stu-
pidly, weariedly, made preparations to go home.
Mrs. Ewing stopped him.

"You haven't asked me to tell you why Mr. Ewing
went to Atlanta," she said.

Dully he asked why he had gone away with his
daughter in such a critical condition, what she had
meant by her cryptic remarks over the telephone.
She spoke gladly.

"I couldn't tell you over the telephone," she explained. "If anyone had been listening, it would
have been bad for all of us. He went to Atlanta
this morning—it's yestiddy morning, now—to **do**

two things. First, to warn you not to come back to Central City until things has blown over, because he'd heard threats against you. And most of all to see the Gov'nor!"

"See the Governor for what?" Kenneth asked.

"Why, to get him to do somethin' to protect you!" she cried as though amazed at his ignorance in not seeing.

"Protect me?" Kenneth echoed with a rising, questioning inflection.

"Yes, to protect you. Y' see, he knew She'ff Parker couldn't be depended on 'cause he's in with this gang 'round here. He knew the only chance was through the Guv'nor."

"But why should *I* need protection now?" Kenneth asked wonderingly. "Good God, haven't these devils done enough to my family and me already?"

She explained patiently as though talking to a child. Neither of them realized the unusualness of their situation. Both had forgotten race lines, time, circumstances, and everything else in the tenseness of the moment.

"*B'cause the Ku Kluxers are after you!*" she whispered.

"Why should they be after me? I've done nothing! My Lord, I've tried in every way I could since I've been back in this rotten place to keep away from trouble——" he declared querulously.

"Wait a minute an' I'll tell you!" she interrupted him. She took his arm and led him into the next room where they would not disturb Mary. "Roy

[294]

heard them talking about you and cursin' you out about some kind of a society you've been formin' among the nig—the coloured people. He told 'em they oughter let coloured men like you alone 'cause you were a credit to the community. *The nex' mornin' he foun' a warnin' on the front po'ch from the Kluxers, sayin' he'd better stop defendin' niggers or somethin'd happ'n to him!*"

"Oh, that's all tommyrot, Mrs. Ewing!" Kenneth declared in a disgusted and disdainful tone. "These silly night-riders wouldn't dare do anything to your husband! I don't believe they'd even try and do anything to me!"

"You mustn't talk that way!" she sharply broke in. "They'd do *anythin'*! Roy says She'ff Parker's one of 'em, and a whole lot mo' of the folks you wouldn' believe was in it!"

Kenneth's voice became hard and bitter.

"Mrs. Ewing, I've tried—God knows I have—to keep away from trouble with these white people in Central City. If they bother me, I'm going to fight —you hear me—I'm going to fight—and fight like hell! They'll get me in the end—I know that— but before I go I'm going to take a few along with me!"

He left her standing there and went back into Mary's room. He secured his bag and started down the stairs. Mrs. Ewing ran after him and caught him just as he opened the front door. She had to seize his arm to hold him, as he was impatient to be gone. He felt as though he never wanted to see a

white face again as long as he lived. He did not
know, nor did Mrs. Ewing, that several white faces
were looking at them as he stood there with Mrs.
Ewing clinging to his arm.

"You will be ca'ful until Roy comes back, won't
you, Doctor?" she pleaded.

Promising her impatiently, without even compre-
hending what he promised, he ran down the steps,
eager to get home.

CHAPTER XXIII

KENNETH did not see the dark forms that crouched like tigers in the shrubbery on either side of the long walk that led to the gate. But as he reached the ground, he turned just in time to see a shadowy body hurl itself upon him. Instinctively his right arm shot outwards and upwards. His clenched fist met flush on the point of the jaw the man who had attempted to hurl him to the ground. His would-be assailant gave a deep grunt and fell to the ground at Kenneth's feet.

Before he hit the ground, however, Kenneth found himself surrounded by a cursing, howling crowd. He lashed out blindly—hitting wherever he saw what seemed to be a form. Madly, desperately, gloriously he fought! For a time he was more than a match for the fifteen that assailed him. He did not know that they had expected to take him by surprise. The surprise was now theirs. He heard a voice shout at him in rage: "Sleepin' with a white woman, eh! You dirty black bastard!" With superhuman strength born of hatred, bitterness, and despair, he lunged at the speaker. Almost at the same time that his fist landed in the man's face, his foot went into his stomach with a vengeance. He put into the blow and the kick all the repressed hatred and passion the day's revelations had brought forth.

It seemed to him he had been fighting there for hours, days, months! The odds fifteen to one against him—his strength was as of the fifteen combined. No Marquis of Queensberry rules here! He knew it was a fight to the death, and he yelled aloud for sheer joy of the combat! In the darkness his assailants could not lay hands on him, for he was here, there, everywhere—hitting, kicking, whirling, ducking blows, jumping this way and that—a veritable dervish of the deserts in his gyrations! One after another his opponents went down at his feet! Windows began to be raised at the tumult. Shouts and cries of inquiry filled the air. But still Kenneth fought on.

At last he saw an opening. Out went his fist! Down went the man who met it with his face! Shaking off one who sought to grasp him from behind, Kenneth stepped over the body of the one who had just gone down before him, and, like an expert half-back running in a broken field, darted out to the sidewalk. Fifty—forty—thirty—twenty—ten—five more yards and he'd be in his car and away! At last, he reached it! Feverishly he wrenched open the door! He started to spring in! They'd never get him now!

A shot rang out! Another! Another! Kenneth's arm flew up. With a low moan he sank to the street beneath the car. He tried to rise. He couldn't.

The bullet had shattered his leg! On they came, howling, gloating fiendishly—their rage increased by the mess they'd made of what was intended should be an easy job! Kenneth saw them come! He groaned and tried to draw the gun from his hip pocket. It hung in his clothing, pinned down as he was! If I only can get one or two of them, he thought, before they get me! On they came! The gun stuck! They had him! They pulled him out from beneath the car! . . .

The next morning, in a house in the coloured section of Central City, there sat a girl. . . . Her eyes were dry. . . . Her face was that of despair. . . . Her grief was too deep for tears. . . . In her lap there lay a soft, white, lustrous, fluffy mass. . . . It looked like cream charmeuse . . . looked like a wedding-gown. . . . A woman entered the room. . . . Her eyes were haggard. . . . Around her shoulders an apron. . . . She'd put it on, thinking it a shawl. . . .

"Honey! Honey!" she cried. "Mamie was sleeping . . . so I ran over a minute.". . . She put her arms around the younger woman tenderly. . . . The dam broke. . . . The relief of tears came. . . . Hot, blinding, scalding tears rained down on the soft mass that now would never be used. . . . And the women cried together. . . .

In the newspapers of the country there appeared the same day an Associated Press dispatch. It was sent out by Nat Phelps, editor of the Central City *Dispatch* and local agent for the Associated Press. It read:

ANOTHER NEGRO LYNCHED IN GEORGIA

CENTRAL CITY, Ga., Sept. 15.—"Doc" Harper, a negro, was lynched here to-night, charged with attempted criminal assault on a white woman, the wife of a prominent citizen of this city. The husband was away from the city on business at the time, his wife and young daughter, who is seriously ill, being alone in the house. Harper evidently became frightened before accomplishing his purpose and was caught as he ran from the house. He is said to have confessed before being put to death by a mob which numbered five thousand. He was burned at the stake.

This is the second lynching in Central City this week. On Thursday morning Bob Harper, a brother of the negro lynched to-day, was killed by a posse after he had run amuck and killed two young white men. No reason could be found for their murder at the hands of the negro, as they had always borne excellent reputations in the community. It is thought the negro had become temporarily insane.

In a telegram to the Governor to-day, Sheriff Parker reported that all was quiet in the city and he anticipated no further trouble.